"THIS IS YOUR LAST CHANCE TO WALK AWAY."

"I will return tomorrow, and we will take a ride through the park?"

"Hmm ... it sounds wonderful, but my uncle will never agree to you courting me."

"I see. I shall contrive a plan to persuade him, then."

Sophia stood up, prompting the earl to rise. She could hear Uncle Hugh's heavy footfalls in the hall. By now, one of the servants had informed him that an infamous rake was in his drawing room, paying addresses to his niece. Stepping around the table, she stood directly in front of the earl.

"I already have a plan. Are you certain you wish to see this courtship through to the end? This is your last chance to walk away."

Saunton's eyebrows drew together in confusion. "Yes ... I am certain."

Sophia stepped closer, noting his pupils dilated as she approached him. Out of the corner of her eye, she saw the tall form of her uncle stepping into the drawing room. With a deep breath, she leapt into the earl's arms, springing up on her toes to throw her arms over his wide shoulders, and kissed him full on the lip-

For more information, contact author Nina Jarrett. www.ninajarrett.com

ALSO BY NINA JARRETT

INCONVENIENT BRIDES SERIES

TO REDEEM AN EARL

INCONVENIENT BRIDES
BOOK TWO

NINA JARRETT

Babooks.

PROLOGUE

*M*iss Hayward fluttered her eyelids much like a crazed butterfly.

"La, sir! You flatter me," she simpered.

Lord Richard Balfour, the fourth Earl of Saunton, resisted rolling his eyes at the young lady's empty-headed flirting while he twirled her across the crowded ballroom. He had quickly discovered that his dance partner, Miss Hayward, was a proper miss and not very bright. He could not be happier that this waltz was coming to an end as the closing strains of music echoed through the great, gilded ballroom of the Astleys' stately home on the River Thames.

She was an attractive young woman with red-blonde hair twisted in a coronet around the crown of her head. Her complexion was silky and clear, her arching brows framed stormy blue eyes, and her nose was delicate and straight. Under ordinary circumstances, he would find her alluring, but he knew he must be on his best behavior with innocent young misses. Marriage was a permanent state of affairs, and he needed to be certain he could bear the presence of the young woman whom he would wed. He could not allow himself to be allured.

His expectations for his future marriage were not high, but Miss Hayward was simply too silly to consider permanently saddling himself with the vapid chit. Nevertheless, he must admit he enjoyed clasping her slender waist; her rosewater scent and the feel of her slim, warm body beneath her white silk gown were causing him to wonder if he had made a mistake ending things with his last mistress in preparation for his return to the marriage hunting grounds. It had seemed well-advised to make an effort to look sincere in his courtship attempts, if only to ensure fathers would be receptive to his suit, but Miss Hayward's heated skin below his hand was drifting his thoughts in a decidedly carnal direction.

The Season of 1820 had officially begun, and Richard could already feel the onset of bone-deep boredom when he contemplated the months ahead. If only his former betrothed, Miss Annabel Ridley, had not seen fit to hare off across the country to marry his cousin, the Duke of Halmesbury, in a fit of pique. He would have been married already with an heir well on the way, but instead he was forced to attend these endless events of polite society to seek a new bride he could tolerate.

Endless small talk, nauseating orgeat, and watered-down lemonade, along with a parade of vapid girls ruthlessly molded by their mothers into perfect young ladies. Their only flaw was ... there was not one interesting personality to be found amongst the lot of them, which was why he had chosen irrepressible Annabel to be his wife in the first place. Was it too much to ask to wed a woman with whom he could conduct a reasonably intelligent conversation? Tonight, the feminine pickings certainly suggested that was the case.

Pity Miss Hayward was such an utter flibbertigibbet, or he would alleviate his boredom by steering her out to the terrace to steal a kiss from her delectable lips.

* * *

MISS SOPHIA HAYWARD was a great observer of people, especially men. She had to be in order to have avoided marriage for the past three Seasons—four if she successfully traversed this current Season without receiving a marriage proposal. Observation was key to her plans because she had a sizable dowry which undermined her efforts to remain unmarried. How much of a dowry she had, she was unsure because her uncle, who served as her guardian, was notoriously tight-lipped and protective of his family members, as had been her grandfather before him.

Her keen observational skills accounted for why when the Earl of Saunton, the very wealthy but infamous libertine who was now searching for a wife, requested this waltz, Sophia had intuitively leaned into her silly debutante act. The act she had honed over the past three years.

Her *ingénue* act involved eye fluttering, insipid language, and very dull small talk about needlework, the need for many shades of ribbon, and the fine selection of gloves in the shop she had visited that day.

However, for the other type of gentlemen, the ones who were searching for a docile and proper wife and who seemed attracted to that sort of behavior, she used her bluestocking act to sound disgracefully intellectual, which involved her detailed analysis of Shakespearean works, the need for the many hues of roses yet to be cultivated, and the fine selection of classical literature at the bookshop she had visited that day.

The two strategies were surprisingly similar, albeit at different ends of the intellectual spectrum. The art was in knowing which particular strategy to employ, and being sufficiently subtle to ensure her aunt and uncle did not hear about any untoward behavior from the gentlemen in question.

To his credit, Saunton was the former type of gentleman. Just when she had begun listing out all the ribbons she had collected over the years, he had desperately diverted her mindless chatter to a discussion of horseflesh. It was amusing to Sophia to note how his eyes had glazed over and his charming smile had become fixed in place, as if painted on his face with an artist's brush. Clearly he had already lost interest in her as a prospective bride, which suited her just fine.

Sophia could not deny that the gentleman was devilishly handsome, with his dark brown curls, long thick lashes framing his distinctive green eyes, and athletic build, with no hint of padding beneath his tailored clothing. He possessed pearly white teeth and perfectly proportioned, sculpted lips, which made her ponder what it would be like to kiss him. Saunton was easily the most attractive man at the Astleys' ball.

Nevertheless, she steeled herself to pay no mind to the pleasing warmth of his elegant fingers emanating through their gloves as he clasped her hand to lead her in an admittedly graceful waltz. For he was the very worst of husband prospects, devilish being an apt description, not to mention that she was doing her best to avoid the noose of matrimony altogether, despite her nagging aunt and persistent uncle who believed their primary duty as her guardians was to see her be married off *safely*. She was no fool; she had seen what marriage had done to her mother, and there was nothing *safe* about her mother's untimely demise. Nay, she planned to bide her time until she could claim her dowry to live independently.

Sophia exhaled a sigh of gratitude that the dance had ended, while Lord Saunton dropped a curt bow in visible relief.

Plastering a polite smile on her face, she kept a vapid look in her eyes while he deposited her back with her aunt and cousin at the edge of the ballroom. He dropped a curt bow to her aunt before parting ways.

It would seem her strategy to dissuade his interest had been successful, although she could not deny that an ill-advised visit to the terrace, to discover if his sculpted lips were as kissable as they appeared to be, would serve as a pleasant interlude. It was unusual for her to have thoughts like this, but Saunton was an unusually handsome man with an amiable smile and playful manner that were very ... appealing. And she could appreciate that the gentleman was known to never gamble, to drink in moderation, and to manage his estates with financial acumen, which were attractive qualities given the circumstances of her papa's death.

Even so, Lord Saunton was a rake not to be trusted, and she was not looking for a husband, despite her aunt's and uncle's best efforts. Playing bland had been easy in his company because he was so easy to read that all she had to do was bat her eyelashes and flirt in a vacuous manner while pretending to listen to him talk about the weather and riding. He certainly made use of his stables, if his conversation was anything to go by. She shared his interest, but she had stopped herself from displaying any useful knowledge—she had no wish to attract his attentions.

Sophia considered with no small amount of weariness that the evening had only just begun and there were yet hours of polite talk and awful orgeat to endure.

Together with her cousin, she watched the lengthy quadrille from the edge of the ballroom where they fluttered their fans while the heat of the room continued to rise. The smell of pomades blended with perfume and the music itself sounded loud and shrill, but perhaps it was just her mood. She attempted to relax, but she was not fond of large gatherings and she had many more of these ahead of her to dread. Perhaps it was the vague whispers about her long-departed parents that made it so, or perhaps she just did not like crowds, but she wished she could be at home reading a book or enjoying a stimulating conversation in the library with her cousin Lily. Even a dinner with a manageable number of people would have been more pleasant than this.

Turning to her closest friend and confidante, Miss Lily Abbott, she deliberately glanced toward the terrace. Her tiny cousin, with her huge brown eyes set in a delicate elfin face, immediately understood her meaning. Turning to her mother, Sophia's aunt, Lily paved the way for their escape.

"Mama, I believe my hem is coming loose. Sophia and I will find an alcove to mend it and be right back."

Lady Moreland waved her gloved hand in assent as she continued to gossip with the turbaned Lady Astley, whom Sophia did not personally know, nor did she care to because the elderly woman was haughty and vile with nothing pleasant to say about any of her guests.

Breathing sighs of relief, Lily and Sophia swiftly made their way from the crowded ballroom to push open the fogged-up terrace doors. Laughing softly, they spilled out into the cool spring night.

The sounds of music and chatting muted when the doors swung shut, and they walked to a far corner so they might remain hidden on the grand balcony overlooking the vast lawn sprawling down to the river's edge.

* * *

IT WAS NOT SO MUCH the quadrille he had just danced, but rather the insipid dancing partners he was seeking to escape that had driven Richard out to the balcony, where he deeply inhaled the cool spring air in relief.

The crowded Astley ball was the first of the Season and so far had proven to be long and tiresome. His dances were an unceasing procession of pretty, empty-headed misses without an original thought in their heads. He just needed to find one that was … well … full-headed—or even half-headed—and this hunt would be over.

He reached into his pocket for his silver cheroot case, an infrequent indulgence of his, when he overheard female voices from the far end of the terrace.

"What a travesty of an evening! There is not one interesting gentleman here. Spoilt, entitled bores and rogues, every last one! I thought I might fall asleep from the tedium during one dance, not to mention I danced with at least three *gentlemen* who I know for a fact, due to Lady Astley's wicked prattle, are keeping mistresses. What business do *they* have seeking a wife?"

Richard smiled to himself as he took in a puff of cheroot smoke, listening to the tirade and the heavy sarcasm threading the word *gentlemen*. Now, this sounded like an interesting girl, who roasted an entire ballroom of peers in their absence.

"Perhaps they will reform for the right bride?" A second woman had chimed in, this one clearly a romantic optimist.

"Lily, you are such a naïve romantic. Polite society is hypocritical, not to mention unfair to women. King George is not even cold in his grave, and his son is rumored to be arranging to put Queen Caroline on trial for her affairs when his own infidelities are legendary." Richard looked around to

7

ensure no one could hear the injudicious girl. The chit would be ruined if someone overheard her disparagement of their current monarch.

She continued, mimicking in a husky, lowered voice, *"I will be king, but you will be tried, harlot wife! Be careful not to trip over my mistress there by the door. Or the one behind you. No, no, do not sit on the bed. I will never hear the end of it if you sat on Mrs. Fitzherbert's favorite hiding place. Don't worry, Maria, you can come out from under the bed now. It's just my ridiculous wife. I will get this awful woman out of here before she squashes you beneath the mattress."*

The second girl giggled as Richard choked back a laugh.

"Shhh, Sophia! If anyone hears you talk this way, you will be ruined." Richard was glad to hear one of the girls had sense.

"Oh, horrors! I will stop receiving invitations from people I do not like and be forced to live outside of polite society as a spinster with only an unspecified dowry to keep me company. Oh—wait—I cannot think of a more glorious death than to leave the *ton* behind!"

Richard smirked at the cynic's sentiments, wishing he had danced with this opinionated debutante. If he must marry, he should minimally save himself from a boring girl to ruin his breakfast every morning for the rest of his life. A woman like this one could brighten his meals. And, he reminded himself, he could still fill his evenings with far more delightful company than a dutiful wife, even if she happened to be half as entertaining as this girl. He just needed to get this pesky duty to marry and sire an heir taken care of so he could get back to his real life.

He scowled at the intruding thought. Damn Annabel Ridley for delaying his marriage plans with her willful reticence to fill the accepted role of a stoic wife who looked the other way when a man did what he was wont to do—albeit when he was not in the company of ladies. Damn her for her prudish ideas of monogamy and marital fidelity. Marrying his cousin, the Duke of Halmesbury, just because of Richard's little indiscretion with the kitchen maid still grated. His fault for trying to marry a naïve country noblewoman who did not understand how marriages of the *ton* were conducted.

Richard was brought back to the present by the current conversation.

"But, Sophia, what of Lord Saunton whom you danced with earlier? He is ever so handsome," the second young woman urged. Richard started at hearing his own name. He had danced with the satirical shrew?

The first girl, the acerbic one, snorted. "You jest! Lord Richard-Can't-Keep-His-Breeches-On Balfour, the infamous Earl of Saunton? Not only is he the most arrogant peer in the realm, he also happens to be the randiest, most despicable peer in the realm! It was all I could do to politely bat my eyelashes and smile genteelly at his banal small talk. If I were to marry a cad such as Lord Saunton, I would need to hire only old, ugly housemaids just to save myself from the horror of his dallying right under my nose! Not to mention saving poor housemaids from his attentions so that they would not be coerced into ruinous relations for fear of being dismissed. Lord Saunton is a licentious blackguard, and I have nothing but pity for the poor chit who is stupid enough to accept his hand!"

Richard froze, his cheroot hovering inches from his mouth. He dropped his hand; breathing suddenly pained him as he stepped farther back into the shadows, his heart squeezed in wounded remembrance.

Somehow the girl's words had struck him in the chest, freezing the blood running through his veins. Was this how people saw him? And had housemaids only accepted his attentions out of fear of dismissal? He had not dallied with

9

many maids, especially not since the incident in the Baydon Hall stables when Annabel Ridley had caught him with her kitchen maid eighteen months earlier, so how had this chit heard about his trysts?

His late mother's voice echoed in his ears—a ghostly voice from the past. *"Lucas is such a heartless cad. If he must dally with other women, could he at least respect me enough not to break my heart in my own home with my own servants? I do not know what I will do if this situation continues! Perhaps I should get rid of all the attractive ones. And the young ones. Or, perhaps, all the women on our staff."*

Richard's mother had been weeping to her sister over tea in the blue drawing room. A mere seven years old, Richard had been hiding behind a sofa when they had interrupted his playing with his pewter soldiers. He had all but forgotten that sad and confusing afternoon until this moment. He was not sure he even knew what the conversation had meant at the time. Unfortunately, he now definitely understood the long-ago discussion. That afternoon had been only weeks before she grew ill and faded away, as if she had not the will to fight for her life.

Oh, my God! Am I an awful, laughable caricature of my father?

Richard grimaced when he recalled his own unfavorable thoughts of his former betrothed's condemnation just moments ago. How she had broken off their betrothal after discovering him in the stables with Caroline, the kitchen maid. Like a clap of thunder shaking the earth, in a terrifying moment of clarity, he realized just how wrong his behavior toward Annabel had been.

Trembling, he leaned back against the wall. His knees had gone weak, and he did not trust himself to be able to stand.

The girls on the balcony came around the corner, having finished their conversation, to return to the ball. The taller of the two women, the clever but caustic chit, stepped into the light spilling from the ballroom doorway. He knew it was Sophia of the sharp tongue as soon as he saw her. She was the so-called empty-headed miss, Miss Hayward, who had danced with him earlier. He was struck by how wrong his first impression of her had been. The tricky minx had fooled him regarding her level of intelligence and depth of personality.

Her friend followed, a teeny little thing with rich brown hair whom he did not recognize. In that moment, however, he would barely recognize his own mother returned from the dead because he had eyes only for the heartless, truthful termagant who had just shattered his illusions as a pleasure-seeking cad. How could he have been so wrong about her? This was no shallow miss. This was a sharp-witted girl who saw too much. Her stabbing remarks had cut him to his very soul, which was bleeding out while a bloody ball continued in the background—the sound of merriment a jarring accompaniment to his sudden onslaught of conscience and humiliation.

Richard shrank back, ashamed to be seen in this moment of his rude awakening. He prayed to remain unseen in the shadows, with the ballroom lighting now falling in their eyes, and breathed his relief when they looked straight into the ballroom while they exited the terrace.

He needed to escape the suffocation of the Astley ball and looked around for a route through the garden that would lead him to his coachman in the mews. His need to be alone overpowered him.

With his mother's words echoing in his head, he confronted the fact that he was well on his way to becoming the replica of his libidinous father, who had caused his mother such misery that she had not the will to live.

Was this the man he had become? Was this who he

wanted to be? Had Annabel, his former betrothed, and Halmesbury, her husband, been correct in disparaging his behavior? He was afraid these questions answered themselves.

His mind reeled as the long-ago memories whirled through his head. His father driven mad by the pox because of his indiscriminate taste in lightskirts, cyprians, wicked widows, housemaids; all were welcome in the late earl's bed, which led to his painful death years earlier. Richard had barely managed to keep the shameful affair private.

His own aversion to contracting a similar disease had resulted in his profligate use of sheaths, and his rejection of doxies of any class, but it had not resulted in tempering his pursuit of carnal relations. While his cousin, the duke, who had married his betrothed in his stead, could probably count the number of women he had bedded on one or two hands, Richard suspected he would need a minimum of eight hands, plus perhaps the toes on his feet, to count his conquests despite his so-called higher standards in avoidance of dread illnesses. Mayhap an acceptable number of paramours over a lifetime, but he was only just turned seven and twenty.

He *had* become a shadow of his father, albeit a more fastidious version. His mother, had she lived to see this day, would be ashamed—nay, *wounded*—by his debauched way of life. Viewing it from that perspective made him feel … unclean.

Richard was unsure what he was going to do with his unwanted enlightenment, but the answer was not at this infernal rout. Nor was he fit to keep company; he felt pallid and his hands were shaking with the shock of his sudden and unwelcome awareness.

He needed to be alone to gather his wits. A maelstrom of unpleasant emotions and regret racked his body.

Precisely why the girl's words had evoked his long-forgotten parent's presence from his murky youth, he was unclear. But evoked it had been, and he knew if his sweet, loving mother stood before him in this moment, he would have been unable to look her in the eye and defend the man he had become in her long absence from this world.

CHAPTER 1

*S*ophia was enjoying an early respite in the Moreland breakfast room. She liked to start her morning before her aunt and uncle appeared at a fashionably late hour, and sometimes her cousin joined her unless they had been up late at a ball the night before.

It was two days since the Astley ball, but Lily had not yet recovered from the late hours and frantic schedule of preparations her mother paced her through. Aunt Christiana was determined to see both her daughter and Sophia married off forthwith, this being her cousin's second Season and Sophia's fourth.

Arriving early meant she could enjoy the cheerful, well-lit room in quiet, with a cup of tea, a book, and a full plate of eggs, ham, and fruit.

She inhaled the aroma of the Indian leaves and looked up from her book to sip her tea and take in the decor, which always lifted her spirits.

The walls were covered in azure damask silk above white wainscoting. Over the white marble fireplace, a gilt mirror reflected the morning light from the sash windows into every nook and cranny of the room. It was so refreshing to savor these quiet moments alone before her uncle's family descended. Later in the day, her brother, Cecil, might make an appearance, but it was unlikely. The Morelands were hosting a ball that night, and he avoided polite events for the most part, favoring time spent gambling and carousing with his questionable friends.

It saddened Sophia to think of her older brother following in their father's footsteps. He had learned nothing from their father's death years earlier—brought about by the stress of his high-stakes wagers and excess drinking—nor from the grief that had overtaken her mother in the aftermath, resulting in an overdose of laudanum. Sophia's uncle, as her guardian, was vague on the details, which made her speculate whether her mother's death within just weeks of her father's was not so much accidental, as perhaps deliberate.

It was because of her parents' passing, more than ten years earlier, that she and her brother Cecil had come to live with Lord Hugh Abbott, her mother's brother, and his wife Lady Christiana Abbott, along with her two cousins. Her uncle had been generous, taking Cecil in along with Sophia despite no direct relationship to each other, Cecil having been the child of her father's first marriage. Papa left his estate bankrupt, and Cecil had still been a boy at school when tragedy had found them.

As a young girl, Sophia had determined she would never become her mother and had vowed to her cousin Lily on her very first night at the Abbott home that she would never marry a man who partook in gambling. Husbands could fritter away the wealth and happiness of a young woman while she had little or no recourse.

Certainly, Sophia did not harbor a desire to fall in love with a man who could not walk away from a wager. Indeed, she did not wish to fall in love with any man at all. Love led to heartbreak and leaving one's only child alone, relying on the kindness of family to offer protection from the harsh realities.

Just three more Seasons to endure before she would inherit the money from the trust directly, without a husband. With her dowry under her control, she could finally start her real life, which was why she sat refreshing herself on Shakespeare's work to prepare for her bluestocking performance at tonight's ball. She liked to quote lesser-known verses to turn away the more ardent bucks who might be tempted by her alluring dowry.

She licked a finger to turn a page, sipping her tea when, without warning, her aunt strode into the room. Sophia's heart promptly sank. She had hoped to avoid her single-minded Aunt Christiana this morning, who would have courtship and marriage foremost on her mind.

"She's in here, Lord Moreland!"

Sophia's heart sank further. Clearly she was cornered and would be forced to talk about marriage plans outnumbered two to one.

Lord Moreland hurried in, his tall form filling the doorway. He brushed his thick, graying hair back from his temple. "Good morning, Sophia. Enjoying your breakfast?"

Sophia gave a resigned smile as her aunt and uncle came to sit at the table set with a white tablecloth, silver, and cheerful blossoms in tiny vases. Two footmen came forward to serve the viscount and his wife with tea in delicate china cups.

Sophia dearly loved her adopted family, but they were frightfully conventional. Lord Moreland would do anything to protect his family, but in his mind that meant marrying Sophia off to a safe and proper gentleman while Lady Moreland was obsessed with her niece and daughter marrying gentlemen with the best connections. Being trapped alone with the two of them meant she could not escape The Conversation. The one that took place at the beginning of every Season and grew lengthier with each passing year as Aunt Christiana grew progressively more frantic to marry Sophia off before she was placed firmly on the shelf as—horror of horrors—a spinster!

Sophia appreciated their concern, but she had no intention of falling in line with society standards in order to be acceptable, so she had learned to be wily in her avoidance of the fate they planned for her. She did not wish to upset them, so did her best to not engage in direct conflict. This morning was turning out to be an opportunity to practice her diplomacy. Again.

She should have eaten her meal rapidly before finding another room to hide in.

Stupid move, Sophia, not predicting your aunt would choose the morning of the Moreland grand ball to challenge you!

Her aunt added sugar to her tea and stirred. Uncle Hugh stared at his tea with a perturbed expression, as if he was not sure what to do with it, probably reminiscing about his customary pot of morning coffee waiting for him in his study. Perhaps the viscountess had waylaid him in a similar manner to accosting Sophia at her breakfast. Aunt Christiana was not usually awake this early in the morning, so she must have planned ahead to waylay the two of them.

Her aunt sipped her tea, arching an elegant brown eyebrow pointedly in her husband's direction.

Uncle Hugh cleared his throat. He was to lead the way, then.

Keep calm, Sophia. Do not show any reaction and take your time responding so that you may lead the conversation to your desired outcome. With that reminder, she closed her leather tome and put it aside. Then she looked to her uncle expectantly.

"Now, see here, Sophia. It is high time we saw you settled in marriage with a household of your own to manage."

The words sounded rehearsed, which meant her aunt had made him practice what they were to say. Sophia repressed a grin.

She parried. "Why, Uncle, am ... am I no longer welcome in the Abbott household?" Sophia widened her eyes in dismay, letting her lower lip quiver ever so slightly.

Hugh Abbott's square, gentle face immediately fell. "Never, no, never, my dear niece. You are always welcome here. We love you like you are our own ..."

He fell silent as his hand came up to rub his jaw, groping for words to repair the inferred slight as he threw a panicked expression at his wife. Sophia watched, careful to hide any evidence of smugness. The first point might belong to her aunt for cornering her so early in the day, but the second point was hers alone for turning the tables.

Uncle Hugh was floundering; thus, her aunt would now be forced to lead the charge without much help from her husband, who believed he had hurt his beloved niece's feelings.

Such sentiment did not overtake Aunt Christiana. An elegant woman in her forties, she was a tough and determined opponent despite her lack of intellectual interests. Sophia knew not to underestimate her tenacity. Politely, she looked to her aunt, who was now scowling in displeasure at her husband, likely for being so easily manipulated. Squaring her jaw, she turned back to face her niece.

"Sophia, at the Astleys' the other night, Lord Saunton asked you to dance, but then deposited you right back with me. I know he is searching for a wife, and he admires intelligent women like yourself. He is ever so wealthy. I hear his estates are thriving and he never gambles. You must make an effort—"

"No!"

Sophia and her aunt both turned in surprise at her uncle's unexpected interjection. His face was a thundercloud of undisguised ire. "The earl is a scoundrel, and he will not lay a finger on someone under my protection. How could you allow them to be introduced, Christiana?"

Clearly her aunt and uncle had not sufficiently prepared for The Conversation. While her aunt responded in hissed tones to her husband's interrogation, Sophia grabbed the opportunity, her toast, and her book. Pushing her chair out, she made a hurried departure before they could turn their attention back to her. The handsome young footman, Thomas, stationed near the door, pressed his lips together to prevent a smile as she headed toward the threshold. Throwing him a saucy wink could not be helped, which caused the formidably large servant to snort a laugh. He threw up his hand to his mouth to pretend a sneeze when she exited into the corridor, a flurry of embroidered white skirts marking her path as she strode briskly away. Her aunt would have to find her another day.

* * *

RICHARD HAD CONCLUDED it was finally time for him to become a real man. Nay, a gentleman.

The morning after the Astley ball, he had accepted he was either on the road to becoming a changed man or he would become a grotesque caricature of the late earl. Realizing he was well on his way to becoming a shadow of his callous father—a true scapegrace who had driven his mother to her untimely death—was the prod he needed to evaluate what he wanted from his life, who he wanted to be.

Over the past two days, he had finally acknowledged that he had hurt his longtime friend and former betrothed, Annabel, with his cavalier treatment of her feelings, not to mention his rakish pursuits. Despite his newfound shame, he was now grateful that his cousin had rescued Annabel by stepping in to marry her in his stead. Richard may have railed against him at the time, but Philip had been a true gentleman. Annabel deserved a real marriage, but Richard would not have changed his ways to be worthy of her.

He must make changes in his life to become a man worthy of the title *gentleman*. To be a man his mother would be proud of. In light of which, he had begun to make these changes, but he had a lot of worthless behavior to atone for. He hoped he was up to the task, that it was not too late to correct his course and become a better man. He also hoped it was not too late to earn the regard of a worthwhile woman.

Miss Sophia Hayward of the cutting remarks was never far from his thoughts. Her forthright manner beyond the public eye reminded him of his prior relationship with Annabel before he had ruined their friendship. No one had ever delivered such a thorough dose of truth to him before. Granted, Miss Hayward was not aware of having done just that. She was a determined young woman, and he … If he could convince her to reveal her true self with him, perhaps …

The thought of seeing the intriguing lady again that evening was ever present, but that was hours away. In the meanwhile, he would meet with his man of business because it was time to put inquiries into motion. He needed to discover if his past immoral liaisons had produced any new responsibilities, despite the care he had taken to not father any bastards. He had never considered such a consequence, and now he was desperate to know. Regardless, he had a long string of apologies to give and financial recompense to pay.

21

Before his meeting, Richard rang for his butler in his study. He gave Radcliffe a list of the housemaids he had dallied with, much to his chagrin. Fortunately, there were only two girls from his own household, both of whom had flirted coyly with him before he had succumbed to temptation over the past year or two. Sadly, finding a woman to bed had never been problematic. Many were all too eager to throw themselves into his arms—or lap—and he had never been one to turn away a good, wholesome offer of that nature.

He informed Radcliffe that he would pay them each a handsome amount that would provide them with financial comfort and asked the butler to locate suitable new positions for the girls, if they so wished. The hawkish butler would bring the girls to him one at a time so he could meet with them to those ends.

His conscience told him he needed to take responsibility, and for his own sanity, he knew he must clean house if he was going to embark on a new way of life. Richard did his best not to wince during the discussion, but Radcliffe showed no reaction, the impeccable English butler that he was.

Or he already knows about the girls.

Richard steeled himself against this unwanted thought.

He intended to go courting in an honorable manner, so it would not do to have his past indiscretions dusting the banisters, reminding him he did not deserve this second chance he was striving for in order to become the man his mother would have been proud of.

Once he had met with the two maids and arrangements were made, his man of business had arrived for their meeting, where they were now ensconced for his fourth uncomfortable discussion of the day. Richard sat at his desk, pensive as he stared at his bottle-green wallpaper, and waited for his man of business to comprehend his instructions.

Johnson was staring at the list in his slender hand, visibly disconcerted. He was a competent man, integral to Richard's financial success, who looked inordinately like a banker with his bulbous forehead, meticulous black hair, and tidy, close-shaven beard lining his narrow jaw. They had worked together for some years, but Richard had just in that moment realized he had no knowledge of Johnson's life. Did the man have a wife? Dependents? Richard had always found that women and men alike were eager to please him, so he had never felt compelled to inquire after such things. Johnson was more than happy to work long hours, for which Richard paid him very well, but did he steal the man's time from his family?

"My lord, respectfully, I am going to repeat back my understanding of your instructions, so I am perfectly clear on what I am to do."

Richard cleared his throat. "Go ahead," he said hoarsely as he fidgeted with his tight cravat. Odd, the cravat had felt like a perfect fit when his valet had first tied it, but now it was a hangman's noose squeezing his throat shut.

Johnson continued in a strangled voice. "I am to seek, with the help of runners if needed, four housemaids with whom you—*ahem*—dallied over the past several years. Two of which you do not recall their names, but only their descriptions and their respective households where you encountered them. I am to establish their current circumstances and report back to you. We will then arrange a meeting so that you may ... apologize ..."

Richard filled in the awkward silence. "I will meet with them discreetly to apologize for my past behavior and offer them a financial settlement to recompense them for my disrespectful advances. If any of them are in untenable circumstances, we will establish what improvements they would like to make and assist each one to take the needed steps to set them up in improved circumstances."

Johnson looked aghast but managed to respond, "Then once these housemaids—"

Richard interjected, "I do feel that if I did ruin them, they would be the most immediately in need of assistance due to their lack of financial resources and connections."

Johnson cleared his throat. "Indeed. Then I am to continue the investigation and locate a further eight widows in order to determine their current situations, along with any consequences from your past … relationships."

"That is correct. I did not include any courtesans or any women I found to be more debauched than myself when we …"—*frigged*—"interacted, for I determined that I was not the cause of their ruin and that responsibility fell to someone else. After all, the list must have a finite end point, don't you think?" Richard gave a hollow laugh.

Johnson echoed him with his own lifeless laugh. "Yes, my lord. *After all*, an infinite list of amends would require infinite access to funds."

Richard and Johnson both looked away, each finding the furnishings in the room far more fascinating than the endless parade of women in Richard's past. Turned out, this redemption business was difficult. Needing another's aid in the redeeming was as mortifying as he had expected it to be when he first contemplated this restorative rite.

He had met with his cousin, the Duke of Halmesbury, for his advice early that morning. Fortunately, he had not encountered his former betrothed, Annabel, during his visit. Halmesbury was visibly appalled by his scrawled list of paramours, although Richard had not revealed their names. It had been a prop for their conversation regarding Richard's quest to take responsibility for his actions. Showing his cousin the actual list? *Now that*, he thought to himself with a healthy dose of irony, *would be the height of poor taste*.

Richard blushed as he thought of the earlier meeting and shifted uncomfortably in his chair. Really, his cravat felt awfully tight for some reason. Thankfully, the duke had given his wholehearted support of the endeavor and provided excellent guidance on what forms of amends would be appropriate for the various situations Richard might contend with.

Whether it be him or Johnson, one of them would need to break the stilted silence soon or this would become … decidedly embarrassing?

Taking a deep breath, Richard exhaled and spoke. "I need regular reports and, of course, you will let me know when I have a meeting to attend."

Johnson nodded, tucking the lists safely into his portfolio.

A thought suddenly struck Richard. "Johnson, instead of taking my lists with you, copy them out for yourself and leave me with the originals. I wouldn't want something to happen to them and have to make the lists again." He cleared his throat, and then, thinking to lighten the mood, continued with an attempt at a smile. "Please."

Johnson's eyes widened, apparently spooked. "Please?" he repeated back.

A fresh wave of shame hit Richard. "Please," he confirmed with firmness.

Egads, how pompous had he been with Johnson in the past that the man was astonished by Richard's rudimentary display of manners? This restoration of honor business was proving to have endless ramifications for his peace of mind, he feared. He was not sure he liked his new heightened awareness of what other people thought of his behavior. But it was imperative that his quest begin before he attended Viscount Moreland's ball tonight. He wanted to see Miss

Hayward, but he needed to be armed with some sort of defense when he next encountered the young lady.

* * *

SOPHIA STOOD at the edge of the ballroom, watching the colorfully attired dancers twirl in time to the music. She had never had high hopes for her first Season. She had vaguely hoped she might meet a gentleman and marry for love, then experience the newfound freedoms one attained as a married woman. However, the more her brother's poor choices over the past few years had mimicked those of their late father, the more Sophia had grown fearful of being trapped in a marriage such as her mother's. Her indistinct hopes had quickly turned into a determination to avoid marriage at all costs. Not that she could let her uncle and aunt know of her decision because the conversations would be endless and trying, so instead she had developed her two strategies for gently repelling would-be suitors.

Now into her fourth Season, it promised yet again to be evenings filled with dreary small talk, mindless conversations, and fine-crafted performances on her part. Parliament, in its infinite wisdom, had determined that the 1820 session would run longer than usual, stranding the peerage in London during the odorous summer, which she found terribly disheartening. Not to mention the gossip regarding the new king's plans for an ill-conceived trial of Queen Caroline. Hopefully, Sophia's slight anxiety at being forced to engage with sizable crowds would dwindle due to prolonged exposure as the year wore on.

Fluttering her dance card, she mused that the novelty presented to her when she first arrived was turning out to be useful to cool herself in the crowded ballroom. Aunt Christiana's friend, Lady Astley, had recently returned from

Vienna where such a *Programme du Ball* was the height of fashion, so now that word had spread about them, they would likely appear at all the events this Season as hostesses attempted to outdo each other.

Her thoughts were interrupted when she realized someone was standing beside her. She sighed, pasted on a smile, and turned to see who it was. It startled her to come face-to-face with Lord Saunton, undeniably handsome and unquestionably morally bankrupt. Her heart—and her smile—sank as he greeted her and reached for her card. Had she not already repelled the man at the Astleys' ball?

"I see your next dance is available," he said in his smooth baritone. "May I have this waltz with you?"

Belatedly, she curtsied. "Of course, my lord."

Lord Saunton led her to the center of the ballroom. As he moved into position and took up her hand in his much larger one, he spoke unexpectedly. "I have been thinking of you."

Sophia's head whipped up in surprise. She looked at him, stunned. Too startled to catch herself, she blurted her thought out loud. "Why?"

Lord Saunton laughed sheepishly. "You are more direct than I remember from our last dance."

Sophia inwardly cringed. "La, my lord, I am flattered you remembered our one dance together." She hastily executed a flirty flutter of her eyelids.

He grinned and chided, "Now, now, Miss Hayward, I preferred it when you were direct. It was not the dance that was unforgettable, it was your unfettered thoughts about my character that you shared with your friend on the balcony."

Sophia blanched as she frantically tried to recall what she had said to her cousin Lily about Lord Saunton that night.

"Do not be concerned; you gave me pause for thought. Consequently, I have made a decision. Several decisions.

And, as a result, I was thinking I would like to call on you tomorrow?"

Sophia shook her head. *No, no, no, no!* This was a horrible turn of events. Her aunt would literally skin her alive if she failed to accept such an invitation. From an earl, no less. This couldn't be. She could not get involved with an incorrigible rake. She couldn't get involved with anyone! During their first dance, she had made a point of boring the earl to avoid garnering his attentions. Now she was memorable? *It would not do. It would not do at all!*

"Sophia?" She winced at his intimate use of her name. In a lowered voice, he spoke again. "Sophia, please say yes. I will not embarrass you or tell your aunt if you do not agree." Wait! Was he reading her thoughts? "I would very much appreciate the opportunity to call on you, and I would like it to be with your permission."

She stared at him as they spun around another couple. "I dislike cads," she whispered.

Lord Saunton sighed. "That is fair. You are a beautiful, intelligent woman ..."

Sophia's jaw fell as she stared at him with rounded eyes. She was?

"... and I promise to treat you with the utmost respect if you allow me to call on you. Please grant me the honor of a little time in your company, as I would like to get to know you better."

"Why should I believe that? About respecting me, I mean?" She strived to sound confident, but she feared she merely sounded breathless.

He looked down into her eyes. "Subsequent to learning your critical thoughts on my character, I have decided to grant generous assistance to the *poor housemaids* you spoke of, and I am working to be a better man. I was wondering if you could help me."

Sophia was so astonished by his inappropriate words, she stumbled. His powerful hands corrected her so no one could see her slip. In befuddled shock, she heard herself speak. "That is splendid news, but given your promise not to inform my aunt …" She paused to await his confirmation. He gave a slight nod. "No, I would not like to be courted by you."

Disappointment flickered across Saunton's face, then determination. "I understand, and I have no wish to force my attentions on you. I did not expect this to be easy. However, I am resolute to learn more about you—the intriguing young woman who caused me to see the error of my ways. Tell me, Miss Hayward, do you believe it is possible for a man to change?"

Sophia thought for several moments about the unexpected question while he continued to move her across the floor. "He can get sick; he can get well. He can make poor decisions, and he can make astute decisions. I have seen men change for the worse, so logic dictates if a man can get worse, he must be able to become better."

Saunton looked down at her, a flash of respect in his eyes. "I am glad to hear you say that. I am yet a young man who has just awakened to discover himself guilty of selfish behavior. I have to believe that it is never too late for a man to change, or I will go mad. My cousin, Halmesbury, who partakes in philanthropic works, assures me that a man can make amends for his past in order to build a new future, so this is what I am doing. Do you believe in second chances, Miss Hayward?"

"I would never deny a man's right to try to correct his path." Sophia could not recollect a conversation of such a direct and intimate nature. They were discussing something truly meaningful, and the man was baring his soul to her, if he was to be believed.

"Then know your words had a profound effect on me,

and I would like—nay, I *need* you to promise me a dance at the Yardley ball so I may try once more to persuade you?"

His eyes searched hers, so much hope reflected in their emerald depths. Sophia's breath caught with the intensity of the moment as their eyes remained locked. The sounds of the ballroom faded away as she became lost in his gaze. No man had ever riveted their attention so fully on her, and it was throwing her, and what she thought she wanted, decidedly off-balance. She felt as alluring and powerful as he suggested with his words.

Swallowing hard, her voice a mere whisper, she heard herself say, without quite making the decision to say it, "I promise."

A genuine smile, displaying pearly white teeth, relaxed his face. Sophia could not help dropping her gaze to his full lips. Good Lord, he was compelling when he smiled with such warmth. While her heart careened out of control, she wondered what she had just done. *What harm could another waltz possibly do?* Feeling the increased beating in her chest, she worried that a single dance could do far more damage to her vow to stay unaffected than she could possibly conceive. Yet she could not bring herself to regret her decision to see him again.

CHAPTER 2

*A*fter her waltz with Lord Saunton, he returned her to her aunt's side, who watched him walk away with a calculating gleam in her chocolate brown eyes. Aunt Christiana was not a bad person. She was, however, ruthless in pursuing her goals, and her current goal was to see Sophia married to a well-connected gentleman. To be fair, Sophia's parents and their tragic end might have been to blame for inspiring her aunt's single-minded focus.

Standing in the crowded ballroom with people continuously brushing past stirred Sophia's customary anxiety within large gatherings, mounting to an uncomfortable level. Oddly, during her dance with Lord Saunton, she had not even noticed the other dancing couples despite their proximity. He had profoundly distracted her with his intimate conversation.

As her anxiety rose, she looked around for her cousin, thinking to escape to the terrace.

"Lily's dance card is filled the entire night."

Sophia started. The uncanny announcement from Lady

Moreland made Sophia wonder if she had spoken her thoughts out loud moments earlier.

"It would behoove you to make an effort, Sophia. You could be married before the end of this Season," her aunt continued. Sophia breathed a sigh of relief. She had not spoken out loud; her aunt was continuing The Conversation.

"Indeed, aunty. I need to visit the necessary and then I shall return."

Her aunt nodded, her eyes fixed on her daughter, who was dancing with Lord Baxton, a man with an obnoxious laugh whose love of snuff was nauseating. She hoped her cousin was holding her breath. Sophia quickly walked off toward the necessary, but when she was sure her aunt's attention was still focused on the dancers, she veered off down the corridor toward the library, which was her favorite room in their London home. She needed a moment alone to clear her thoughts and settle her nerves. *Blazes*, there were too many people in the Moreland townhouse tonight.

Once she reached the library, she quickly made for the annex in the back. Finding one of the library steps, polished mahogany about the size and shape of a large armchair, she sank down to the parquet floor to lean against the back of the solid furnishing which would hide her from any guests entering the room.

She drew a deep, calming breath and closed her eyes, enjoying a quiet moment alone with the sounds of the orchestra dampened by the distance and thick walls. Here in the library, she could once more hear her own thoughts.

Her encounter with Lord Saunton came to her mind as she thought about what he had said. He was making reparations to former paramours and seeking to change his character. A large undertaking for such a man, all because he had overheard her mockery on the balcony. It seemed incredible.

Why would her words affect him to that degree? Would his change of heart last, or was this some sort of momentary whim that would pass by the end of the week? He was known to make sound financial decisions and, according to rumor, had tripled his family's fortune since inheriting the title while he was a young man at Oxford. That would imply that if he truly decided to change, he had the intelligence and fortitude to do so. But he claimed she had been the impetus for such a life-changing decision? Barely anyone knew she existed, other than her immediate family, and no one had accused her of inspiring them before today. Was it truly possible for her to have influenced such an important man? It was heady to consider that her words had created such an impact. She was usually shielding herself from society; few had heard her voice her true opinions, and it was gratifying to think she had inspired a rake to change his morals.

Sophia heard approaching footsteps. She quickly moved to tuck her skirts in behind the enormous steps. It would not do to be caught alone in the library, which could start a scandal depending on who was entering the room. Luckily, the annex was poorly lit at this time of night, and she was unlikely to be spotted from the main room.

"Hayward, why the hell did you have me come tonight? I am not even on the damned guest list, and when Lord Moreland saw me enter, he was glaring at me in a most unwelcoming manner."

Sophia frowned in confusion. Her brother was there tonight?

"Leech, I beg your indulgence. I have news that will benefit both of us greatly. Did you happen to see my sister?"

Lord Leech? Sophia's eyebrows shot up in surprise. She saw the man infrequently at social events. A scrawny, sallow man with unkempt brown hair and a thick mustache, he flaunted a wicked reputation in that he had married two heiresses over the past few years, both of whom had coincidentally died within months of the nuptials under suspicious circumstances. He was either a very unlucky man, or, more likely, a despicable villain who had managed to get rid of his wives in favor of their fortunes, but left no evidence of his foul activities. None openly accused the lord of murder, but many whispered about it in speculation.

Unfortunately, Leech had some powerful friends, so he still moved within society despite his gruesome reputation as a possible wife-killer. On the other hand, fathers were no longer offering up their daughters to the fortune hunter in exchange for a title.

"The tall girl with the reddish-blonde hair and unbecoming white gown standing with your aunt? She looks worth a turn in the gardens. What about her?"

Sophia's lip curled in disgust at the thought of accompanying this reprobate to the gardens.

"That's her. Miss Sophia Hayward. A right spoilt little princess. It happens I was in my uncle's study and stumbled on some interesting documents."

"Stumbled? More like you searched his office. Gambling debts getting a little too deep to manage, Hayward?"

"Nothing I can't deal with. Now let me tell you what I uncovered. The late Viscount Moreland, Sophia's grandfather, apparently did not trust my father. When the marriage contracts for Sophia's mother were negotiated, he made the rather unusual move to establish a trust for the new Mrs. Hayward and any children resulting from the union. As it was in a separate trust, neither my father nor any of his creditors could make any claim on it. The old man ensured that his daughter and his grandchildren would be taken care of irrespective of my father's financial management skills, which were very poor because he was a degenerate gambler."

Sophia threw a hand up to cover her mouth for fear she would chuckle. Her brother had the temerity to call their father a degenerate gambler? That was rich considering his strong-arm tactics to seize her pin money for his own gambling habits.

"The point is, Sophia is the only grandchild from the union and the old viscount must have been overly focused on preventing my father from controlling the funds because it did not state the protections for his grandchildren beyond that. It would appear that his solicitors did not think past the initial issue they were addressing since, from what I understand, the entire trust will go to her husband if she marries, which so far there has been no risk of. The silly chit can't attract a man." Sophia narrowed her eyes at her brother's nasty words. That was deliberate on her part, *thank you very much*!

Leech responded, "How much are we talking about?"

"Fifty thousand pounds."

Sophia clamped both hands over her mouth to prevent the exclamation that struggled to burst forth from her astonishment. The two men were both silent.

Finally, Leech whistled through his teeth. "That's incredible. The Abbott family must be plump in the pocket. Why has someone not snatched her up, then?"

"The Abbotts are very protective, and they have kept the size of her dowry a secret. Uncle Hugh must have an abhorrence of fortune hunters after my father ran through the marriage settlement and gambled all his income and assets away before dropping dead during a high-stakes card game."

"And Moreland's only sister died of an *accidental* laudanum overdose because of her weak nerves after that incident." Sophia winced at the sarcastic emphasis as Leech implied anything but. "Pity the mother passed after birthing a brat, or you might have had grounds to argue that the blunt should drop on you as the heir of your father's estate."

Sophia shivered, icy tendrils of fear coursing through her veins. They were speaking about her never being born, and she suspected the idea of her not existing was part of the plan to be discussed. She had always known there was not much love lost between her and her brother, but it hurt to learn how little regard he had for her.

"If I were to help you marry her, I would want a guarantee that you would split the dowry with me."

"What sort of help?"

"I can introduce you. And, when the time is right, I can let you into the house so you can take the little baggage to Gretna Green. I read the terms of the trust, and there is nothing the viscount can do once she is legally married. The trust will be paid out because she is the only remaining beneficiary."

That her brother would ally with the man to see her wed, with the possibility of her premature death in the bargain, spoke to how little Cecil cared for his younger sister. Sophia struggled to calm her breathing as terror twisted in her stomach. There were few things that frightened her, but her brother and his dedication to gambling, the lengths he would go to for money—there was no question he could follow through with the plan he was suggesting to Lord Leech.

She listened carefully as they reached an agreement about how to exploit her, and there was no doubt in her mind that her freedom and her life were at risk. She had learned years earlier that her older brother, who bore a marked physical resemblance to their father but did not wield his charm or pleasant manner, was ruthless in taking advantage of her. Any hopes she still held that one day they would repair their relationship were well and truly laid to rest.

When she had first come out in society and started

receiving a larger allowance, Cecil had cornered her in her room. Twisting her arm behind her back until tears filled her eyes from the pain, he had demanded that she hand her coin over. She finally gave him the reticule hidden in her dressing table. He took it along with the silver-backed brush and mirror that had belonged to her mother. When he walked out the door, she had called out that Uncle Hugh would not be pleased. He had immediately walked back in, grabbed her by the shoulder with one large hand, and punched her hard in the stomach with the other, which had dropped her to her knees as she wheezed for air. "If Uncle Hugh hears about this, you will regret it, little sister. More than you ever regretted anything before this day."

Sophia had believed him. A direct confrontation with Cecil would never have worked. He was too large, ruthless, and without conscience; his drinking had already mottled his skin as a very young man, and his eyes showed no signs of life in their reddened, watery depths. Her sibling was a man trapped in liquor and ungodly pursuits who lived only for himself. He was on his best behavior with Uncle Hugh because the viscount paid him a quarterly allowance, so the Abbott family had not noticed how low he had sunk. The Abbotts' heir, Aidan, might have noticed the decline, but the two men spent little time together. Cecil had been at Harrow at the time of Papa's death before moving on to Cambridge, while her cousin had attended Eton and then Oxford, which for some reason beyond Sophia's understanding meant they did not have much in common.

Unwilling to be a victim, she had quickly learned to hide any items that she refused to lose to his vices, and hoarded the majority of her pin money in her hiding places. The next time he came for her, she handed her reticule over without complaint, and when he questioned the value of the coins contained within, she blamed her aunt for insisting she purchase gloves and accessories for her wardrobe. Fortunately, her brother had not credited that his little sister could be lying, nor did he possess a firm grasp on what ladies paid for their trifles, so he accepted this after tossing her room for any items of value. She learned to outwit her nasty brother without him becoming wise to it. Eventually he left her alone as the amount of blunt to be gained from her became too little to bother with.

Now, however, there was a promise of twenty-five thousand pounds to lure his interest. There was no possibility that anything would distract or dissuade him from such a prize. Sophia knew she was in serious jeopardy as she listened to the men leave and debated how long she should wait before she should risk leaving her hiding place to rejoin her aunt. Her future was in imminent threat, and she would need to devise a plan, but first she must return to that infernal ball.

* * *

"WHAT DOES your brother think he is doing?" hissed Lady Moreland. Sophia looked at her aunt in puzzlement, then followed the direction of her gaze. Cecil, with Lord Leech in tow, was weaving through the bystanders on the edge of the ballroom in their direction.

"It looks like Cecil is going to introduce Lord Leech to you. You either must dance with him or make an excuse and sit out the rest of the evening. Let me see your dance card, Sophia." Her aunt sounded desperate as she took up the card tied to Sophia's wrist, fanning it out and then audibly groaning when she saw the empty slots.

"Listen here, girl, you injured your ankle and are sitting out the rest of the evening!" Aunt Christiana whispered intensely as she searched Sophia's eyes for assent, squeezing her arm in desperation. "Yes?"

Sophia breathed a sigh of relief. There would be no support from her family for Cecil's attempts to bring her and Lord Leech together. "Yes."

A lively country dance was in full swing when the two men reached them. Cecil introduced the unsavory gentleman, and Lady Moreland did her best rendition of a polite but disapproving mama, which both men ignored.

Once pleasantries were exchanged, Lord Leech turned his malevolent eyes to Sophia. They were a strange amber color, nearly yellow, that reminded her of a snake. His strange eyes flicked over her face and bosom in a manner that made her skin crawl, before his gaze returned to hers. The icy depths contained no hint of humanity as he reached for the dance card tied to her wrist. "Miss Hayward, your brother's description of your beauty does you no justice. Shall we take a turn around the ballroom?"

Sophia pulled her arm away, not wanting to feel his touch. "La, my lord! I am so flattered by your esteemed attention. Alas, I just turned my ankle a few minutes ago and I can feel it swelling as we speak. I am afraid there will be no more dancing for this evening."

A muscle ticked along Lord Leech's jaw as if he clenched his teeth. "How unfortunate. Perhaps I could have the honor of a dance with you at the Yardley ball, then?"

"We shall see," interjected Lady Moreland. "We will not know any more about the injury until the physician is called. Best not to make any plans."

Leech's eyes twitched to look back at her chaperone. "Of course, my lady."

Bowing deeply, Leech and Cecil made their departure. Both Sophia and her aunt exhaled in relief as they walked away.

Lady Moreland shook her head. "I am deeply concerned about Cecil if he is spending time with someone such as Lord Leech. What could they possibly share in common?"

"Nothing worthwhile," Sophia said tightly, her stomach tied up in knots of fear. "Nothing worthwhile."

CHAPTER 3

*R*ichard watched from his study window while Caroline Brown descended from the carriage he had sent for her. He guessed this was her first time visiting London, at his request, and based on her expression, she found the city overwhelming. She had probably never seen so many people, buildings, horses, heard so much sound, smelled so much humanity. London was more … everything. She appeared quite out of sorts as she stared up at the four towering stories of Balfour Terrace, stretching five bays wide. Visibly gulping, she headed toward the servants' staircase.

"Mrs. Brown?" Although the window muffled the words, he could just hear them. His man, Long, called her by her courtesy title, a privilege of being a housekeeper in a respectable household, but to Richard's knowledge she was not a Mrs. *Merely a secretly fallen woman because of unfortunate encounters with me, so mayhap some similarity with married women, albeit only in the bedroom.*

Long assisted his man of business with Richard's vast holdings, and he had sent his loyal agent to find the former

41

maid at the home of her employer days earlier. His man would have invited her to London for an audience with Richard, who had been expecting their arrival for some hours.

Out in the street, Caroline looked back at Mr. Long in question.

"Lord Saunton has invited you as an honored guest." Mr. Long held up his hand to indicate the way up the steps toward the front door. Richard could just make out her eyes widening in surprise as she stood undecided. "Please, come this way, Mrs. Brown."

Fidgeting nervously, the young woman most likely pondered her low status while she considered the front door. A common servant who had worked hard and raised her station to that of housekeeper in a doctor's household after Richard had nearly destroyed her future two years earlier. She was fortunate that after betraying Miss Annabel Ridley, her mistress had seen fit to find her a new position. Annabel would have been well within her rights to dismiss the kitchen maid without a second thought.

Richard could only assume the young woman to be confused by his invitation, but he had sent Long because the man could be most persuasive. He wondered how she had organized her affairs to accompany Mr. Long to the great city of London. Truly, she would have no idea why she was here, and she must believe that she had no business walking in the front door of a fine home such as Balfour Terrace in the famous Mayfair district.

"Mrs. Brown, the earl insisted you are to be treated as a guest. He will be most displeased with me if he learns you entered through the servants' entrance."

The young woman reluctantly rejoined him and ascended the steps out of Richard's view. Long reappeared shortly, descending the steps toward the carriage.

"Mr. Long?" Richard heard Caroline call out in an alarmed tone.

Her companion was halfway down the front steps. He stopped to look back.

"Are you not joining me?"

"Nay, Mrs. Brown. I will return to escort you back to Filminster, but I have errands to run. The earl and his staff will take good care of you in my absence."

Richard assumed the woman must have looked anxious from the cajoling that followed that statement. "Don't worry, Mrs. Brown. I think you will be pleased to hear what his lordship has to say." Long gave an encouraging smile. Evidently, he succeeded in allaying her fears because he nodded a goodbye and continued his descent.

Richard turned back to his desk, anxiously checking his cravat and tailcoat. He could not deny he was nervous about this meeting.

A few moments later, there was a knock at the door. "Come in."

Radcliffe entered. Behind the butler, Richard could see Caroline peering into his study with an expression that mirrored his own internal ferment. "Mrs. Brown is here to see you."

The young woman grimaced behind the manservant before being shown into the study. She came to a halt in the middle of the lavish room, looking around in bewilderment.

Richard pasted a smile on his lips and stepped around his desk to give a short bow. In a surreal moment, he thought about Caroline's perspective—what she might be thinking as her eyes flittered over the bottle-green wallpaper, the white trim, the polished mahogany desk and matching shelves. Her gaze rested for a moment on the set of plump wingback armchairs, upholstered in a cheerful ivory fabric patterned with rich greens, reds, and golds, before skittering to fall to the rug, which she stared at pensively.

"Mrs. Brown?"

Caroline whipped her head back to him. Richard was careful not to smile the characteristic glib smile he used to seduce women, but schooled his face to display concern.

"Mrs. Brown, are you all right?"

"What am I doing here?" she whispered.

Richard looked over her shoulder. "Radcliffe, please bring tea and refreshments. Mrs. Brown must be exhausted after days on the road. Mrs. Brown, please take a seat?"

Carefully, he took her by the arm and steered her to the seating area, urging her to sit. She plopped down in a daze. After a moment, she untied her bonnet, placed it on the end of the table between them, and smoothed her hair with a trembling hand.

"I am sorry for the suspense, Mrs. Brown. When you hear what I have to say, it will be worth it, I assure you." With that, he took the seat opposite, his fingers drumming on the arm of his chair while he collected his thoughts.

"I summoned you to London because I wanted to make my ... apologies ..."

Caroline frowned in confusion.

"First, please, tell me how you have been since I last saw you?"

Caroline cleared her throat. "I am ... fine, I suppose. Miss Ridley—I mean, the Duchess of Halmesbury—and Mrs. Harris assisted me to find a new position as a maid with the local doctor after she ... caught us ... *meeting* ... in the stables." She mirrored his own state of agitation with her awkward mumbling. They both well knew the disreputable circumstances of their last encounter. "Since that time, the doctor's housekeeper retired, so I was promoted to running his household. So I guess everything has worked out for the best."

"I am so glad to hear that." Richard did not reveal that he had gathered this information on her before the meeting. She was clearly distressed. "I wanted to apologize to you … for my seduction … or perhaps a better word would be my interruption of your life."

Caroline looked at the earl, aghast. "Apologize, my lord?"

He cleared his throat uncomfortably, tugging at his cravat. "It was not well done of me, seducing you under your mistress's nose. And, after she found us, I did not step in to take any responsibility for you. If Miss Ridley had not decided to find you the new position, you would have been destitute, and I am profoundly embarrassed regarding my behavior with you."

"I … see. I cannot blame you for the decisions I made, my lord." Caroline dropped her head, shame reflected on her face. What he had done to this young woman, it was her secret burden to bear that she was a fallen woman. Fortunately, those who knew about her trysts with him had elected to keep the affair private.

"That is generous, but I do blame myself. I had considerable experience that I brought to bear when I seduced you. Not to sound conceited, but few women would have resisted."

"I see. While it is very kind of you to apologize, is that why I am here in London? It seems to me you could have sent me a letter to state your apology and spared yourself a great deal of trouble bringing me here."

"No … I wanted to apologize in person and to make an attempt at amends. I wish to make reparations … in the form of funds. Funds you could use to change your current circumstances or could be a means to your retirement in the future. I was thinking of putting two hundred pounds in your name."

Caroline gasped. Richard knew that two hundred pounds was a fortune for a woman in her position. His earlier meetings with similar women from his past had proved quite—

"No."

No? What on earth? "No?"

"No. It would make me feel like a kept woman. I did not engage in relations with you for funds."

Richard's chest tightened in dismay. Would she not allow him to make amends? This was unexpected. He needed to assist her in some way to free his soul, but— "But Mrs. Brown, I want to do this. To take responsibility for my actions as I should have done—"

"No. I accept your apology, but I need something else ... not a payoff."

Oh, thank the Lord! She had a request of some sort. She was not merely refusing a small fortune.

Richard leaned forward eagerly. "There is something I can assist you with?"

"I do not wish to sound presumptive, but Miss Ridley and I were friends. Did you know that?"

He frowned. "I did not."

"I came to work in her household as a girl. Miss Ridley gifted me a book, and when she discovered I could not read, she taught me. She also taught me numbers and showed me how to manage an accounting book. She purchased me fabrics, and she prepared me ... to follow my dreams."

"Dreams?"

"Yes, milord. Miss Ridley promised me that once she was married to you, she would help me with an investment using her pin money. She was to assist me in purchasing a dressmaking shop. We discussed finding one in a market town. I could not ... I could not believe I betrayed her in the manner that I did. It was … so utterly foolish. I have worked hard since the stable incident to prove to myself that I was ever worthy of her support. Now you say you want to make amends. *That* is the path you interrupted."

Richard sat back in his armchair, stunned. Not only had he betrayed Annabel and ruined a vulnerable young woman in the process, he'd also permanently severed the close friendship shared by the two women and laid waste to all of their hopes and plans. He really was a blackguard of the worst sort. In light of the new information, he was truly humbled by Annabel's integrity in doing right by her former friend after the incident and respected Caroline's current bravado.

"You wish to own a dressmaker's?"

"I do, my lord."

"Well played, Mrs. Brown."

She gave a nervous smile in response.

He thought about it for several moments. "I will task my man of business to work with Mr. Long to locate an appropriate shop, and I will loan you the funds to purchase it. The loan will be interest-free, and you can repay me from your profits. Will that do?"

Sheer joy blossomed, a smile spreading across her face while tears welled in her eyes. "That will do," she croaked out.

Richard cleared his throat, his eyes prickling in response, which he furtively blinked away. "I am so happy to hear that. Thank you for the opportunity to remedy this, Mrs. Brown. And for agreeing to come to London to see me. I am … quite heartened to have this chance to talk with you."

Caroline appeared too overcome to speak. She nodded in acknowledgment and looked relieved to hear Radcliffe return with the tea tray. Richard realized she needed time to compose herself after making her impudent demand. He was infinitely grateful she had agreed to come, and even more grateful that she was allowing him to assist her in her dreams after the damage he had wrought on her young life. Women were so vulnerable within their society, and since his rude awakening, he had been battling with self-loathing for his predatory behavior. With each of these meetings, his conscience was eased, and he looked forward to the day he no longer had to squirm in discomfort for his callous and depraved past.

Speaking with Radcliffe to give her the time she needed, Richard felt well pleased with her audacious negotiation in response to his proposal to rectify his past mistakes with her. Caroline was going to own a dressmaking shop, and he was responsible for improving a young woman's circumstances instead of worsening them. Richard observed from the corner of his eye when she did a happy bounce on her chair at the unexpected turn of events and smiled in secret pleasure to have done something so momentous for a woman he had wronged.

Malevolent yellow eyes stared into her own as she fought for breath from the crushing weight on her chest. Struggling, she tried to scream, but no sound escaped her lips. "You are all mine now, Sophia," whispered Lord Leech while panic assailed her. "Soon we will reach Gretna Green ..."

Sophia sat up in a cold sweat. It was the fourth time tonight, not to mention the previous three nights of sweat-soaked nightmares. Panting for air, her hand sought under the pillow on the other side of the bed. When her hand made contact with the cold steel of the knife she had been bringing to bed since the night of the Moreland ball, she blew a sigh of relief. Taking hold of the knife, she quietly slipped from her bed to check her room once more. First, she padded over to the door to verify that it was locked and the chest she had dragged in front of it was still there. Then she felt carefully in the dark to verify that there were still three china figurines carefully balanced along the edge to fall, shatter, and raise her from her sleep if anyone tried to break through the door.

Once she was certain the entrance was barred, she carefully made her way to the windows across the room. She checked that each one was securely locked, each with a figurine placed on the ledge to fall and sound the alarm if Cecil or Leech attempted to climb through one of the windows.

This was her new nightly routine. She stayed awake until all hours securing her room and then checking and rechecking it. She was exhausted beyond anything she had ever experienced before, but she was not going to wake up a trussed-up victim in Leech's carriage headed north to the Scottish border.

Sophia climbed back into her bed, her eyes wide open in fear.

The problem she now faced was that Cecil could enact his plan anytime. Now, six months from now, or even next year, and it would still work in his favor. It was not whether Sophia could hold out and defend herself. Eventually, she would let her guard down, and Cecil only needed one opportunity to snatch her along with a willing conspirator, and her freedom would be gone forever. And, considering who his current co-conspirator was, her life could very well be forfeit. As long as she remained unwed, she remained a target for such a plot.

If she approached her uncle to inform him of Cecil's plans, the viscount would likely insist she immediately marry someone suitable to secure her safety. Or, in an effort to protect her, her freedoms would be further curtailed. And, if she did not marry, there was little to stop her brother from continuing to plot her abduction to Gretna Green because there was nothing her uncle could do to prevent the dowry from being paid out in the event of her marriage. As Cecil had figured out, it was possible consent was not required for his plan to proceed. Sophia was hazy on the details, but from what she understood, all her brother needed was a wedding in Scotland conducted by someone willing to turn a blind eye to any reluctance on the part of the bride.

None of these possible outcomes were appealing. The common thread was her lack of control and her inability to choose her own course in life.

For the first time in her life, she wished ... she wished ... she had a protector. A husband who did not care about her large dowry, but who cared for *her*. Someone who did not imbibe like her father or her brother, and who possessed his own wealth so did not require hers. Someone who could make her feel safe. Someone who could stand up to, and protect her from, her despicable brother. Someone of her own choosing.

Her thoughts wandered over to a certain devilish earl. Did Saunton drink to excess? Would he be willing to stop drinking altogether if she requested it? Surely he had little interest in her dowry? From all accounts, he had walked away from last Season's wealthiest debutantes after a single dance because he had not found what he was looking for.

Now he was expressing his interest in her, and the amount of her dowry was a closely guarded secret. Perhaps she should hear him out, as he had requested. She did not think she could handle many more nights like this one. Her nerves were shot, and it had only been four nights and three days. She was uncertain how much longer she could live under this strain, and thus far, she had failed to think of any alternative plan to evade her brother's plotting.

* * *

RICHARD WAS anxious to see the young woman again. He had thought of Miss Sophia Hayward many times since their last dance together. The young woman of sharp mind and tongue who was so different from the women of his past. There was a quality about her that called to him. An intuition that he would never grow bored with this unusual creature.

He stood on the steps descending into the Yardley ballroom and sought her fair, oval face and distinctive hair coloring in the crowd of dandies, debutantes, and watchful mamas.

He did not know what it was about the young woman that stirred his senses, but since that night on the balcony, his thoughts kept returning to her. He wanted to touch her face with his bare hand. Take possession of her full lips and discover if she was as honest in her kisses as she was in her brutal assessment of his character.

Finally he found her, standing across the ballroom near the terrace doors with her aunt standing by her side. He descended the steps to make his way over to her. Perhaps she would be more receptive to his suit this evening.

* * *

SOPHIA SCANNED THE BALLROOM, looking for Lord Saunton. Would he be there as he had promised? She felt quite desperate to see him after another restless night. She needed to find out if he was serious in his interest. Her very life might well depend on that interest.

As her eyes skimmed through the crowd, she suddenly spotted her brother. And Lord Leech. They were headed in her direction. If she wanted to dance with Saunton tonight, she could not refuse a dance from Lord Leech, because she would be required to sit out every subsequent dance if she turned him down. Desperate, she stepped behind Aunt Christiana to pencil Lord Saunton on to her dance card. Then, before she had second thoughts, she penciled him in for the next dance after that. Now she just needed to find him before Leech found her.

"Aunt?"

Lady Moreland turned to her. Sophia gave a quick nod of her head, and Lady Moreland looked in the direction she gestured and hissed. "Leech is headed toward us! Go to the necessary." Sophia looked at her in surprise. "Now, go now! They have nearly reached us."

Sophia briskly walked away to find the necessary. She would stay in there all night if she needed to, but then she would miss Lord Saunton. Perhaps she should just keep walking the room until she found him? Mind made up, she started a circuit of the room, glancing back to ensure she knew where Cecil and Leech were. She was startled to find them right behind her. Panicked, she attempted to dart forward, but her brother stepped out in front of her, his bloated face red from his exertions to catch up with her and his reddish-blond hair lank with perspiration. He pulled a handkerchief from his pocket to dab at his damp forehead.

"There you are, Sophia dear! Lord Leech is quite adamant that he must have a dance with you."

Sophia paled but kept her face composed as she glanced over to Leech. She curtsied, noticing that Leech's yellow eyes were as sinister in real life as they appeared to her in her dreams. He gave a cursory bow. "Miss Hayward, I have not stopped thinking of you since we met. May we take a turn around the room while we await the next dance?"

"I would love to, but I need to refresh myself and then my next dance is already promised, my lord."

Leech looked skeptical. He reached out and grabbed her

wrist before she could prevent him. Looking down at her dance card, he looked up at her and sneered. *Sneered!*

"Lord Saunton? I do not believe he is even here tonight, and you are certainly not his sort. Are you sure you did not write in his name yourself?"

"Quite sure, Leech." Saunton's deep velvet voice interrupted. Sophia nearly wept with relief when his handsome face appeared beyond Leech's shoulder. Brushing past the bristling gentleman, he came to stand by her side and bowed.

"Are you ready, Miss Hayward?"

She gave a nod. More ready than she had ever been.

Leech was not so easily dissuaded. "I will see you for the next dance, Miss Hayward."

Saunton flicked his eyes over Leech in a disparaging fashion. "I don't think so, old chap. The next dance is mine, too. Miss Hayward is quite captivating, and I have concluded that I am ... well, captivated, I suppose. And then it will be time for supper, I believe."

Leech gasped and Sophia's heart quickened at the news that Saunton intended to dance with her twice. It confirmed he was serious in his pursuit of her, practically announcing to the world that he had found the young woman he might wed. A third dance would be, for all intents and purposes, announcing the nuptials. Inhaling deeply, Sophia took the arm Lord Saunton offered her and accompanied him farther into the ballroom.

"You said the chit had no earnest suitors, Hayward!" Leech's low hiss made it to her ears, causing Sophia to smile widely as Saunton took hold of her hand and placed his gloved fingers on her waist. She had never been so happy to see any man before.

As the waltz began, Saunton looked down in her face. "If Leech is attempting to court you, there must be a sizable dowry involved?"

Sophia bit her lip, unsure of what to say.

"You wrote my name in? Was it because you promised me or to avoid Leech?"

"Both. I have been waiting for you, but you never appeared."

Saunton's eyes flickered away. "I ... was getting up my nerve. I was trying to think how to persuade you to allow me to call on you tomorrow. Now we are engaged for two dances, which will cause society tongues to wag in speculation."

"I already decided to accept your request if you made it again."

He looked incredulous, but pleased. "You did?"

"I want to learn more about this crusade to redeem yourself. Does it include drink?"

"You mean spirits?"

Sophia nodded.

"I only drink spirits occasionally. When my betrothed married the Duke of Halmesbury, I enjoyed a last hurrah and then mostly lost interest. I was never that fond of the consequences of drinking, and I find I like to keep my mind clear."

"Truly?"

"Truly. Does that make me a more desirable suitor?"

"It does."

Saunton's distinctive green eyes blazed. "So, I am to call on you tomorrow? And we will talk? I mean ... talk openly?"

Sophia inclined her head. "We are well beyond propriety, are we not?"

Saunton's face broke into the warm expression from the night of their last dance, his delight palpable as he gracefully led her through the steps of the waltz. Sophia's heart skipped a beat as her gaze narrowed on his sculpted lips and she wondered ... what would it feel like to kiss such a handsome rogue? Saunton must have read her thoughts because his gaze grew heated, falling to her own lips in response.

Nervous, she flicked the tip of her tongue to moisten them, and was taken aback to hear a low growl emitted by the earl while his eyes riveted to the path her tongue followed. It would appear the gentleman fostered a sincere interest in her as a woman. The knowledge caused a tingling response to shoot through her body, her nipples tightening uncomfortably at the thought of his mouth on hers.

Sophia was quickly becoming accustomed to the idea of this man taking on the role of her protector, now that she accepted it was a credible escape from her dilemma.

CHAPTER 4

The following morning, Sophia walked into the drawing room with Nancy in tow. Saunton's eyes flicked toward the elderly maid as he bowed to greet her. "Miss Hayward, I was thinking we might take a drive through the park."

As Sophia curtsied, she smiled and shook her head. "Nay, Lord Saunton, I arranged for us to talk in private, as you indicated we had intimate matters to discuss today."

Lord Saunton narrowed his eyes in confusion as he stared pointedly at the old woman beside her.

"Nancy is hard of hearing, aren't you, Nancy?" Sophia directed her question to the short maid with the full head of gray hair pinned under her mob cap in disarray.

"Too fancy? I don't think so, miss. I think you look like a perfect young lady!" Nancy responded with a perplexed expression.

"Nancy was my uncle's nursemaid when he was a boy, and he is very attached to her. Fortunately for us, she does not wish to retire, so the household accommodates her limited communication abilities," Sophia explained before raising her voice. "NANCY, WHY NOT SIT HERE AND WORK ON YOUR MENDING?"

"Bending? I don't really do much bending anymore, miss."

Sophia blinked, her head beginning to ache at the strain of talking to the beloved but exasperating maid she had sought out thirty minutes earlier to attempt to explain that she would chaperone a visit.

Nancy blinked back, and several seconds of silence ensued before she said, "I think I shall sit here in this chair by the door and do some mending."

Sophia beamed her approval, nodding enthusiastically before any further conversation was encouraged. Turning back to Saunton, she saw his handsome countenance relax into a relieved expression. He stepped forward to hand her a bouquet of hothouse flowers with a bow. She smiled in pleasure at the gesture, thanking him warmly. He gestured to the seating area. "Shall we, Miss Hayward?"

Accepting his invitation, she strode forward to take a seat on the hard, silk-covered sofa and primly folded her hands into her lap—the picture of maidenly modesty. She had no intention of being proper this morning, but if Nancy looked up, she would not find any cause for alarm.

As Saunton flicked the tails of his wine-colored tailcoat to take his seat, Sophia could not help but notice that the infamous rake boasted a masculine form that was near perfect, with a flat stomach and powerful thighs encased in buckskin breeches. His black and brown Hessians were polished, his shoulders broad, and his silky, curling hair brushed his white stock. She had heard him compared to Lord Byron, but she personally thought Saunton had a friendlier and more approachable demeanor than the arrogant poet she had heard tales about.

"Tell me about your crusade of amends, my lord."

"I have been meeting with the women of my past to apologize and make reparations. It has been unexpectedly uplifting to do so." Sophia was uncertain what else to ask on this subject, so she moved on.

"Are there any children from these past encounters?"

Saunton grimaced. "So far, I have been fortunate. The precautions I took were effective."

Sophia wondered what precautions one could take to prevent children, but she refrained from asking, not wanting to reveal her ignorance.

"And you are seeking to court me with a view to marry?"

Saunton's eyes glowed with a fierce hunger. "I am."

"Are you sure ... I mean, about me? You barely know me. How do I know you won't lose interest next week when you meet another woman?"

He frowned at this. "Never. I have only been interested in marrying one woman before you, and I have been seeking a wife for some years now. You are not like anyone I have met before, and now that I have started on this road, I will not be turning back. Once I make up my mind about something, very little will dissuade me from a course that I have chosen for myself, and you ... you fascinate me."

Sophia felt her cheeks warm with pleasure. To be the single-minded focus of such an attractive man ... it was overpowering. She fidgeted in her seat as heat pooled in the region of her lower belly. "We do not have much time, so tell me why I should accept you?"

Saunton leaned forward in his seat, his face earnest. "I will allow you your freedom. As my countess, you may do anything you want and I will support you, as long as you are at my side."

"Anything? What if I do not want to host balls?"

"Then we shall forgo balls. Is that what you want?"

"I am not fond of crowds, so I would prefer to hold

dinner parties and small events. What if I wanted to write a book?"

"Then you shall write a book. Do you have one in mind?"

"I do not. What if I wanted to hold salons and invite intellectuals to our home?"

"Then I shall greet our guests and take part in your discussions. Whatever your heart desires. My only requests are that our marriage be a true partnership and that you provide me with an heir."

"Why should I believe you?"

Saunton chuckled, sitting back in his seat as his eyes swept over her face. "I am famously unconventional, am I not?"

Sophia nodded.

"I need an interesting woman to keep me in line. And for the first time in my life, I want … ardently desire … to be kept in line. You will have to trust me, but I am taking the same leap by trusting in you. I am trusting in you to be your true self, to speak your mind, and to contribute to a wonderful future together."

Sophia stared at him thoughtfully as she recalled Cecil and her sleepless nights. Then she considered taking a chance on the earl. She knew deep down she was an untraditional woman and she needed an unconventional husband if she were to marry and remain true to herself. There was no one more unconventional than the strange Earl of Saunton who spoke to her so candidly.

Here she stood at a crossroads—she could spend another night terrified in her room, or she could take a leap and hope that he was strong enough to catch her. There were no guarantees that their relationship would work, but it sounded so awfully appealing to try. To help the gentleman forge a fresh path. It sounded infinitely more appealing than evading the murderous Lord Leech over the coming weeks or months.

"How do we proceed?"

"I will return tomorrow, and we will take a ride through the park?"

"Hmm … it sounds wonderful, but my uncle will never agree to you courting me."

"I see. I shall contrive a plan to persuade him, then."

Sophia stood up, prompting the earl to rise. She could hear Uncle Hugh's heavy footfalls in the hall. By now, one of the servants had informed him that an infamous rake was in his drawing room, paying addresses to his niece. Stepping around the table, she stood directly in front of the earl.

"I already have a plan. Are you certain you wish to see this courtship through to the end? This is your last chance to walk away."

Saunton's eyebrows drew together in confusion. "Yes … I am certain."

Sophia stepped closer, noting his pupils dilated as she approached him. Out of the corner of her eye, she saw the tall form of her uncle stepping into the drawing room. With a deep breath, she leapt into the earl's arms, springing up on her toes to throw her arms over his wide shoulders, and kissed him full on the lips.

As Sophia's soft body landed against him, Richard staggered back in confusion, firing with heat when her lips found his. Apparently, forging a genuine connection with a compelling young woman lit his passions to unprecedented heights. Without his usual glib armor, his soul was laid bare and Sophia's innocent, inexperienced mouth laid waste to his defenses as a surge of pure desire invaded his senses. Sophia was the earth and he the helpless moon trapped in orbit. His blood soared as he hungrily devoured her lips in return. He could not get enough—

"WHAT IS THE MEANING OF THIS?"

Richard fought through his befuddled thoughts as he became cognizant of Sophia's last words before she flew into his arms and robbed him of his sanity. Releasing her slim waist gently, he slowly turned around to find an angry middle-aged lord who was as flushed in the face with anger as Richard's own must be with newly awakened passion. Groggily, Richard realized he had just been maneuvered into compromising Sophia. He knew she was a clever girl. He could only be grateful she had verified it was what he truly wanted before forcing him to propose.

He rubbed a hand over his jaw and then dropped a respectful bow. "Lord Moreland, I wish to marry your niece."

Lord Moreland ignored his declaration. "Sophia, where the hell is your chaperone?"

A bleating snore echoed throughout the drawing room. Lord Moreland swung around to find Nancy sleeping in the chair by the door. He spun back.

"*Nancy* is your chaperone?" he growled at his niece.

Sophia looked unrepentant.

"Well, there is no foul. I am the only one who saw—"

"Lord Moreland!" The viscount's face fell.

"Now see here, dear—" Turning to the doorway, he attempted to placate his wife. He failed.

"Lord Moreland, an *earl* wants to marry your niece. I suggest you hear him out!" The viscountess was magnificent in her demands as she swept into the room. Richard mused that this was becoming a glorious muddle, but it was acceptable to him if he wound up betrothed.

"Christiana, he is a notorious rake!" The viscount was not yet defeated, it would seem.

"Lord Moreland, I suggest you hear what the earl has to say." The lady's voice was steely.

The viscount turned to Richard and demanded in a surly tone, "Are you not a rake? Why should I even consider allowing my niece to marry you?"

"A reformed rake, my lord." Although Richard outranked the man, he decided discretion was the better part of valor in this instance, so he acted as the man's inferior. "Your niece has captivated me from the start, and I have been putting my affairs in order."

"Affairs!" The man responded with something between a snort and a sound of disgust. Richard could not blame him.

"Perhaps affairs is a poor choice of words. I stand before you, a reformed man, seeking your niece's hand in marriage."

"What kind of reformation results in a man taking advantage of a woman under her guardian's roof?"

Richard was stuck for words. He could not very well reveal Sophia had flung herself into his arms. "I … I was … overcome."

"Lord Saunton was overcome when I accepted his proposal, Uncle Hugh."

Lord Moreland looked slightly mollified by Sophia's announcement. "Is this true?"

Richard inclined his head in agreement.

"Is this about her dowry?"

"No, my lord. Whatever funds Miss Hayward brings to the marriage can be settled on her and our future children. I would be more than happy to settle additional funds in the marriage contracts for her future and to provide her with pin money out of my estates."

Moreland relaxed further. The subject of funds appeared to be a sore point. Richard vaguely recollected that Sophia's father had been an unwise gambler, which was rumored to have led to the premature death of Moreland's younger sister.

"Lord Saunton should arrange a special license while the two of you negotiate the contracts," Sophia advised. Richard shot a look at her. She shrugged at him with an innocent look on her face. "There is no choice but to see this through as soon as possible. Now that his lordship has engaged in such scandalous behavior!"

Lord Moreland humphed.

"You have no choice, husband. It is what Sophia wants," a pleased Lady Moreland piped in. It appeared she supported the union wholeheartedly, which was fortunate because Lord Moreland was seriously considering ejecting Richard from his home, if his expression was anything to go by.

"Niece, is this what you want? There is no need to worry about a scandal, and I will not require you to marry this reprobate just to avoid gossip."

"I am certain, Uncle Hugh. I wish to marry Lord Saunton," Sophia reassured her uncle before muttering something under her breath. It sounded like she said, 'forthwith,' which gave Richard pause. He wondered why she was so eager to tie the knot after trying her best to get rid of him on earlier occasions.

"Then Saunton and I best go to my study to discuss terms."

Richard's heart hammered in fearful excitement. He had not expected matters to proceed so rapidly, but it appeared he would be married to the lovely Sophia before the week was out. Doing his best to look repentant, he followed Lord Moreland from the room, but not before winking at Sophia to express his agreement with her manipulation of events and enjoying the answering smile that spread across her face in acknowledgment.

* * *

By the time Richard returned home to meet with his man of business, he was trembling with nervous elation. He was finally getting married to an invigorating and intelligent young woman, with a sharp tongue to act as his moral compass. The fact that she made his pulse race was a delightful discovery that settled any lingering doubts about his monogamous future.

He poured himself a drink from the crystal decanter. "I have been most fortunate thus far, Johnson." He raised his glass in a toast. "Here is to good fortune holding out." He turned around.

Trepidation assailed him when he saw the nervous expression in Johnson's darting eyes.

"What is it?" he groaned. "Don't tell me good fortune has not prevailed?"

"Her name was Kitty. Kitty Smith," Johnson croaked.

"Was?"

"My lord," Johnson began, and then paused as he wrung his hands. "*Ahem.* Do you recall 'sweet blonde, five foot, about three and twenty years of age, worked at Duke of Rosbury's castle in Kent in 1815'?"

Richard blanched and gave a curt nod.

"Kitty Smith died in childbirth in March 1816. She refused to name the father. Her son, Ethan, lives with Kitty's aunt and her family in Derby. He—*ahem*—has dark brown hair and green eyes ..." Johnson's ramble ended. "My lord," he remembered to interject.

Johnson shifted uncomfortably from foot to foot, his demeanor most unhappy.

"The boy is four years old?" Richard whispered. Johnson gave a quick nod.

"Any chance he is not mine?"

Johnson looked away and coughed discreetly. "The house staff in Kent knew of no liaisons, despite being offered a reward for information. They did indicate that Kitty handed in her resignation about two months after the summer house party, which comprised mostly gentlemen from London. From what they said, Kitty was enamored with the peerage and they suspected she had fallen for the glib lines of one of those guests. They considered she was a good girl, properly raised."

Richard could hear his heart thudding loudly in the ensuing silence.

"And what of the aunt's circumstances?" Richard finally asked.

"She is married to a tenant farmer and has six children of her own besides Ethan. They appear to be a relatively successful and upstanding household. The aunt and her husband would be willing to hand him over to the father's care if promises were made to maintain their family connection. She wants to know about family visits before she will acknowledge parentage."

Richard had not thought that a man could experience two earth-shattering life revelations within the span of less than a week. He had been wrong.

"Green eyes are not common," he choked out.

"No, my lord."

Looking at his reflection in the glass cradled in his hand, Richard recognized, more than a little nonplussed, that he, in fact, knew of no other men in his acquaintance with green eyes.

Drawing a deep breath, silently he prayed that Sophia would not call off the wedding at this news. He would not blame her if she did. She certainly deserved better than him. However, his duty to the boy was clear. He was ashamed that strangers brought up his son, while he did not even know of his existence. There was only one honorable move to make, and that was to claim his child and take responsibility for his upbringing and future.

"Return to the aunt and offer them one of my smaller unentailed properties in gratitude for all they have done to take care of my ... my ... son," he croaked. He fought to compose himself before he continued.

"The estate is to be held in trust while the steward apprentices them in the managing of the estate. We will arrange visits over the summer so that the boy may join them. He is to come stay with me, and I would like to interview prospective nursemaids to look after him. I will inform Radcliffe to prepare the nursery, and perhaps we have someone suitable on our staff to promote to that position. My boy must receive the best—a loving hand to take care of him as we become acquainted." It gratified him to hear the decisive ring in his voice as he spoke. He sounded more confident than he felt.

Staring at the tumbler in his hand, he recalled that Sophia would prefer it if he did not drink. He was to be married and answer to another person, which was startling enough. Now he must think about a son—a living, breathing four-year-old boy who would enter his household with needs and expectations.

"Damnation!" He roared and threw his cut glass across the room, where it shattered in the fireplace. Johnson jumped.

"How do I tell Sophia? I pray she still wants to marry me after this devastating turn of events! What lady of the *ton* would marry into a family with a bastard son in residence? What a sham of a life I have led! How can I make amends for such thoughtless interference in people's lives? If only I had kept my breeches buttoned, but I had to be an insouciant prick with another man's household and my son, his mother, and now my betrothed bear the consequences!"

He spun toward Johnson. "Tell me that no one knows of this disaster except for the boy's family?" Before Johnson could answer, Richard threw his hands up in despair.

"Never mind, all of polite society is going to notice that I have a son living in my household before the Season is over. They will call him that, you know? They will call him a bastard through no fault of his own!" Richard paced as his mind reeled with complications. *"This is hell!* I have let so many people down. Leave me, Johnson. I need time to wallow in self-pity before I throw myself on Sophia's mercy. *Richard, you fucking idiot!"* he yelled at himself, a maelstrom of emotions breaking over him in waves.

Johnson took his cue to scurry out the door, his relief palpable. Richard sank into a chair, dropping his face into his hands. He had been so careful not to sire any children, but his promiscuous activities had caught up with him and now he learned he had a son living without a father all these years. He was so ... so ... mortified by his selfish carryings-on.

CHAPTER 5

*P*eregrine Balfour sauntered into Richard's study where he was sitting with his head in his hands, lamenting his past. He raised his head to glare at the languid gentleman who was pouring a French brandy at the sideboard.

"Where the hell have you been, little brother?"

"A vivacious widow held me in her clutches."

"For more than a week?"

"She kept me captive in her bed. I barely escaped with my life," quipped Perry.

Richard groaned, dropping his head back into his hands.

"What the hell is eating you? It's too early in the day to be soused, surely?"

"I have not been drinking. You have missed a great deal in the past week," Richard complained. "I needed you, but I had to make do. Fortunately, Halmesbury was available."

"The duke? Whatever plagues you must be serious if you braved his front door with your Annabel in residence. He did not throw you out?"

Richard ignored Perry's attempts at humor. "She is not

my Annabel—she is all his. I am making changes. I made a list of women I have wronged, and I am setting matters to right."

Peregrine turned to stare at him, his mouth agape. "You can't be serious, old chap?"

"Deadly serious. Halmesbury assisted me in your absence with ideas of how to make reparations."

His brother looked him over with mild disgust. "What brought this on? Have you fallen in love or something just as daft?"

"I don't know about love, but I did find a young lady I wish to wed. That I *will* wed. On Monday morning. She gave me cause to rethink my life, but mostly she forced me to confront that I was becoming … our father."

Perry's eyes flared in shock before he walked over to slump into an ivory armchair. His face was haunted as he stared into the distance. His sibling could have been his twin, they looked so much alike. Unfortunately for his younger brother, Richard knew his father had been particularly cruel toward Perry, although he was hazy about the details because he had been attending Oxford while Perry remained at home with tutors. His brother never discussed what it had been like to live in proximity to the mad earl in his final years. Their father had refused to send him to Eton, as was tradition, preferring to keep his spare within his household to torture in some manner that Richard could only guess at. Even a mere mention of the old man made Perry morose and bitter.

"I … see." Perry shook his head as if to clear his thoughts before he looked over at Richard. "If making amends to the women of your past is proving so painful, why are you doing it?"

"It is not painful. It has been a wonderful experience, very uplifting. I am reclaiming my life … stitching my soul back together one apology at a time. Until today ... I just received dreadful news. It must be faced, but I do not know how it will affect my wedding. I want to marry Sophia, but I do not know if she will reject me when she learns that ... that ... that I have ... a son."

Perry shot up to sit on the edge of his chair. "What? I thought you took precautions?"

"Apparently precautions do not always work out the way one might hope. I will be fortunate if this turns out to be my only child."

"What are you doing about it?"

"He is being collected and brought to London. What the blazes do I do about Sophia?"

"Does she know? About your past and the possibility of a child?"

"She does ... but she knows nothing of ... Ethan." Richard felt a flutter in his chest as he spoke the name of his son for the first time. *I am a father!*

It could not be comprehended. How could he be a father? What if he was as terrible a parent as his own father? Richard dismissed that concern. No one could be as terrible a parent as the earl. The correct question was, could he do better at it than the aunt's family who had taken in Kitty and Ethan?

"Well, I for one do not know why you would want to get leg-shackled, but if she is aware of the potential consequences of marrying your sorry arse ... I say tell her about the boy after the wedding."

"Perry! This is not how I wish to begin my new life."

His brother shrugged. "Then tell her and take your consequences."

Richard groaned and dropped his head back into his hands. "Please do not talk of consequences. I am dealing with consequences from every direction. What the hell was I thinking when I ran amok with these women? Why could I have not emulated Halmesbury and practiced some restraint?"

Perry pulled a face. "Halmesbury did not have our father to act as an example to lead him astray. It is a wonder you have any of the restraint that you do possess. I seem to recollect … never mind. I cannot dredge up memories of father's hedonism. It is making me nauseous to think on it."

"Truly? You think I have shown restraint?"

"Oh, brother, I *know* you have shown restraint. Now, are you going to show me this list and tell me what you have done thus far? It sounds like quite the lark."

* * *

SOPHIA BRUSHED out Lily's hair in front of her cousin's dressing-table mirror. She had convinced her cousin the day of Richard's visit that, because she would depart the Abbott household soon, she should sleep with Lily in her gigantic bed so they might spend as much time together as possible.

She hated lying to her best friend. Perhaps she would tell Lily the truth once the wedding was done and the entire matter was a *fait accompli*. Until then, she did not wish to burden her cousin with the knowledge that Sophia was terrified of her desperate brother assisting Leech to steal her from her bed on the eve of her wedding. She was sure she was being excessively cautious, but it was so refreshing to sleep without fear the past few nights and she enjoyed the extra time with Lily.

The Abbotts were good people, and they deserved to be free of the worry that her situation with her depraved brother would cause them. She had taken care of the problem, and she could not deny a thrill of excitement that she would marry the earl in the morning. Once she had decided on her new course, she had become quite taken with her future, married to the handsome lord and, perhaps, assisting him in his project to restore his honor. It sounded far more entertaining than being society's oldest debutante or a ward in another family's home.

Lily giggled. "You are tickling me!"

"You are too ticklish. What will you do when you receive your first kiss? Twist about and lose your breath?"

Lily's enormous eyes widened in trepidation. "You think? That would be a disaster!"

Sophia chuckled at her younger cousin. "You are such an innocent! Please never change. And, no, you will figure it out with the right beau." She leaned down and gave the girl a swift hug. "I love you, Lily. I will miss you."

"That is good, for if Mama does not relent on pushing me into the path of every well-connected man in London, I may have to come knocking on your door."

Sophia smiled at her in the mirror. "Just promise me you will not settle for someone unsuitable? I want you to be happy, cousin."

Lily shrugged. "It will all work out."

She smiled at the girl's optimistic outlook. Lily always found the silver lining. It was one of her most endearing qualities and helped balance Sophia's more jaded point of view. It was why they were such good friends.

She plaited Lily's hair. They had dismissed their lady's maid hours earlier and were up late, talking the night away. It was the last time they could spend this sort of time together. Tomorrow Sophia would be a married woman, and their relationship would shift to something new.

In the distance, she heard the tall case clock down the hall toll twice.

"Two in the morning! We need to get some sleep, or I shall marry with dark circles under my eyes!"

She tied Lily's braid in a ribbon and hustled her cousin to

the bed. Sophia made her way around the room to extinguish the lamps while Lily used the steps to crawl into the bed. Sophia had no need of the steps, being several inches taller than her petite cousin. She strode over and pulled the sheets back.

"WHAT'S THE MEANING OF THIS?" The shouting, along with scuffling sounds, was coming from the hall.

She glanced at Lily in confusion, who stared back at her in consternation.

"That sounded like Papa."

Sophia nodded in response as dread crept over her. She had thought she was being overly cautious when she bribed the footman, Thomas, to sleep in her room with coin and the promise of a position in the Saunton household if his current became forfeit because of his cooperation. Now, with the commotion out in the hall, she was alarmed that her caution had been warranted. She ran over to the door and opened it a bit, noticing Lily join her while she peered into the dark corridor.

"Where is Sophia?" Lord Moreland cried out.

Sophia swung the door wide and stepped out into the hall, where she found Thomas holding on to a squirming Lord Leech whose eye was swelling shut.

Uncle Hugh appeared fearful but exclaimed when he caught sight of her, clutching his chest as he inhaled in relief. "Oh, thank the Lord! Niece, where have you been?" He was dressed in his nightclothes and barefoot, evidently running out of his bedchamber after the initial scuffle between Leech and the footman.

"I was sleeping in Lily's room."

"What? Why? And what was Thomas doing in your room?"

"I asked him to sleep there … in case."

Uncle Hugh scowled. "In case what? Were you aware this ... this ... *lech* was going to sneak into your room?"

Sophia bit her lip, ashamed that she had not informed her uncle what had been happening under his roof. She had not wanted to burden him with the worry, and she wanted to take care of her own problems to maintain some tenuous control over her choices, but the concern etched on his face ... Perhaps she should have told him what Cecil had planned. Her fingers tugged nervously at the cotton of her night rail. She felt awkward in her half-dressed state, but she doubted anyone was noticing her attire given the situation at hand.

"Sophia! Tell me, what is this about? Why is this depraved lunatic in my home?" Uncle Hugh gestured with disgust toward the squirming Lord Leech, who was muttering in indignant outrage at the servant holding him fast.

Aunt Christiana hovered down the hall in the doorway to her chamber, tying her dressing gown nervously, but she moved toward the gathering. "Sophia, what is this?"

Lily took hold of her hand and squeezed it. "Did you expect Lord Leech, Sophia?"

Sophia shook her head in disbelief. She could not believe Cecil had tried to go through with his plot. She was utterly grateful she had taken the threat seriously, or even now she could be tied up in Leech's carriage, racing out of London with no one the wiser that she was absent until the morning.

"Unhand me or you will regret this!" The despicable Leech chose that moment to interrupt.

Her uncle turned to glare at the man. "Charges can be brought for breaking into a peer's home, and even you cannot sweep such a matter under the rug. I, too, have powerful friends, Leech."

Leech fell silent at the threat. Turning back, her unexpectedly fierce relative gestured for Sophia to talk.

"Cecil ..." she began, then stopped.

Uncle Hugh walked forward to grasp her gently by the shoulder. "Tell me! What has happened?"

She took a deep breath. "Cecil learned about the terms of my dowry and plotted with Leech to exploit them." She waved a hand toward the outraged lord, still detained by the much larger footman whose powerful arm wrapped around Leech's trapped arms and waist. "They planned to kidnap me to Gretna Green to force the trust funds to be released."

Uncle Hugh grunted in dismay. "Oh, my God!"

He rubbed his jaw with a hand as he paced back and forth for several moments. Finally, he came to a stop and glared at her. "Is this why you were so willing to marry Saunton?"

Sophia nodded. "But ... I still want to marry him. I realized I will not be safe without a husband. Cecil could strike an agreement with any fortune hunter. Saunton does not care about my funds, he only cares about me—for some inexplicable reason he has settled on *me*, but I know it is not for the want of funds."

Silence followed this pronouncement for several moments.

"What the blazes do we do now?" Uncle Hugh walked over to Leech to flick his eyes up and down over the heaving, struggling form. "You, sir, are utterly repulsive. Absolute dregs!"

Leech glared at him, his yellow eyes glowing eerily in the dimly lit corridor. "You will regret treating me this way, Moreland!" he spat.

"My only regret, Leech, is that I did not have my servants throw you out when I saw you sneaking into my ball the other night! Can you believe it was to prevent a scene? Had I any idea of the threat you are to my niece—"

"Uncle Hugh, we will have to let him go. It will only cause a scandal to ..." What did one even do in a situation like this? Calling for a runner or taking the lord to a magistrate would be more ruinous to her own reputation than to his once word got out.

Her uncle took a deep breath and spoke to Thomas. "See Lord Leech out and do not be gentle about it. If he happens to hurt himself on the banisters on the way out … well, that is what happens when you steal into another man's household. Do not hesitate, Thomas. Leech cannot complain to the authorities"—Moreland gave the lord a speaking glance—"because he will have to explain how he came to be at the tender mercies of a footman in my household at two in the morning."

Thomas grinned in delight. He dragged the struggling man away, his voice carrying back to where the Abbott family stood with Sophia in a huddle. "Oops, did your head hit that wall? So sorry, milord."

Lord Moreland turned back to find his family staring at him in consternation. "Good Lord, I wish that Aidan was back from Paris to assist me with this disturbance."

"I think you are doing a fine job, Papa!" Uncle Hugh's face relaxed in response to Lily's encouragement.

"You will all go to bed. I will take charge of securing our home and discover Cecil's whereabouts, but there is a wedding in the morning, so you must rest." He raised an eyebrow in question. Sophia nodded to reassure him that this remained her desire. He nodded in acknowledgment and took his wife's hand to settle it on his arm. "Come, my dear. We have a wedding to attend in a few hours. I shall take care of this situation, but now it is time for you to return to your chamber to get some sleep."

Sophia realized her pulse was racing as she and Lily returned to the bedroom, her breathing rough with shock at what could have happened while Lily led her to sit on the bed.

"Why did you not tell me about Cecil?"

Sophia looked up into her cousin's innocent eyes. "Mostly, I was … embarrassed. You have a wonderful brother who would kill any man who tried to harm you, and I … I …" To her horror, she burst into tears. Lily leaned forward to embrace her.

"Oh, Sophia, I am so sorry. You can share my brother! If Aidan were here in London right now, he would give Leech a sound beating!"

Sophia laughed through her tears. "Thomas looked more than happy to mete out some justice on the way out. And he had already gotten a few punches in by the looks of it."

Lily grinned in response as she continued to hug her. "Good, that vile man will think twice before involving himself in any more plots. As it is, I am sure he will be forced to stay out of sight for a number of days with that face of his marred by bruises."

Sophia nodded with a wan smile. Returning to a more serious frame of mind, she dried her eyes. "I know our grandfather was doing his best to look after his family, but the trust he set up … it did not take into account reprobate brothers and villainous lords who might take advantage of the terms."

Lily sighed. "It is most fortuitous that you attracted Lord Saunton, I think."

"I hate that as a woman with few legal rights, I must rely on someone else to protect me, but I could not think of another way. Cecil could attempt this again at any time. Marrying a man of my choosing seems the only way to … to be sure that I maintain control of my own future."

Lily gazed at her. "I think you are able to protect yourself, cousin. You found a way to deal with this situation, and I think no matter the circumstances, you are resourceful and would always find a method to survive any situation. Not like me. I have never needed to fend for myself. But you, you are a heroine!"

Sophia raised her arms to hug her cousin back. "You silly girl, you have been reading too many novels. I am just doing my best to be my own person."

"Your best is admirable, Sophia. I could never be so brave on my own. You took steps to protect yourself *and* you found a handsome husband who admires you. You are most clever and courageous, cousin! Are you going to tell me how you learned of Cecil's plot?"

Sophia grimaced. "Can you believe he is involved with Lord Leech? The man is despicable."

"He is a villain right out of a gothic novel. I could not believe it when I followed you into the hall and learned he snuck into our home. But tell me what happened. How did you know?"

They climbed back into the bed, and Sophia put out the light while she told her cousin about the conversation in the library. Lily gasped in horror. "I had no idea Cecil was so … so …"

"Evil?"

"Yes. I wonder what Papa will do about him. He takes family responsibility seriously, and I think Cecil is in for a world of trouble. Why is he so greedy? I thought Papa was quite generous in taking him in and providing him with an allowance. He treated him like his own family!"

"I think Cecil has been gambling away his funds … more funds than he actually possesses. He is hell-bent on pursuing our father's footsteps, it would seem. He has been on a downward path since our father died. Maybe before, for I do not know what he and my father might have gotten up to together."

Lily was silent for several seconds before responding. "I am very glad the men in my family eschew gambling. And I am glad you came to live with us. And I am even more glad that Lord Saunton took an interest in you. You already solved the problem, you clever woman!"

Sophia smiled into the darkness. She, too, was grateful for Lord Saunton's interest. She reached up to touch her fingers to her lips, remembering the feel of his mouth on hers when she took that irrevocable step to compromise herself. This may have been a shocking evening—a shocking week—but tomorrow she would wed the devilish lord and she would begin a new life far, far, far from her brother's influence. In fact, she would probably never need to see Cecil again.

CHAPTER 6

*I*t disgruntled Sophia to see Cecil waiting in the vestibule. It was time to leave for Balfour Terrace and, apparently, Uncle Hugh had decided Cecil would still be attending the wedding for the sake of appearances.

Her brother looked pale and glared at her malevolently before casting his eyes back to stare at the floor in resentment. It appeared Uncle Hugh had already spoken with him about the prior evening's incursion. She wondered if Cecil had spent the night in his room because there had been no sign of him when Leech was caught. The whiff of hard liquor seeping from her brother meant he must have gotten soused after letting Leech into their home. Perhaps a sign that he had some conscience, then? Not that Cecil ever needed an excuse to drink.

His presence that morning suggested that he was doing his best to hold on to his allowance and connection to the viscount, who was taking full advantage of his desperation to keep up appearances.

Thinking of the evildoer, Leech, being bruised and battered this morning brought a small smile of relish to her lips. The man had been hoisted with his own petard, for which she harbored no regrets. It could have been her, bruised and battered, if she had not taken measures to protect herself.

Uncle Hugh entered the entrance hall, swinging his head around as if he was counting up family members. "Everyone ready to leave, then?"

Aunt Christiana sighed. "After the events of last night, I am more than ready to see our girl safely wed. And the sooner we are done, the sooner I can return home to take a lie-down. I missed much sleep."

The older woman appeared peaked. It made Sophia ever more certain she was making the right decision to wed Lord Saunton. Her adopted family did not deserve to be exposed to such villainy of the kind Cecil had visited on them. With Sophia wed, the risk would be terminated.

It was a sad state of affairs that once a woman wed, she lost all rights to her own income and possessions, but she felt she had found an excellent resolution to the problem that her dowry in trust presented. And if Lord Saunton thought he could change his mind and return to his philandering ways, he would discover that she did not tolerate such behavior. But the earl seemed sincere about his efforts to alter his course, and she was certain she could assist him to find his way. His issues were far easier to solve than drinking and gambling, especially when taken into account with the fact that he was taking calculated steps to correct his past mistakes, which demonstrated his commitment to his crusade of redemption.

Uncle Hugh frowned in concern at his wife. "Are you all right, dear?"

Her aunt smiled. "I am happy to marry Sophia off to such a well-connected peer. It will be quite the relief to know she will be taken care of. Losing a little sleep is a small price to pay for such a prestigious event."

Her uncle broke into a smile. "I had my reservations about allowing this marriage, but I had time in the past few days to get a report on Saunton. He is considered quite moderate in how he spends his money and, from all accounts, has expanded the wealth of the Saunton estates and investments considerably since inheriting the title. He assured me he has every intention of seeing our niece happy and healthy. I think this is a good match, wife. My apologies for doubting you."

The entire family was evidently relieved to marry Sophia off today in order to end the threat of a scheming brother and any future fortune hunters he may ally with. Except for Cecil himself, of course. Sophia was quite looking forward to the security that marriage to Saunton would bring.

Aunt Christiana beamed in response while Uncle Hugh took up her gloved hand to press a kiss to her fingers. The two of them stood staring at each other with loving gazes, causing Sophia and Lily to fidget. The cousins looked at each other, and Lily quirked an eyebrow at Sophia in silent remark. Sophia shook her head and exhaled a brief chuckle of discomfort.

"I think the carriage is waiting for us, Papa. I trust *Cecil* is not traveling with us?" Lily pointedly interrupted the moment between her parents.

Uncle Hugh looked over at Cecil with distaste. "No. He is making his own way to Balfour Terrace. *But he will be on time.*" The menacing tone made Cecil straighten in agitation.

"Yes, my lord."

With that, Lord Moreland ushered the women out the door to the carriage awaiting them.

* * *

RICHARD FIDDLED with his pristine cravat while Peregrine stood grumbling under his breath across the library. His brother was still coming to terms with his hasty wedding and complaining about having a woman underfoot in their family home. He even mentioned finding rooms, but Richard interjected that they were family and Perry's place was in this ridiculously large family home. His brother relented but asserted he would stay at his clubs frequently in order to pursue his pleasures.

Richard shrugged in nonchalance, but secretly he hoped that his path back to honor would, mayhap, inspire his brother to rethink his own course. Richard was very much afraid that his own debauched history had infected his younger brother immeasurably, or, at least, done nothing to mitigate the damage their father had done to him.

Richard paced, switching his thoughts to Sophia. He needed to pull her aside before their vows and inform her about Ethan. She deserved to have an opportunity to cancel the wedding if she wished. Richard had conducted his negotiations with Lord Moreland without seeing her for the past few days. He wanted to do the right thing and inform her about his son, but at the same time, he was strangely reluctant to impart the news. He grew more and more certain that any sane woman would immediately screech and run from him. The terrible scandal would affect her life in ways he could not imagine. Many would turn away from him and his family due to his recognition of his son, openly residing at Balfour Terrace.

He would adroitly explain his presence, perhaps claiming Ethan was his ward, because that was the way of polite society. But everyone would still know Ethan was his natural born son, especially if the boy turned out to resemble him as much as Johnson had intimated.

Richard felt light-headed, nauseous even, with the stress

of confronting Sophia with the news. Mayhap his brother was correct and he should inform her after the wedding? Sophia knew something like this might come to light. *But you assured her no progeny had been uncovered just a few days ago in the Moreland drawing room.* Then the delightful hellion had thrown her supple body against his to kiss him, the sensation of which was ever present on his lips and his mind since that astonishing moment.

No, he must inform her. She must have the right to choose if she wanted to become the *de facto* mother to a four-year-old bastard son.

Grrr!

Perry called out from the other end, "If the idea of being wed is making you growl, it is not too late to find a way to break the contract."

"Ha ha. I think it would be easy to reach a mutual agreement to have the contracts canceled. I simply tell her about Ethan, and Lord Moreland slaps me across the face as they all storm out with much shouting and weeping."

Perry raised his eyebrows. "A reactive bunch, are they? Then it sounds best to get the cancelation moving ahead."

Richard shook his head. "Perry, I want this. I want to marry Sophia. She is an interesting young woman, and I am certain you will grow to like her."

His brother huffed in disgust and turned to stare out the French doors into the garden, his arms folded to show his ire at the nuptials.

Richard stared at his brother, not knowing what to say to reassure him they would still be brothers, that their relationship would not be altered. Then he recollected he needed to speak with Sophia and started pacing in agitation once more.

"The wedding party has arrived, my lord," Radcliffe intoned from the doorway.

"Right. I will come greet them, then." Richard followed the butler out, his stomach twisting in nervous excitement.

Lord and Lady Moreland stood in his front vestibule, looking very proper. The cousin, a Miss Lily Abbott if he recollected correctly, was a diminutive fairy staring up at the artistry of his Italian frescos with open-mouthed delight, while a thickset man with the same reddish-blond hair as his betrothed stood detached from the family, appearing quite belligerent. He briefly wondered if the gentleman protested the union before his eyes found Sophia, and he was robbed of thought. She was beautiful. Exquisite. Dressed in an indigo pelisse which brought out the red highlights in her blonde hair, the blue glints in her eyes, and the warm tones in her silky skin. He was speechless with wonder. This intelligent, vivacious young woman had consented to marry him, and he was awed.

Reminding himself to draw breath, he hurried forward to greet the party.

After brief pleasantries, he bade his butler to show them to the library and to collect the vicar from the drawing room. As the family passed him, he shot out a hand to gently grasp Sophia by the arm. "I would like to speak to you for a few moments, Miss Hayward."

She hesitated and then stepped aside as her family continued down the hall.

"Miss Hayward, you are … well?" Richard asked, finding himself rather ill-prepared to talk with her. For some reason, her appearance was causing his tongue to tie up, and he felt intimidated. What on earth? She was not the most beautiful woman he had ever encountered, although she was very comely. It was the sparkling life in her eyes. He dearly wanted to earn her good opinion, more than he had ever desired it from anyone. It was … disconcerting.

Sophia looked up at him with her large blue eyes and gave a nod. "Yes, my lord."

"Please, call me Richard. We are moments away from being wed." *Maybe. If she does not run screaming into the street.*

She smiled, the corners of her eyes creasing slightly. "Richard." A shiver of pure pleasure ran through him at the sound of his name on her lips. *Richard, you have something to tell the young lady!*

He sighed deeply in resignation at the intruding thought. Sophia's face would twist into anger, she would yell for her family and depart his home, never to give him a second thought other than to gossip about 'that awful Lord Saunton and his vile ways.'

He opened his mouth to speak, but choked on the words. He tried again. "I ... I ... do you have any doubts?"

Sophia tilted her head, her eyes filled with concern. "No. Do you?"

"NO!" Richard shook his head violently. Calming himself, he spoke with more composure. "No. I have looked forward to this all week."

"As have I."

He paused in consternation. "You have? But ... what about my past?"

Sophia nibbled on her lip. "This has been a strange alliance we have forged, has it not?"

Richard nodded numbly. There was no denying that the progress of their relationship was odd.

She continued. "I find you interesting ... and unique. Your crusade intrigues me. I did not think I would ever marry, but I have changed my mind and I am ready to embark on an adventure with you."

She gazed at him with such earnest admiration that it caused his heart to squeeze painfully. It was so ... sincere. It made him want to be worthy of her regard, to have her look at him with that expression for … well … forever.

Screwing up his courage, he asked the question burning through his mind. "And what if I make mistakes … or it turns out there are consequences to my past? What then?"

"We shall deal with it."

His jaw fell open. He was stunned. This girl was so unlike the people he was accustomed to associating with. She reminded him of Annabel Ridley, or rather the Duchess of Halmesbury now, but this relationship with Sophia was different. Perhaps he could have found this with Annabel if he had stripped the veneer of his charm off to reveal himself as a flawed man. With Sophia, he revealed himself and, instead of flinching or shying away, she seemed to be attracted to his honesty. Closing his mouth, which was still hanging open, he leaned down to press his lips against hers. She mumbled in surprise, but, to his delight, kissed him back.

He should be honest, explain the consequences of which he spoke, but then … then he would have to stop kissing her and take the risk that she would reach her breaking point of allowable consequences. She sealed her fate with her sweet esteem, and he could not let her go. She was vital to the healing of his soul. He should tell her, but he could not bring himself to do it. He *would* tell her … he would *tell* her … *tomorrow*.

So, instead, he ran his tongue along the seam of her lips to coax her to part them and let him in to explore her sweet mouth. He groaned in delight when she complied, stealing his tongue into her silky depths and hardening with the sensation. Her body was so soft, so supple, and so perfectly fitted to his own as his arms stole around her to sweep her into a close embrace. Feeling her arms sneaking up around his neck, he sank into the pleasure of the young woman's caress while her hands slid through his locks.

* * *

As their kiss deepened, Sophia sensed that Lord Saun—nay, Richard—wanted to tell her something. But the truth was, if that something would potentially affect their wedding, she did not want to hear it. Perhaps she was a gambler, just like her father and her brother. Perhaps even her mother had been a gambler at heart, wagering her future on a marriage to such a man. Regardless, Sophia's impulse was to throw caution to the wind and embark on a new life with Lor— Richard, whose heavenly kisses and caresses in that moment were greatly encouraging her … impulse. Still, whatever consequences he feared, they would confront together. Her decision was made, and she was ready to proceed.

Then an alarming thought went through her mind. She leaned back to look up at him. "You do not have some … unmentionable disease?"

He stared at her in dazed confusion, apparently struggling to make sense of her words as their kiss ended abruptly. Sophia tried again. "The consequences … is it a … dread disease? Like … the p-pox?"

He burst out laughing. "Young ladies should not know or speak about dread diseases. But, no, I am healthy."

She blew an unladylike puff. "Oh my, that is a relief! And if you wanted a proper young miss, you should not have pursued me. I did my best to dissuade you."

Richard smiled down at her while letting her go. "You are very sweet."

"I am not being sweet. I am being quite selfish, I assure you. I do not wish to contract the pox!"

Richard chuckled again. "Neither do I, Sophia, neither do I. Shall we?"

He offered her an arm, and she took it so that he may lead her to the site of their nuptials.

What a very strange week it had been. And now she would wed, hopefully for the only time in this life, which made a strange week even stranger. She could not help but think that life would never be dull with Lord Richard Balfour, the illustrious but sullied Earl of Saunton, and she hoped fervently that she was correct as he escorted her through his grand London townhouse. He was unlike any other man of her acquaintance, and it fascinated her to discover where their path together would lead.

THEIR VOWS TOOK place in the library overlooking the gardens. Sunlight streamed in through a wall of French doors edging the length of the room. Everyone was in good spirits. Everyone, that was, except for the aloof Mr. Peregrine Balfour who barely said a word, and, of course, her own seething brother who stood apart from the wedding party, glowering near one of the French doors. When not scowling at her directly, Cecil spent most of the ceremony with his back turned to glare into the gardens. Sophia ignored him. He had created the situation with his greed, and she was unwilling to assume any of his guilt.

Aunt Christiana sniffed into a handkerchief that Uncle Hugh had handed to her during the vows. She and her aunt might not see eye to eye about a woman's role, but Sophia appreciated the older woman stepping in to mother her, always doing what she thought was best for Sophia's future.

Lily was particularly fey, taking in the vows with an expression of sheer joy. Her large brown eyes that dominated her dainty face were lustrous, and she glowed with the light of a thousand candles. There was no doubt that her cousin was happy for the fortuitous turn of events, especially now that she knew about the grave danger facing Sophia.

Lord Saun—Richard—*I need to become accustomed to his name ... we are marrying, after all!*—Richard stared down into her face with reverence, looking not at all like a depraved libertine but an enthralled youth, never taking his eyes off her. She did not quite know what to make of it; his green eyes glowed with admiration in the well-lit room. She could drown in his soulful gaze, but she was mildly uncomfortable. She wanted to assist him with his crusade, but she was not a savior, and she hoped his ideal of her would measure up to his expectations.

The ceremony ended and the wedding breakfast began, with the unlikely gathering of personalities sitting around the breakfast table. Her aunt and uncle talked with the vicar, while Lily chattered to Sophia. Perry, as Richard called him, picked at his eggs and ham while swallowing down endless cups of coffee and speaking little unless Richard addressed him directly. Perhaps his brother was recovering from a night of drinking?

Cecil was in the foulest mood, stabbing at his plate aggressively to make loud clinking noises with the cutlery. It was quite ill-behaved, but a minor offense compared to his other transgressions. That her brother had not said a word, even to greet the earl, did not bother Sophia. He was no longer her problem, and Uncle Hugh would address the matter.

She reserved no doubts that Lord Moreland was dealing with her sibling because the Moreland title was synonymous with family. Both her uncle and her grandfather before him were dedicated to safeguarding their household, which had proved very fortunate for both Sophia and Cecil when their parents died within weeks of each other. She still could not believe that Cecil had thrown away such a loyal family connection for the sake of high wagers and spirits.

Shaking her head, she decided she would not waste any

further thoughts on the scapegrace, so she turned to Richard only to find him once again staring at her. She shifted uncomfortably.

"You look ravishing today," he murmured in her ear, his heated breath sending tingles along her skin.

"Um … thank you?" Sophia could not claim to be familiar with compliments from handsome men. She had spent much of her time dissuading them of any interest.

"I hope you like the ring? We can get another if you wish?"

Sophia looked down at the gold band on her finger in a floral design of diamonds and sapphires. "I love the ring!"

"It belonged to my mother."

Sophia felt her cheeks warm with pleasure. It seemed a high compliment to bestow his mother's ring on her.

"It would seem neither of our brothers are happy to attend our vows this morning." Richard tipped his head toward where Perry and Cecil sat side by side in silence across the table.

"Peregrine did not desire our match?"

"Perry did not desire any match. He is not a … relationship person. He is having difficulty understanding why I set my current course, but I am hoping in due time he will realize the advantages of clean living and healthy kinship. We never experienced a proper family because my mother passed away when he was just a few years old and my father … was … um … not a family man. Even I hardly remembered my mother until you said … what you said on the terrace. I hope between the two of us we might influence him over the coming months."

Sophia perked up at the thought of a second challenge. The truth was, she was rather bored living with the Abbott family. They were all so even-tempered and moderate. No one ever needed her help. Growing up with her parents, she had been needed, especially by her mother, who would grow quite despondent during her father's long, unexplained absences. Sophia had made it her mission to cheer her sorrowful mama by bringing her gifts, such as handpicked flowers, and reading to her novels or poetry. Sophia missed the sense of purpose she had experienced as a child to lift everyone's spirits and bring the family together.

The Balfour family needed her, and she could not deny the rush of resolve and intention that filled her at the thought of assisting her new family. To be sure, the idle life of a viscount's ward and heiress had bored her since she had completed her schooling and found herself with nothing to do but prepare for social events. And read, of course.

Now Richard was offering her not just a chance to manage her own household, but to bring his family together. What a delightful challenge to fill her days with a sense of responsibility once more.

"I would like that."

Richard looked surprised for a moment, then grinned. "You are an exceptional woman, Sophia Balfour."

He grabbed the hand resting beside her plate and brought it up to his lips to press a soft kiss to her fingers, the contact sending a fissure of warmth up her arm. "I am glad to hear that because I insisted Perry continue to reside at Balfour Terrace. He shouldn't feel displaced by our marriage. I did not know if you would object to his presence."

Sophia shook her head. "I look forward to learning about Perry ... and ... you."

"Then you shall. But today you will only learn about me. Once this breakfast is over, I plan to spend the day alone with you. I have a surprise for the moment your family departs."

Sophia experienced a rush of pleasure at his words. Richard was taking their marriage seriously, and it felt validating to be the focus of a handsome and fascinating man. Suddenly, she wanted the breakfast to be over so she could be alone with … with her *husband*. She restrained a sudden desire to fan herself at the thought of being alone with a man who was not her direct relation for the very first time. Would he be in a hurry to bed her, or did he have other plans?

CHAPTER 7

*T*wo hours later, Richard ushered her out of his —*their*—townhouse to a waiting curricle with a matching pair of chestnut bays swishing their tails in the crisp spring air.

"What is this?" she queried in a breathy voice. She smoothed her pelisse and the ribbons of her bonnet, nervous about her first time in an open-air vehicle. She had never gone driving with a beau, having avoided courtship for so many years, and a thrill of excitement ran through her that she was to do so now with her handsome husband by her side. Although, anyone who saw them together in the curricle would likely assume he was merely courting her with this traditional method, for a drive in an open-air carriage did not require a chaperone. To her knowledge, the gossips were not yet aware of their unexpected union.

Richard turned to her. "I never had a chance to woo you. With how events transpired, I feel I owe you a courtship, which will be even better now that we are wed and do not require a chaperone. Shall we get to know each other?"

Sophia was dumbstruck. It was so … so thoughtful. A shy

smile spread across her face, and she nodded. Richard lifted her into the carriage while the tiger in his knee-length coat stood politely looking away while holding the team. Once Richard walked to the other side and embarked to take hold of the reins, the servant moved to the back and mounted the rumble, causing the curricle to shift into a new position. She gasped slightly at the shift of balance, shooting a hand out to grab the edge of her seat. The lightweight curricle was a very different experience from the large family coach she was accustomed to.

Richard shot her an encouraging grin, then deftly guided the horses into motion. Soon they were driving through the light traffic in Mayfair. When they entered a congested street into Berkeley Square, she realized where they were heading. Although she had never desired a courtship before this strange turn of events, suddenly she felt giddy with delight.

"You are taking me to Gunter's?" she exclaimed.

Richard smiled as he continued to drive the horses patiently through the square, heading for a line of trees and railings where several curricles and phaetons were parked. Ladies perched in their shaded seats, while a number of foppish lords leaned idly against the railings and observed the square.

"I have never been!"

Richard turned his head in surprise, before straightening to look back at the street he was navigating. "Never?"

"Lady Moreland receives visits, and she pays calls on her friends, but she rarely goes out in public. Mostly we go to the modiste, the haberdashery, and occasionally the theatre or opera. My cousin and I are sometimes allowed out with servants in accompaniment, but we always use the opportunity to go straight to the bookshops. Which is to say, I have passed by this square, but I have never stopped here."

Richard appeared pleased at this news. "I have chosen

well, then. Every lady should visit Gunter's before she weds, but at least we got you here before—" He stopped, then lifted a hand to rub his neck in slight embarrassment. *Before our wedding night*, she supposed was the end of that sentence, experiencing a quiver of delight that he anticipated the evening.

Richard brought the curricle to a stop by the trees. The tiger descended from the rumble and came forward to help place the carriage under a large tree, the branches of which extended out to provide welcome shade from the midafternoon sun. Then the servant moved a respectful distance away to lean against a tree far apart from the patrons of Gunter's.

To her surprise, Richard remained seated and did not disembark to go stand with the other lords, who were staring at them with curiosity. She recalled, from the various gossip between her aunt and her friends, that he had not openly courted any woman before, although he had been hunting for a wife for several Seasons. There had been a rumor that he had been jilted by the daughter of a baron in Somerset, but that must have been two Seasons earlier, if recollection served, and no other woman was rumored to have caught his eye. She wondered briefly about the broken betrothal. It was likely that his philandering might be the cause of the rift, considering that his crusade to redeem his honor had just begun, according to him, the night of the Astley ball when he overheard her criticism. The woman in question had purportedly wedded Richard's cousin, the Duke of Halmesbury, in his stead. *Should I ask him about it?* No, she decided. This was a day of courtship, not the time to discuss difficult topics.

"You are the first woman I have brought to Gunter's." Richard leaned in to inform her. "We may raise some eyebrows, and gossip that I am courting you will run rife throughout the day until news of our wedding gets out. As far as these gentlemen know, this is merely an outing with an eligible young woman."

Sophia giggled. The gossips would get their conjecture wrong today.

"How does this work, then?"

"A server will come out to take our order for ices, then bring them out to us. We will eat them, return the dishes, and when you are ready, I have another destination in mind."

"And you will not join the lords over by the railings?"

Richard shook his head. "I am not here to visit with the fashionable set. They come here to be seen, but today is for learning about my bride so that we may begin our life together. Have you had an ice before?"

"I have not. What do you recommend?"

"I despise the Gruyère cheese, so do not order that. Perhaps ..." He thought for a moment. "... the chocolate cream ice?"

Her mouth watered. Feeling like a naïve young debutante rather than a woman who had navigated three Seasons and wed that morning, she nodded enthusiastically. "That sounds lovely."

Richard turned away upon the waiter's arrival and ordered a chocolate and a maple cream ice. When he settled back on his seat, he commented to her, "You may try my maple ice, if you like. It will cause quite the rumpus." He gestured toward the other carriages and lords. She looked around and realized that the ladies and gentlemen were openly gawking in their direction and talking amongst themselves. Apparently the very eligible Earl of Saunton was the subject of much speculation, especially since his companion was a self-designated wallflower whom barely anyone had paid attention to since her come-out four years earlier.

"Pay no mind. Nothing useful is ever said." Sophia looked back to find Richard gazing at her with slight concern in his vivid green eyes.

She shook her head. "It is a little daunting to be so closely scrutinized, but I do not usually concern myself with gossip. People should live their lives based on what they feel is right. I do not care what others' thoughts might be about my decisions."

His face relaxed. "I am glad to hear that. Your connection to me ... it may expose you to a great deal of gossip."

She put out a hand to cover his gloved one. "Do not concern yourself. I was well aware of your reputation when I first encountered you. Which reminds me, I must apologize."

He frowned slightly, perplexed. "For what?"

"You overheard me mocking you about rumors that I paid attention to."

His gaze shifted away, clearly troubled. "Your words were warranted. I am fortunate to have overheard them, or I would not have decided to change."

"Richard?" She waited for him to look back at her. "I cannot have worked such a miracle. On some level, you must have been ready to shift your course. The reparations you are making ... they were your decision. *You* are the one doing the work."

Richard stared at her for several moments. Eventually, he nodded in agreement, but Sophia perceived he was still directing criticism at himself. Her husband was going to require patience so that he might heal and rediscover his self-respect. She felt honored that he was involving her in his transformation. He was an important man who affected thousands through his estates and leadership. It was a terrifying responsibility to aid him in his endeavor.

Their ices arrived, and their discussion moved to their family histories while they spooned delicious, melting ice. As promised, Richard took up a portion of maple cream ice and brought it to her lips to sample. The chatter spiked as their observers witnessed the inappropriate sharing, but Sophia smiled up at him and accepted the offering with relish. Damn the gossips! She was sharing a wondrous afternoon with her new husband, and they could go to the devil.

Soon they left Berkeley Square, and he drove the curricle to Hyde Park. Once there, he disembarked and then reached up to lift her from the curricle and settle her onto her feet. They walked along the Serpentine, passing couples and families on the banks of the river as he showed her some of his favorite spots. The entire day was magical, and she regretted its end when they returned to the townhouse and he sent her up to her new chambers to prepare for dinner.

* * *

THE DAY HAD BEEN a great success. Richard's bride was relaxed in his presence, and they had spent the day learning about each other. The ennui that had plagued him for years had been steadily dissipating since his initial encounter with her. With each apology he made, with each step he took toward Sophia, a little more life and energy loosened within him. His soul had been frozen in darkness, but now he was thawing out to feel more alive with each passing day.

He laughed to himself as he climbed the stairs after dinner. The flashes of discomfort and shame about his past still hit him unexpectedly, but they were lessening, and he was astounded to find he was optimistic about the future for the first time in many years.

Soon he would join Sophia in her bedchamber to enjoy a tender wedding night with his bride, an event which he had imagined endlessly since she flung herself into his arms and sparked the delightful passion between them.

He reached the hall leading to his bedroom, whistling while he walked the long path. Hard work was still ahead of him, but every step he took brought him closer to a peace of mind he had never expected to find. He was learning that true joy was only possible with a clear conscience, and he was eager to continue clearing his.

Opening the door into his bedchamber, he was engulfed in a shocking wave of cheap perfume. He stopped short, trying to make sense of the gagging scent. His rooms smelled like a bordello.

"Milord, we have been waiting for you," said an unfamiliar, purring voice. Richard spun toward the bed and choked in horror when he found three scantily dressed lightskirts with dyed hair and rouged cheeks laying on his bed in numerous wanton poses.

"What is this? Who are you? What are you doing in my rooms?" His voice was urgent, for he was thinking about Sophia preparing for bed in the adjoining room. Panic raced through him. He stormed across the room and attempted to carefully but firmly haul one of the women from his bed. He shivered when a cloud of stale sweat, gin, and cheap perfume assailed his senses. "You must go! Now! My bride is in the other room!"

"But we were hired to take care of you, and we know how to do it." The blonde doxy of advanced years trailed her fingers down his arm suggestively while Richard tried to think. He disliked the women of ill repute who were to be found in pleasure palaces and cheap bordellos around the city, and he never stepped foot in such places. They reminded him of his father and the stench of his rotting flesh when the old man had been wasting away from the pox. His father once magnanimously hired two such women when Richard turned fourteen, informing him he was a man now. Richard had spent the night hiding under a bed in one of the guest rooms to avoid them. *Living hell, did something similar happen to Perry while I was away at Oxford?* His brother refused to attend any clubs where he might encounter such creatures.

Choking, Richard grasped another woman by the arm and gently tugged her from his bed, hoping the other two would follow. Pasting on a charming grin, he attempted persuasion. "Ladies, I am afraid someone misinformed you regarding my need for you. It is time to depart! Immediately!" The woman he had drawn from the bed was shuffling along with him, but her hands were fondling him simultaneously. A vivid recollection of his father's hedonism hit him. He could not expose Sophia to this. He needed to get them out of there.

Where was his valet?

Damnit! Sophia could arrive any—

He froze, squeezing his eyes shut when he heard the sound of the adjoining door opening. Slowly, he turned around to find Sophia staring grimly at the women still on his bed, with their nipples peeking up over the tight bodices of their gowns and at least one naked leg sprawled on display. Then her gaze settled on the doxy in his arms, who was trailing her hands over him like the tentacles of an octopus.

"Sophia, this is not what it looks like." Her blue eyes met his to stare directly into his soul for what felt like an eternity. She tilted her head as if to ask a question.

"The young lady can join us if she wishes, but it will cost extra, milord." The slurred voice interrupted them from the direction of the bed, followed by a loud cackle. He swallowed his antipathy at the perpetrator of this cruel joke. He could not believe his innocent bride was witnessing this depravity.

A hand crawled over his thigh toward his groin and he

swiftly caught that hand with his own before the woman groped him in front of his new wife.

A clear voice cut into the drama of the moment. "Richard, pay these ladies their coin so they may be on their way."

Had he heard her correctly? Perhaps his thoughts were befuddled.

Pay these women? Pay *these* women to leave. *Pay* these women to *leave*!

She was brilliant. His bride was a veritable genius! In retrospect, he was a fool. Why did he not think of offering them coin to be on their way? Inhaling in relief, he let the lightskirt go while he grabbed for a purse. Clutching it in his hand, he ran over to the bed.

"Time to go, ladies! I shall give you two—no, three guineas a piece to come downstairs with me!" The drunken women stared at him with bleary eyes before slowly rising from the bed. It was a fortune. Enough to pierce their cloud of gin-soaked stupor.

He would pay them more if they would move quicker. He handed coin into their hands, their fingernails chipped with grime underneath. What friend would think this humorous? Who would play such an ill-conceived prank on him? Had they known it was his wedding night—*would Perry do this as a lark?* He immediately brushed that thought aside. Perry would rather pull out his own teeth than come within speaking distance of these women. His brother abhorred lightskirts and favored licentious widows. *Do I need to talk to Perry about what happened while I was away at university? What did Father do in my absence?*

The welcome sight of Richard's valet appeared at the door.

"Shaw, we need to show these young ladies out." Richard wanted to personally escort them out of his townhouse to ensure that they left. And to question them downstairs. He swung his head in Sophia's direction. She gave him a nod; it appeared she understood his need without him voicing it.

"You shall find me in my chambers when you are done, my lord."

Richard was relieved, but also concerned. Why was she 'my lording' him? *Ballocks!* This day had been so promising, but now it was going to be a very long, very disappointing evening.

Courage, Richard.

He must deal with this. Only then could he return to explain the situation to his bride.

One step at a time. *One* step at a time.

He drew a deep breath. *Take them downstairs, Richard. Then find out how they gained access.*

Only then could the depth of his bride's disdain be established.

One step at a time.

CHAPTER 8

*O*nce he had established very little—other than a cloaked, hooded figure had ushered the women through the mews and into one of the garden-facing doors before leading them to his rooms—Richard returned to his bedchamber. Which reeked.

The cloying scent of cheap perfume, stale sweat, and traces of carnal relations mingled to make his room smell like a bawdy house, or what he imagined a bawdy house would smell like if he ever entered the doors of a house of ill repute. Personally, he had never needed to risk disease, death by knifepoint, or thievery by paying coin for carnal relations. More fastidious women had been volunteering to care for his needs since he was a lad—one of the many privileges of being a handsome, successful peer with an easygoing charm.

Not that he felt successful or easygoing at the moment.

His valet arrived with a swarm of footmen to hurriedly provide a tub of bathing water and whisk away bedding to be cleaned. Richard had already thrown open the windows despite the chill of the evening in order to air the room out.

Once the bath was prepared, he quickly took advantage

of the steaming hot water to bathe the stench off his skin and hair. In his imagination, the odor lingered still, but Shaw assured him that he currently smelt delightful. He was uncertain if the man was funning him with his droll words, but the servant stated it with no trace of humor.

Clothed in loose cotton trousers and shirt, he donned a dressing gown and approached the adjoining door to Sophia's chambers. There he stood for several moments, his forehead leaning against the door. What was he to say to her? He could not explain what had happened because he barely understood what had happened. His bride must think him the very worst type of depraved libertine. Worse even than his own father.

All his hard work building a relationship with her, destroyed by some unknown figure … presumably a so-called friend who was utterly lacking in taste. Mayhap he had done too many terrible deeds in his past, and this was his penance. Perhaps his cousin was wrong, and it was far too late for him to amend his ways. Perhaps he should go sleep in a guest room and leave his bride alone. He dreaded entering the room to find her embittered toward him after their enchanting day together.

Inhaling deeply, he accepted he was well on his way to relying on her esteem, and he felt angry desolation at how their day was ending. Nonetheless, the problem would not evaporate on its own. He must confront it now before it worsened.

He knocked on her door.

* * *

IT HAD TAKEN Sophia only a moment to register her groom's distress when she entered his rooms. She quickly ascertained from his expression, and his general demeanor, that

105

he was not involved in inviting the women into his chambers.

Had he done such a thing in the past?

Hearing the quiet knock on the adjoining door, she sprang up from the bed to race across the room on her bare feet and open the door. She found her husband on the other side, looking worn out. And well-scrubbed, his hair damp.

"I am so sorry. This was not planned." His voice was gruff, and Sophia took pity. Claiming his hand with her own, she drew him into the room and over to the seating area.

"I know."

He frowned in confusion.

"It only took a moment to realize you did not possess the look of a man with an agenda. You looked like a man in a blind panic."

He chuckled dryly. "That would be an accurate description of how I was feeling."

"Did they come on the wrong night?"

Richard's head bobbed up in surprise. "What do you mean?"

"I thought perhaps ... this was an old meeting you forgot to cancel. Or a standing arrangement had not been ... well ... called off? From before. When you ... I mean, you only recently decided to change your ways ... Perhaps this is how you spent your evenings ..." She trailed off, feeling silly.

"No! I never paid coin for ... that. I would never risk my health on ..." He took a deep breath to continue. "Apparently, some acquaintance of mine thought it would be amusing to play a lark on me and showed them to my rooms. If I find out who exposed you to this, I will kill them with my bare hands. Radcliffe is downstairs questioning the servants to find out if any of them assisted with this ... this ... invasion of our home."

Sophia stared at him for an eternity, not sure what came next.

"Sophia, I do not think this is the night to celebrate our wedding." Richard turned away to glare at the wall.

She could see his point. He still appeared disturbed, and the wonderful rapport they had built earlier in the day was missing. They sat together in their dejected silence while Sophia pondered what to do. She wanted to assist him, to play a part in his restoration of honor. This seemed like a moment that she should show her mettle in some way, to somehow mitigate this disastrous night. Show some kindness to alleviate his mood.

"Perhaps ..."

His eyes found hers. "Perhaps?"

"Perhaps you would care to lie in my bed with me? Just to sleep?"

The regret in his eyes eased, and he exhaled, appearing more relaxed. "I ... I would like that very much."

Sophia stood and took hold of his hand. She walked over to the large canopied bed with him. Dropping his hand and then her dressing gown on the floor, she quickly climbed under the coverlet, then watched him remove his own robe and climb into the bed with her. She turned away on her side while he extinguished the lamp, and under the cover of darkness, he slid closer to her and tentatively placed his hand on the flare of her upturned hip. She pressed back against him, feeling his tension slowly fade.

She closed her eyes. It had been a very long day, and she was exhausted. Their troubles would need to wait until the morning, despite her yearning to feel his lips on hers once more. For tonight, she must be satisfied with the warmth seeping into her body from his proximity.

* * *

SLEEPING near his bride without taking advantage of her had been torturous. His body denounced the depravation for hours while his conscience gripped the reins. He had not lain with a woman in some time, but that was not the true problem. The true issue was that he had never wanted one particular woman this much, and refraining from bedding her while she lay slumbering in his arms was a torment.

Finally, amid a cockstand he could not control, he had moved his hips away from hers to conceal his ardor until he fell into an exhausted sleep.

Slowly, he awakened and opened his eyes to discover it was morning. He blinked in surprise when he found clear blue eyes staring into his. His bride was awake and watching him closely.

Tentatively, she moved forward to place a kiss on his lips. He shifted in agitation when his deprived body responded by rushing blood once more to his groin. Her free hand came out of the covers and reached to smooth his hair back, and he nearly growled from the pleasure of her touch. She continued to glide her hand down his neck, over his chest, where her fingertips slowly traced over his pectoral muscles. His blood thickened in response to her rapt attention and soft touch while his loins fired in rigid agreement when her fingers dipped to feel the musculature of his abdomen. With great effort, he held himself still to allow her to explore the shape of his torso, but he could not contain low groans as his desire mounted. When he could resist no longer, he raised himself up on an elbow to lean over her, lowering his head to devour her sweet lips. This seemed a perfect moment to—

A discreet knock interrupted his intentions. "Milord, there is an urgent matter to attend to."

Richard lowered his head onto her shoulder to scowl at his butler's intrusion. *What the blazes could be important enough to interrupt me in my bride's chambers?* Belatedly, he recalled the events of the night before.

On second thought, perhaps his butler had cause. Sighing in resignation, he leaned forward to press a kiss against Sophia's forehead and then withdrew from the bed. He donned his robe and went to the door, stepping out into the passage to talk with Radcliffe while shutting the door behind him.

Radcliffe looked a little worse for wear, dark shadows under his eyes, but otherwise his usual tidy self. Richard wondered if his faithful servant had been to bed or if he had been questioning the servants all night.

"A certain guest has arrived early, my lord."

Richard frowned. He was not expecting any guests … other than … other than … *Fuck!*

"My son has arrived?" he asked below his breath.

"Yes, milord."

Richard raised a hand to swipe over his face. He had planned to inform Sophia today about his natural born son and his imminent arrival. He had thought Ethan would not arrive for another day or two. This was too damn early. How could he spring this on her after the terrible night she had endured? How much could one woman be expected to forgive?

He ordered his butler to send his valet up to his rooms to help him dress. He refused to meet his son for the first time in his nightclothes.

One step at a time, Richard.

Swiftly, he walked down the hall to the entrance of his room. Shaw arrived moments later and quickly dressed Richard. Before he had much time to think, he ran downstairs to look for his man of business who had collected his son from the Davis family.

* * *

RICHARD WALKED into his study to find Johnson missing and Radcliffe standing beside a small boy of about four years old. The little chap possessed soft brown locks, and when he raised his face to look at Richard, he revealed the distinctive green eyes of the Balfour family. Richard could not deny that the boy must be related to him.

Richard shifted uncomfortably from foot to foot, trying to decide how to greet his son. Did the boy know who he was, or must he explain their relationship? He was still pondering how to begin when the door behind him swung open.

"Who is this, Richard?"

Richard spun around to stare blankly at Sophia, words escaping him while several moments passed. How had she dressed so quickly?

"Richard, who is this?" Her voice rose to a shrill level, piercing his fog.

Richard opened his mouth. Then closed it when he still found no words to say. She stared at him expectantly, but he was speechless. *Hell! What is this?* He always knew what to say, but this past day was unprecedented. He had no experience to draw on, and he felt exposed emotionally. *Emotionally? What the hell does that mean? When did I begin to wield emotions?*

"Richard, I need to know, who is this boy?" Sophia asserted, maintaining a cheery tone likely intended to prevent the child's alarm, but her smile was tense.

All Richard could think about was that redemption was difficult. Telling the truth was difficult. It was difficult to know what was the right thing to do. Life was complicated. He knew he needed to explain the truth but, though he opened his mouth to speak, still no words would form.

Sophia brushed past him to kneel before the little lad. "Hello. What's your name?"

"Ethan," said the boy. He gave an adorable little bow. "Pleased to meet you."

Sophia stood to give him a solemn curtsy in response. "Sophia," she replied. "I am Lord Saunton's wife. And, who, may I ask, are you to Lord Saunton?"

"Is that Lord Saunton?" asked the boy, pointing to Richard where he stood in pained silence. Sophia nodded. "Emma says he is my papa, and I must listen to what he says. But he has not said anything yet."

"I see. While we wait for your … papa … to speak, perhaps you would like to eat? I am sure Cook could find some milk and perhaps cake to go with it."

Ethan's eyes rounded in delight, and he nodded vigorously in response.

Sophia turned to Radcliffe, who was politely standing by and stoically studying the wall. "Radcliffe, can you see that Ethan finds his way to the kitchens and is well fed?" The butler inclined his head and took the boy by his tiny hand to exit the room.

Sophia waved her fingers to Ethan, smiling. As she turned back to Richard, her smile fell away and she glared at him. "Perhaps you should explain why Ethan thinks you are his father?"

Richard winced as he made his way to the drinks cabinet across the room. Then he recollected his promise to avoid spirits. He brought such chaos into the life of his bride; he owed it to her to attempt to keep at least one promise.

"When you asked me if I had any natural born children, I did not know about Ethan. Later that day, I came home to meet with my man of business, which is when … I was told about his birth." He stared down at the decanter of French brandy with yearning.

Sophia was silent. So silent he was afraid that the silence would stretch out, wrap around the world, and all speech would be canceled for eternity. His own breathing sounded like a cacophony of sound in the deafening silence that—

"So, the people whom I do not like will no longer wish to associate with us," she finally blurted out so loud it made him jump.

"Wait … I do not understand … what?" He turned to face her.

"So, we are to be a scandal. The members of the peerage whom I dislike the most will be the first to avoid us. I may never be required to speak to them again. No soul-draining small talk with my aunt's friends; no chitchat with that obnoxious Lady Jersey or her husband. I can live with that. And our family just grew larger," she finished in a pragmatic tone.

Richard shook his head in disbelief.

"However, I would have appreciated being *forewarned* …" She scowled at him, hands fisted on her hips, then brought a finger up to tap her lips pensively before pointing it at him. "On the other hand, I think I may have dissuaded you from telling me something before the wedding. Was this what you pulled me aside to discuss?"

He nodded ruefully.

Sophia appeared thoughtful until excitement crossed her face. "*Oooh!* I shall spend my evenings with thinkers and literary geniuses instead. I shall be an irregular bluestocking who holds salons."

Richard tried to make sense of what was unfolding before him. Was his wife somehow pleased with the recent turn of events? Her mind zigzagged, not unlike the military maneuver, and he realized his bride was an enigma that he might never fully comprehend, but she would keep him endlessly entertained in the years to come.

He stepped forward and wrapped his arms around her. "You are a wonderful woman. You accept that my son will live with us?"

"Where else would he live? He is your son."

Richard had suspected when he had eavesdropped on Sophia and Miss Abbott less than a fortnight ago that he had met a compelling woman. Now that he held her against his chest and breathed in the scent of roses, he was certain that Sophia was his perfect woman. He could think of no other lady of the *ton* who would have accepted his son into her home.

"And will you be his mother?"

"If he has no mother, I will fill the role in any way that Ethan requires."

Richard let her go and walked over to drop into one of his plush ivory armchairs. He leaned his elbows on his knees in relief. His wife was a revelation, and he felt like he, yet again, had been granted a reprieve. It did not surprise him when she came to stand over him.

"Are you all right, Richard?"

He nodded, clearing his throat in embarrassment at the display of emotion. He reached out to grab her slender hand. "Thank you."

"I know you have a troubling past. But from here on out, can we work together?"

"Yes."

"Are there any more surprises?"

"No."

"Well then, shall we go meet your son properly?"

"Yes."

Richard stood and held out his arm to his remarkable bride.

* * *

IN THE KITCHENS, Sophia met the housekeeper and kitchen staff while Ethan demolished a large ham sandwich that barely fit in his small hands. Once he was done, they brought him back to the study to talk. The child proved to be bright and well-spoken, chattering away about his journey from Derby and all that he had seen and experienced.

Sophia had been remarkable, talking to his son with directness while giving him her full attention, which the boy responded well to. It soon came to light that Ethan could read when he commented on the books on the shelves, and Sophia promised they would visit the library together to select books appropriate for him or, if they could not find any, would visit Hatchards for new stories.

Ethan was exploring the study when Sophia lowered her voice to speak with Richard. "I do not think a nursemaid will be sufficient. I will cultivate the boy's love of learning, but he may require a tutor to keep him occupied. Whoever this Emma is, whom he keeps referring to, she has clearly taught him beyond his years. Perhaps the boy is a genius? Reading at his age?"

"Johnson will bring us candidates for tutors, then. But I do not want my boy to be educated by the kind of men my father hired when I was a child. We must find someone who will foster his enthusiasm rather than squash it."

"Agreed."

Sophia strode across the room when Ethan called her over. Richard watched her crouching to talk with him. He was overjoyed to witness her acceptance of Ethan, not to mention the salve of having her support while he grew to know his son. Although usually a decisive man, he was uncertain of what to do with a young child, but fortunately Sophia was taking the lead.

Richard crossed the study to join them at the shelves

when Sophia beckoned him. He dropped to one knee to join their chat.

"Sophia said that you and I could play chess tonight, Papa!" Ethan looked up at him with an excited, wide-eyed glance and pointed to the chess set that lay forgotten on the shelf. Richard followed his finger to look at the set and perceived for the first time that, as Sophia had pointed out, the four-year-old boy was learned beyond his years if he was interested in a game of chess.

"You play chess?"

Ethan chortled. "Of course. Emma said it would teach me to think and to plan a *strat ... e ... gy*." He drew out the word carefully.

"Do you know what it means to plan a strategy?" Richard asked him.

"It means to play smarter than your *op ... po ... nent*." The boy sounded out cautiously.

Richard smiled down at the boy, an errant rush of warmth causing him to raise his hand to affectionately ruffle the silky locks of his ... *child*. "That it does, Ethan. That it does. Who is Emma?"

The boy looked at him oddly. "Emma is ... Emma." Ethan frowned slightly, then elaborated. "She is my *cuz-zin*. And my friend."

Richard winced, but quickly cleared his face to smile at the boy. Might he have been too hasty ripping the boy from his family? Should he have collected the child himself? Perhaps spent a few days with the boy's family and come to know them, and this Emma, and the life that Ethan had led? Had he been arrogant to send his man of business to collect the boy and make the arrangements?

He was not accustomed to knowing how to treat family matters such as this and feared he may have been ruthless in his single-minded focus to claim his son.

He raised his head to stare at Sophia. She raised her eyebrows in question, but he could not talk about it in front of the boy.

Radcliffe entered the room accompanied by a short, young maid with a wide, pleasant face and dark brown hair scraped back in a bun. Richard thought she might be new.

"Milord, this is Daisy. She has come to work with us from one of your Somerset estates, and she has several younger brothers and sisters. I arranged for her to act as a nursemaid until permanent arrangements can be made."

Richard was relieved as he stood up. He needed to accustom himself to his changed circumstances, so a temporary reprieve was in order.

"Perhaps we can walk with Ethan up to the nursery to see him settled, Richard?"

Accepting Sophia's guidance in the matter, he gave a nod. Taking Ethan by his small hand, he smiled down. "You want to see your rooms, son?"

Ethan grinned and nodded. The boy was sociable and inquisitive. He chattered about the books Sophia would show him later as he tugged Richard into a walk.

Sophia followed them while they walked up the stairs to find the nursery. She looked around with keen interest, and Richard sensed she was noting the rooms and their contents in order to make improvements. Once Ethan started yawning, no doubt the effect of his long journey and hearty meal, she encouraged him to sleep. The boy nodded, swiftly dozing off on his small bed while Sophia quietly instructed Daisy about his belongings, meals, and recreations, along with arranging a time for his promised game of chess with his papa.

Finally, they left the nursery to walk back downstairs.

"Do you mind if I make arrangements to remodel the nursery? I will want to make purchases."

Richard shook his head. "Of course not. I did not expect you to be involved, but I would appreciate your input."

"I think we will need to ensure we spend quite a bit of time with Ethan. It sounds like he has come from a large family and will not be occupied with only a nursemaid to keep him company. I think we should find a nursemaid who is educated and can discuss his books with him. Or even a governess who might continue his studies until he is a little older?"

"I bow to your insights, wife. We will find my man of business so he may begin searching for someone appropriate. You mentioned a tutor might be needed sooner rather than later, so we will discuss our needs with Johnson, but perhaps a governess would be a good start, considering he keeps mentioning this Emma. It is not the done thing, but as you pointed out, we no longer need to concern ourselves with that."

Sophia smiled up at him, her arm woven around his while they walked down together. "This is quite a turn of events. Last week I was a mere ward in my uncle's house, and this week I am a bride and I guess I am standing in as a mother. Who would have predicted such a change in circumstances?"

It was eerie to hear his earlier thoughts echoed, but he smiled at her pleased expression. His eyes lingered on her lips, and he wondered when they might find an opportunity to make her his wife in truth. It did not seem like the day presented much possibility, but the memory of her fingers slowly exploring his body had returned the moment they closed the door on the nursery. Her interest in his son and the grace of her acceptance increased his frustrated desire. He wished he could drag her into one of the chambers they were passing to have his way with her.

CHAPTER 9

*R*ichard led Sophia down to his study, closing the door once they entered. He guided her to an armchair where, to her surprise, he took a seat. She stood by hesitantly, unsure what to do. Suddenly, she felt his hands at her waist as he picked her up and settled her down on his lap.

Squeaking, she looked at him in surprise, noting the rather pleasant experience of feeling his hard thighs pressed against her buttocks. He buried his face in her neck and breathed in deeply.

"You smell so sweet," he groaned into her skin, his lips grazing up to her ear, where he unexpectedly drew a lobe into his mouth and suckled. Shivering in delight, she arched to the side to give him better access while raising a hand to rest it on his defined chest. His mouth explored her, tracing over to her cheek and then pressing against her lips in agonizing stillness. She moaned and leaned in to kiss him, which he quickly took advantage of by slipping his tongue into her mouth to tangle against her own while his large hand idly grazed up and down the flare of her hip. His deep, drugging kisses intoxicated her senses while breathing in his spicy male scent made time itself stand still.

Slowly, he pulled back, giving her sweet kisses before withdrawing to look at her. She opened her eyes and found herself enthralled by his gaze.

"Why did you marry me?"

She shook her head to clear her thoughts. "You intrigued me."

"Yes, but that first time you dissuaded my interest with that vapid act of yours—it was very effective, by the way. When I danced with you the second time, you showed no interest. What changed?"

"I ... did not want to marry. But then my circumstances caused me to change my mind. Once I changed my mind, I realized that your crusade to reclaim your honor intrigued me."

"What circumstances?"

She flushed in shame. "It became clear that the terms of my dowry created an untenable situation in which I was exposed—vulnerable to fortune hunters. As the terms were set long before my birth, they could not be altered. I concluded that the most favorable solution was to seek security through marriage to a man of my own choosing, and I immediately thought of you. Your interest in me appeared genuine."

Richard looked troubled. "Is that the only reason?"

She bit her lip, her eyes focusing on the hand resting on his shoulder. "I ... found you fascinating after our second conversation ... and ... attractive during our first dance," she blurted out, the last in embarrassment.

He grinned in delight, wrapping his arms around her to embrace her close to his body, which emanated heat. He lowered his head to rest on hers, and she gave in to the impulse to burrow into his chest and remain there.

"We should eat soon," she ventured after a while.

"Soon. Right now, I just want to hold my bride before any more excitement can find us."

She smiled at that and settled back down to rest her head on his shoulder. Several minutes passed while she listened to the thudding of his heart within his powerful chest and wondered if he would bed her tonight. Warmth pooled in her belly at the thought.

He spoke in a low, soothing voice. "How is it you knew what to do with Ethan? I am personally at a loss, but you did not hesitate."

"I was a girl not that long ago. A motherless one. I simply thought what I would like in Ethan's place and acted accordingly."

"What about the mothering?" He gestured his head up toward the nursery.

"Lady Moreland is a capable woman. I was older than Ethan when we arrived at the Abbott household, but I thought he would need similar things. Time spent with family, including meals. Something to engage his curious mind. My aunt and uncle are very involved with their family, and I was fortunate to be included. I observed them for many years, so I developed some instincts, I suppose."

"I am impressed. You are quite composed for such a young woman."

Sophia raised her head to roll her eyes. "That does not serve as a compliment. Am I not composed for an older, more experienced woman?"

Richard chuckled, leaning his forehead on her shoulder. "I stand corrected. You are quite composed—period," he emphasized.

His hand idly caressed her belly, fracturing her breathing once more at the exquisite delight of his fingers gliding over her skin with just her day gown and her shift between his hand and her body.

"I am afraid there is something I failed to mention."

Sophia stopped breathing. She had been taking the events of the past evening and this morning in her stride, but she thought she might have reached her capacity for surprises.

"I accepted an invitation to a musicale for this evening. Before I knew I would marry yesterday."

Sophia exhaled in relief. This was a minor issue, then.

"I know you have not had an opportunity to order a new wardrobe befitting a married woman, but do you mind if we attend? The gentleman is a friend, and he has two daughters to marry off. He asked me to lend my support, and there has been no opportunity to speak with him about my getting wed."

Sophia smiled. "I think we can manage that if it is someone you consider a friend. Who is it?"

"Lord Lawson."

"Oh! I heard his daughters are quite talented musically. I think we could enjoy a most agreeable evening."

"I hope you are right. I would hate to sit through pitchy singing and missed notes on the pianoforte. Even worse, if they cannot properly play the harp, it could be a loud and painful evening."

Sophia giggled and swatted his shoulder. "Nay, husband. This is a perfect evening of entertainment. Shall we learn about each other once more? Yesterday the time spent together was enjoyable before ..." She did not wish to recall the awful night.

Richard grimaced in distaste. "Yes, before. I want to apologize for the chaos you have encountered since taking up residence at Balfour Terrace. I would have preferred our marriage to begin differently."

"You could not help that someone played that vicious

prank on you. However, Ethan should probably not have been a surprise?"

"I assure you that I was as surprised as you the past few days. More so."

"Yes, but moving forward ... perhaps you could inform me of such things. I would very much like to be your helpmate in this marriage. My own parents were ... quite broken. Father always kept secrets about his gambling, and his drinking made him difficult to communicate with. And Mother wallowed in self-pity. Lord and Lady Moreland are much closer, and they work together. I would like our marriage to be more like that. A partnership and meeting of the minds."

Richard chuckled. "Quite the revolutionary I married."

"If it is revolutionary to know my mind and to speak my truth, then yes."

"I agree. We will try it your way. You may require patience because I do not come from a close-knit family and I have not had a feminine influence in my life to soften me since I was a very small lad. I will learn."

Sophia stuck out a hand. Richard stared down at it for a moment in surprise.

"Is it not what close friends do?"

"I suppose it is." He shook her hand.

"It is an agreement, then. No more secrets."

* * *

When Richard and Sophia entered the large room of Lord Lawson's musicale, there was a momentary lull in the background chatter. Faces across the crowded room swung to stare at the two of them before talking resumed. Clearly conversation was shifting to the subject of the Earl of Saunton's unexpected nuptials with that Hayward girl.

His bride held her head up high, her arm woven through his own, and they walked in together to greet Richard's acquaintances. They soon found the Morelands and her cousin Lily near a marble column, and they arranged to sit together. Richard bid them to go ahead so he could collect refreshments for Sophia and himself.

The musicale was very crowded. Having located a server amongst the thronging guests, he held two glasses of orgeat, which he loathed but was all to be had, when he was jostled. Stumbling forward, he managed to hold the drinks steady and quickly returned to Sophia.

Taking a seat at her side, with the Abbott family lined up in chairs to her right, he handed her the drink. She pulled a face. Leaning over to him, she whispered, "When we hold our dinner parties and salons, there will not be any orgeat in sight. Must it always be sweet and watered-down?"

"You have not tried it yet," he pointed out.

"You know I am right."

He lifted his glass to take a sip, grimacing. "Indeed, it tastes like watered-down almonds with an excess of sugar."

She grinned in response.

At that moment, Lord Lawson called for the audience's attention. He was a swarthy man with graying hair at his temples, dressed in a black tailcoat, silver waistcoat, and snowy white linen. He introduced his young daughter, Lady Jane, who hurried forward to take her seat at the pianoforte with a daunted expression. Richard could not blame her. This event was very well attended, with more than a hundred guests in the room.

The debutante played the opening bars of an Irish aria which Richard did not recognize, but when she began to sing in a clear, high voice, he breathed a sigh of relief. Sophia had not overstated the Lawsons' musical talent. He settled back in his hard-backed chair, easing into a position that was more comfortable. The seat was not designed for a man of his stature, and he was compelled to drop down to stretch his legs out under the row in front of him.

The music proved excellent, and he enjoyed observing the rapt expression on his bride's face as she leaned forward to listen, tapping her foot in time beneath her skirts while her cousin swayed her head until she received a cutting glance from her mother. Sophia looked beautiful with her red-blonde hair braided into a coronet and soft curls falling to frame her face, which was glowing with excitement.

Richard scanned the crowded room, stiffening when his eyes met those of a wicked widow from his past who was staring openly at him. Lady Partridge had invited him into her boudoir for a single tryst two years earlier. Her prurient tastes had been too rich for his blood and not worth revisiting, so he had avoided her since, but the blonde deviant was currently smiling lasciviously at him in invitation.

He quickly averted his gaze in tacit refusal only to find another former paramour, Lady Wood, sitting next to her weighty, brutish husband. The lady had been a pleasant interlude, but he had sensed great unhappiness below the surface during their time together the previous year. Tonight, her wan pallor and unhappy countenance reinforced the impression and tugged at his sympathies. Lord Wood was not a pleasant man, and he suspected the lady suffered for it.

Clearing his thoughts, Richard looked away before anyone noticed him staring, only to realize that a guest in the row behind was glaring at the back of his head, causing his nerve endings to itch. He flicked a glance from the corner of his eye but did not recognize the dark-haired man. It could well be a husband he had cuckolded.

Richard turned his gaze back to the songbird, Miss Lawson. With his storied past, it was not safe to let his eyes drift around the room. It was deuced uncomfortable to discover the musicale was littered with his indiscretions, and he would happily have stayed at home with his bride rather than be confronted by his mistakes.

Contemplating time with Sophia, his thoughts wandered to later in the evening, when they would leave and head for home. If they did not make love soon, it might become a habit he did not wish to encourage. Sophia and he had enjoyed a pleasant day once the startling arrival of his son had been dealt with. He had shown her around Balfour Terrace, including the gallery where he told her the highlights of his family history. They had met with Ethan and played chess in the library. The boy was still learning the finer points, but Richard was impressed with his grasp of the game and enjoyed showing him moves after their initial match. Throughout the day and during dinner, Sophia and he had successfully rebuilt their rapport and returned to the relaxed state of companionship from the day of their wedding.

Now that the drama had receded, Richard anticipated that this would be the night that they would consummate their wedding vows. He imagined, with relish, undressing Sophia later in the evening when he would discover what she looked like beneath all those clothes and school her in the art of lovemaking. Her eager responses thus far were promising an exceptional compatibility to be revealed in their marriage bed. Mayhap he would suggest they leave at the earliest opportunity. Perhaps he should slip out to request that their carriage be first in line. Realizing how his wayward thoughts would provide evidence of arousal, he diverted his attention back to the music. It had been too long since he had lain with a woman, and he looked forward with heated fervor to bedding his wife as he recalled the feel of her rounded buttocks pressing into his lap earlier that morning.

* * *

Sᴏᴘʜɪᴀ ɴᴏᴛɪᴄᴇᴅ that Richard had left her side, but the popular music was riveting so she did not pay much mind. Which was why she was so startled when he dropped back into the seat beside her.

Leaning forward, he whispered in her ear, "Tell your family you are fatigued, so we will be leaving now." His breath tickled her ear and reawakened the desire initiated that morning in his study.

"But I am quite alert and I am enjoying the music," she protested under her breath.

"The music is nearly over. I ordered the carriage because you and I have unfinished business." Richard moved his hand to the edge of her seat to trail a hand along her hip, using her skirts to hide his scandalous handling of her person. Her heartbeat increased, a rush of pleasant warmth traversing her senses.

"Oh," was all she could think to say, her mind replaying memories of sitting in his lap, touching him. And kissing. Leaning over to speak in a low voice, she told Lily she would be leaving. Her cousin gained the attention of Lady Moreland, who swung her head to look at her in question. Sophia made short work of her excuses and farewells.

Richard rose, and she followed him out. As they walked down the corridor to the front door, he grabbed her hand. She was shocked, swiveling her head around to ensure no one could see them engaged in such impropriety, but there was only a lone footman standing next to the front door, his gaze politely averted to the opposite wall.

Soon, Richard was helping her step up into the carriage. He followed and swung the door closed behind him before pulling the curtain closed. Sliding down the bench, he closed the curtains on the other door, then shifted over to sit beside her. Sophia was breathless with anticipation by the time he caressed her cheek to gently turn her head toward him. His head lowered until he was less than a quarter inch from brushing her lips with his, but he stopped to stare into her eyes. She stared back at him, hungry for his kiss. When he failed to, she finally lost patience and leaned forward to press her lips against his, feeling him smile against her.

He moved to rest his clean-shaven cheek against hers. "I love that you want me. The way you explored my body in bed this morning ... it was beguiling." She shivered in delight as his seductive words stroked against her skin in a whisper, continuing to travel through her blood until they reached between her legs where she throbbed in melting heat. A large hand found her knee where it rubbed gently back and forth, intensifying her body's response. His lips grazed along her cheek to find her earlobe, and she felt his mouth closing over it to suckle gently. She moaned, arching her neck when the errant hand grazed up her leg to rest on her waist, his fingertips fleeting across the curve of her breast.

She moaned again in arousal, pressing closer to him in eager frustration while his tongue traced down her neck to flick at the base of her throat at the frantic pulse beating just beneath the surface. She raised a hand to tentatively rest on his shoulder before giving in to temptation to slide it up his neck to comb through his soft locks of dark brown hair with her fingers. He groaned while his hand moved up to cup her breast, and Sophia discovered just how much he affected her senses when her breathing frayed erratically and blood pounded in her ears in response. She wanted to climb onto him, entangle herself against him like a vine weaving through a trelli—.

The carriage stopped.

Richard raised his head and gently let go of her breast, panting. With a sound of frustration, he eased back on the plump squabs, where he rested his head against the seat to stare at the ceiling. Sophia was uncertain what was happening, but he appeared to be slowly counting. He drew a deep breath and then shifted to sit on the other side of the carriage.

"You will need to get out before me with the help of the footman. I ... need a few moments to recover." He exhaled deeply. Sophia gathered up her wits, which were scattered chaotically, when she heard a discreet knock. The door swung open, and she slid across to grasp the hand that the servant held out to aid her in her descent. Light was cast over the steps when Radcliffe opened the door and waited calmly for her to enter the house, but she stood waiting for her husband who took an interminable time to appear in the carriage doorway.

"Radcliffe!"

"Yes, milord?"

"I need Shaw immediately and send someone to assist her ladyship right away."

It gratified Sophia to hear Richard's urgent tone. It was comforting to observe that his frustration at the recent interruptions was wearing his patience as thin as her own. She smiled with delight when he grasped her hand to pull her firmly up to and through the front door, heading to the grand staircase.

* * *

RICHARD DID NOT WAIT for his valet to make an appearance. Instead, he began wrenching off his tailcoat to throw it across the chest of drawers. His waistcoat followed. Then he sat and tugged at his shoes to drop them before tackling his stockings with impatience. Once he discarded those, he started on his cravat, but in his eagerness to join Sophia, his fingers fumbled and he struggled to undo the knot. With relief, he noticed Shaw's shadow cast across the floor a moment before the valet made an appearance in the open doorway.

"Milord! Let me take care of that, I beg of you." Shaw rushed over. Richard dropped his hands so that the manservant could make short work of untangling him from its grip.

Richard was not sure what had come over him. He had engaged in trysts many times in the past, and normally exhibited a deftness in the art of clothing removal, but since the heated moment inside the carriage, his thoughts were in disarray. All he could focus on was that his lovely bride was in the next room and the memory of her pert breast in his hand. He was demented with lust, his mind engaged in the need to bed this unusual woman who did not care about society's opinion but appeared to care about *him*. Who accepted his newfound child, while rejecting connections with cloying, spoilt peers. Who loved music and despised gossip.

He could not wait any longer. The patient seductions he had engaged in before Sophia were a thing of the past. He wanted to bed his wife. Now.

The moment Shaw loosened the cravat, Richard sprang to his bare feet to storm across the room in his trousers and linen shirt, flinging the connecting door open to his bride's bedroom.

CHAPTER 10

*S*ophia flinched in surprise while the young maid attending her squealed in fright. She swung her head to look over her shoulder at her intruding husband, who stood panting in the doorway. He stepped deeper into the room, closing the door with a careless bang behind him.

"Out."

His demand made the maid flinch.

"But … her ladyship's hair?"

The maid held up a hand filled with hairpins in mute explanation.

Richard inhaled deeply, perhaps to calm himself? Sophia watched him, tall and commanding, which her body responded to in tingling pleasure. Her husband's patience was wearing thin. She admitted to a kernel of delight that the infamously glib lord was exhibiting signs of frustration in his pursuit of her.

"I will take care of her ladyship's hair. Put the pins down, if you will, and leave us."

The servant curtsied, placed the pins on the dressing table

where Sophia was seated, and hurried from the room to close the door behind her.

Sophia chuckled. "Are you satisfied? You frightened the poor girl."

"If she stayed any longer, she would have been far more frightened when I ignored her presence to take you to bed."

"Hmm ... then I am glad you threw her out. Are you going to help me with my hair, husband?"

Richard walked over to her. He raised his hands hesitantly before carefully touching her hair to pull out the remaining pins. Feeling his fingers working through her strands caused frissons of pleasure. She murmured in delight while he continued, her body attuning to his touch in a manner she had never experienced before.

He unraveled her braids so that her hair fell down to her waist. Combing them out gently with his fingers, he leaned down to lift her locks to his face. He breathed in her scent while she remained frozen in melting enjoyment. "So beautiful ..." His whisper was so low she barely caught the words. He came around to clasp her hand in his, drawing her up from the chair while his hungry eyes scoured her from head to foot, causing her nipples to harden beneath the thin shift that was all that shielded her naked body from his gaze.

His eyes returned up to look at her, an intense green as they bored into her soul.

"Are you ready? For ... this? After everything that has happened, I would understand ..." He gestured toward the bed, his face reflecting vulnerability while he waited for her response.

Lifting onto her toes, she placed a kiss on his lips. "I do not wish to wait."

He growled, bending down to lift her in his powerfully muscled arms. "Then we will wait no longer."

He carried her over to the bed, leaving her with a healthy

appreciation of his strength when he showed no sign of effort. He lowered her onto the turned down sheets and stepped back to lift his shirt up and off, tossing it aside while he returned to lower himself over her. Sophia ran her eyes over the sculpted muscles she had explored that morning, breathless with awe at his broad chest and shoulders, with a light dusting of curling hair trailing down into his trousers. His face came over hers, and she stared up into his eyes.

"You are most impressive," she whispered.

"So I have been told." Richard grinned and then winced. "Scratch that. Call it a bad habit. I have no wish to be my past glib self with you. I think I will rather say … thank you." He appeared to be at a loss for words before finally continuing awkwardly. "And you have been impressing me, which is why I have presented myself in your chambers with such a ravenous appetite."

Sophia's eyes went wide. "Ravenous?"

Richard growled. "Ravenous. I cannot stop thinking about you, about your soft skin, and the breathy sighs you make when I kiss you. How you ran your hand over my body this morning, and how much I wanted to …"

"To?"

He appeared to be grasping for words. "To … make you my wife. I want this … with you. You make me feel things I have never felt before. I think … I think I admire you. You know what you want, and you do not hesitate in pursuing it. Even as an innocent woman, you are not afraid to touch me, to explore my body in the manner I wish to explore yours."

She smiled up at him. "I want you," she whispered.

Richard shook his head, disbelief splayed across his countenance. "I do not know why, but I will take advantage of it." With that, his lips found hers in a deep, drugging kiss. His tongue stole into her mouth to find hers, and she was lost in the moment, the feel of him drowning her in a whirlwind of desire while she panted out the very sighs he had admired just moments before.

His hand found her breast once more, and she moaned in ecstasy, arching up to make more contact with his hard body and his large hand. She wrapped a leg around his while her foot caressed up and down his calf as their kiss deepened. Finally he groaned before trailing hot kisses down her neck to lick at the point it met her shoulder, making her shiver and gasp when tingling sensation shot through her entire body down to her toes.

He chuckled against her skin before moving his mouth down to suckle a hardened nipple jutting against her shift. The warm, wet heat of his mouth made her moan and squirm beneath him while his hand lifted to fidget with the edge of her shift. He pulled at the garment to loosen it before exposing her breast.

He raised his head to look down at it before groaning. "I love …" He lowered his head to lick at her pebbled nipple. She whimpered with pleasure, pushing up for closer contact. "You are as perfect as I …" She could barely make out his whispered words, drowning in the shocking delight of him tonguing her nipple while trailing a hand down to find the hem of her garment. She felt him clasping her ankle, where he toyed back and forth across her skin before gliding his hand up her leg.

Sophia pulled his head back, the sensation too exquisite and her need to feel his lips again foremost on her mind. She wiggled down and leaned up to kiss his lips once more while his hand traveled to caress the back of her knee. Exhaling deeply, she slipped her tongue into his mouth as he had done to her and explored it. He made a pained sound before deepening the kiss further.

Vaguely, she grew aware that his hand rested on her inner thigh, but she paid no mind. She was lost in a sea of feeling. His kisses were magical, the feel of his hands over-whelming.

Sophia jumped in shock when he grazed his thumb between her legs, her thighs quivering in excitement at the feel of him against the seam of her sex. Her legs fell open to invite further ministrations, to which he responded with a groan while his warm hand cupped her. She stopped breathing in anticipation before he slowly slid a finger gently through her folds. They were ... slick? Was that normal?

"You are so wet for me," Richard groaned against her mouth. He seemed happy about it. Sophia supposed that answered the question, then. She started breathing again. Heavily. Really more panting than breathing while his fingers explored the creases and folds of her sex, touching a sensitive spot which caused her to keen at the white-hot pleasure that rippled through her.

Richard moved his mouth to her cheek, where she could feel him smiling against her skin while he explored her. One of his fingers dipped into her tight channel where her muscles throbbed, craving ... she was not exactly sure, but his hand was a good start.

His thumb returned to graze the sensitive spot at the apex of her seam while his fingertip continued to seek access to her body. Sophia was mindless with the pleasure of it, grinding into his hand while panting moans of rapture. The pleasure rose and kept rising, making her feverish with exci-tation. "Come for me, sweet Sophia," Richard breathed against her jaw, his tongue flickering over her skin. A wave of sensation hit her, shooting through her so that she wailed her pleasure. She was only aware of Richard, and his hand, and the waves of white-hot pleasure rippling through her body while her intimate muscles contracted rhythmically for several heart-stopping moments. Slowly, she fell from the heights of pleasure back into the sheets of her bed.

Gradually, she opened her eyes in amazement. "That was …" She could find no words.

Richard smiled smugly. Sitting up, he grasped her shift and, with slow deliberation, lightly tugged it up to pull it off her. She struggled up to assist him, realizing that despite the transcendence she just experienced, they were not yet done.

Once he had the garment off her, he tossed it away before slowly examining her naked body with an ardent gaze. He groaned, raising a hand to caress her belly before lowering his head to kiss her mouth. Pulling back, he rose from the bed and made quick work of his trousers and small clothes.

Sophia gasped in appreciation, her eyes riveted to his swollen manhood that jutted proudly. He followed her gaze.

"I am quite pleased we finally reached this stage of our marriage, wife," he growled. Consternation crossed his features when she suddenly sat up and swung her legs over the side of the bed to sit facing him.

"What do you call … it?" She waved a hand toward the impressive appendage.

Concern flickered in his eyes. "Most men call it a cock."

"Hmm … may I touch it?"

Richard closed his eyes for a moment, his lips moving as if he was saying a silent prayer. When he opened them, the intensity of his desire shone to make his green eyes glitter like emeralds in the lamplight. He gave a nod.

"It is not normally like this?" She did not think so. The museum housed several Italian marble statues with fig leaves to cover the area, but it had not appeared they were covering something so … large. He shook his head, words appearing to fail him when she reached out a hand to graze a fingertip across the crown. To her bemusement, it twitched at her touch. Slowly, she wrapped her hand around the shaft and ran it down the length in a caress. It twitched again, and Richard groaned before grabbing her hand to move it away.

"I cannot endure much more of that tonight."

"You will let me explore it another time?" Richard looked at her with something akin to shock before lowering his hands to her waist and lifting her back to lie on the bed.

"We shall see." With that, he raised a knee onto the edge of the mattress and kneeled over her with hunger painted across his face. His lips sought hers while his hand played once more with her breast, and Sophia found her desire returning quickly. He slowly lowered himself down to press his heated flesh against hers. She murmured at the feel of his naked skin against hers, noticing his legs were roughened with hairs when he slid between her own until his cock was resting against her sex.

He raised his head to stare into her eyes. "Are you ready?"

She gave a nod. Her intimate muscles were clenching at the feel of his cock so close.

"You are aware it might hurt the first time?"

She gave another nod. Lady Moreland had taken her aside on the eve of the wedding.

He looked relieved. His hand reached between them, and he took hold of himself to guide the swollen length into her channel. As he entered her, she felt a slight pinching sensation before the feeling of his fullness invading her body overcame her. She threw her head back in wordless intoxication while her body eagerly grasped at his cock.

"Sophia …" Whatever Richard wanted to say was apparently forgotten. Fully sheathed inside her, and his breathing unsteady, he held himself still. After several long, sweet moments of bliss, she opened her eyes. His were closed, and his expression was pained with effort.

"Is that it?"

Richard opened his eyes in shock. "No. I am proceeding slowly so I do not hurt you."

"I am fine. Is there more?"

He shook his head in amusement. "Yes, there is more."

With that, he eased back and then gently thrust back into her. The slow drag out and in was astounding. She threw her head back and wailed. She heard Richard chuckling for a second before he, too, was carried away.

Rippling pleasure returned as he thrust in and out of her hungry body, slowly increasing the speed until she thought she might splinter into a million pieces of thrilling sensation. His hand reached between them to slide against her slick nub. She gasped in response when a new tidal wave of titillation cascaded into another peak of clenching pleasure. She heard herself crying out in a way she had never done before while Richard continued moving, seeking his own peak. Moments later, he groaned while his length spasmed rhythmically inside her, his heat flooding into her.

Richard panted above her before lightly extricating himself from her body to roll onto his side. His eyes were closed, but his large, elegant hand slid across her belly to caress her waist while his breathing slowly returned to normal.

"Was it good?" Sophia asked.

"Very good," murmured Richard into her ear.

"As good as …" She was not sure exactly how to ask what she was curious about.

"Better. Much, *much* better."

"Good." A small smile of happiness quivered on her lips. She was finding she truly enjoyed being married to this outrageous man and, after a chaotic couple of days, they were finding their way in this new relationship. It would seem that she had made the right choice to marry him and life at his side would never fail to provide excitement. She shivered at the delicious exhilaration she had just experienced in his arms.

* * *

RICHARD AWOKE as dawn crept into Sophia's room. Staring up at the swaths of fabric that covered the four-poster frame, he reflected on the wonderful night he had spent in Sophia's bed. Somehow, this woman made him forget his past, forget his mistakes, and made him hopeful that he would become an honorable man. Time with her was paradise compared to the women of his past because she eased his worries just by being near him.

It made him question what he had been doing with his licentious pursuits. Had he been trying to bury deep-seated problems by losing himself in the arms of the many women he had lain with? Sophia made him want to live his life, while earlier women had merely been an escape from it.

He rolled onto his side, preparing to rise, when he yelped in surprise. Standing next to the bed, staring with wide, green eyes, was Ethan, almost exactly at face level.

"Ethan?"

"Good morning, Papa. I have been waiting for you to wake up. Emma says it is polite to let people wake up on their own rather than startle them from their sleep."

"Uh ... good morning."

"I have been waiting for a while. We get up early on the farm, but Emma says people in the city go to sleep late."

Richard let the remarks about the mysterious Emma pass. "How did you find me?"

"I followed your *vah-let*. But when you were not in your room, I tried the other doors. Papa, what is a *vah-let*?"

Richard rubbed his eyes, attempting to gather his thoughts. He was still groggy.

"A valet is a servant who helps a gentleman to dress and look his best."

Ethan's round face scrunched while he thought about this.

"Am I a gentleman?"

Richard froze. It was a difficult question. He wanted to be honest with the boy. Many members of polite society would raise considerable dissent at the idea that Ethan was a gentleman because he bore the burden of unmarried parents. On the other hand, the truest gentleman of his acquaintance was his cousin and friend, the Duke of Halmesbury. Thinking about Halmesbury, he found an answer he was comfortable with.

"A gentleman is a man who is well-mannered and considerate of the people around him. So I would say that you are a gentleman."

Ethan's face split into a wide grin. "I like that. Does that mean I will get a *vah-let*?"

Richard smiled in return. "When you are older, you will get one." He reached out a hand to ruffle the boy's curly hair that looked just like his own. "But only if you do not run off from your nursemaid on your own."

Ethan looked perplexed. "She is to be with me all the time?"

"Yes. She is to keep you safe and ensure you eat."

"Mama said I was welcome to visit any part of the house. Did I make a mistake coming to find you?"

Richard had been sitting up, looking around for something to wear, when he stilled at Ethan's question. "Mama?"

Ethan nodded and pointed to the flowing red-blonde locks spread over the discarded pillow. "I asked Sophia if she was my mama, and she said if that was what I wanted. I never had a mama before, so I thought about it in bed last night. She seems nice, so I would like her to be my mama." The boy's eyes widened with anxiety. "Will she mind if I call her Mama?"

Richard's heart squeezed in a tight grip of emotion. "I cannot say for certain, but knowing Sophia, I think she would like it."

Ethan looked happy with this. Richard suspected he was fortunate to have a four-year-old son who was turning out to be clever and well-behaved with such a calmness of manner. He wondered if the Emma the boy kept referring to had a hand in how well his son had turned out in his parental absence. Shaking his head to clear his thoughts, Richard came to the realization that he was trapped under the covers without a stitch of clothing at hand. He could not climb from the bed until the boy left the room.

"Ethan, could you find your way back to the nursery?"

His child nodded. He moved closer and flung his arms around Richard, who, after a moment's surprise, drew in the slight frame with his free arm to give him an affectionate squeeze. The boy was so sweet and innocent. Although Richard was still growing accustomed to his new role as father, he was experiencing an urge to protect the boy.

After a moment, he let the boy go, and Ethan trotted from the room and closed the door behind him.

Richard rose in a hurry and hunted for his linen shirt, which was lying near the foot of the bed. Pulling it on, he then picked up the shift he had removed from Sophia's luscious body. A rush of heat accompanied the memory, and for a moment, he contemplated returning to bed to awaken her. Brushing this aside, he straightened the covers and laid the shift on top for her to find when she awoke.

Grabbing his trousers from the floor, he loped back to his room where he found a sour-looking Shaw preparing his clothing. "Is there a problem, Shaw?"

The servant sniffed, his thin lips pursed in disapproval. The man's affectations were annoying, but he was the best damned valet in London, so Richard tolerated it. "I am merely concerned that the coat could be irretrievably damaged."

"What? Not with the most skillful valet who ever graced the city of London. If anyone can sort it out, it is you, Shaw."

The man's thin face looked mollified at the praise.

"Milord, I found this in your coat last night." The valet held out a folded paper. Richard frowned, not recognizing it, and he wondered how it had found its way onto his person. Shaw always checked his pockets before taking discarded clothing away, so it must have been from sometime during the day before. He had spent the day with Sophia and Ethan, and not done any work or taken any meetings. He had also not handled any papers, so it did not make sense. And the only time he had left Balfour Terrace was to attend the musicale. Where ... where ... a vague memory took shape. *Where I was jostled while collecting refreshment for Sophia and myself! Did someone bump against me to slip a note into my pocket?* Richard attempted to recall the people who were in his vicinity, but the truth was, the room had been crowded and he had not paid much attention to anyone other than Sophia. He grimaced at the recollection of his former paramours and the men associated with them. Not to mention the unknown man in the row behind who had been scowling at him.

He took the note from Shaw's hand. With a feeling of impending doom, Richard unfolded the paper. His blood ran cold at the threatening words written on the page.

Blazes! Had he entered purgatory? Just yesterday, Sophia had confessed that she married him for security, and now this? What the hell was going on? What was he going to do?

He considered rousting Perry up from his bed to talk, but his brother was still coming to terms with his recent nuptials and was being a bit of an arse. No, he needed to speak with someone else. Someone with maturity and sense. Someone like ... Halmesbury!

The duke would know what to do if anyone would.

His mind made up, Richard resolved to send his cousin a request to meet at White's to discuss how to address the contents of the note. He could not visit Markham House directly with Annabel in residence. The irony that the duke was helping him with his bid to regain his honor, while the duchess was the person he had most wronged with his past proclivities, did not escape Richard's attention. It was a strange situation where he sought advice from her husband, but there was nothing to be done about it. He would still meet with Halmesbury, who had assured him that Annabel encouraged the duke's friendship with himself despite their ongoing estrangement.

Meanwhile, he would organize protection for Sophia and Ethan.

* * *

Sophia awoke much later than usual. Richard had made love to her several times in the night, although he forwent a second coupling, stating that her body needed to grow accustomed. Instead, he had demonstrated a startling method using his mouth which made her cheeks warm to think of.

Humming a popular tune from the musicale the night before, she entered the breakfast room. Several footmen were in attendance, so she assumed her maid had alerted them she was coming down to break her fast. She had met all of the servants over the past two days, yet she noticed a new man standing by the door.

She turned to him for an introduction but hesitated when she took in his appearance. The unknown manservant was several inches shorter than the others. Footmen were usually chosen for their height and handsome features because they were part of a household's display of wealth and status. This man was not only shorter, his livery was ill-fitting, as if tailored for one of the taller men. Sophia hated to be critical, but the man was not … handsome. In fact, he was a bit rough-and-tumble, with his stocky build and a dark shadow across his clean-shaven cheeks. He looked like he might be quite hairy, bearing evidence of the overshadow of a beard this early in the day.

"Hello?"

"Um … milady." He acknowledged her with a clumsy bow. It did not appear he was familiar with the movement. Sophia fought back a frown. Something was off. Also, had the man been inside the breakfast room when she arrived, or had he followed her into the room?

"Your name is …?"

"I am … John, milady." John appeared to forget his own name. Sophia grew ever more suspicious.

"Have you worked at Balfour Terrace long, John?"

The man dropped his eyes for a moment. "Not long, milady. I arrived from one of the country estates recently."

She hated to be rude, but a warning bell was sounding in her head. "Well … pleased to meet you … John." With that, she continued her path to the sideboard with covered dishes.

Sophia was an observer of people—needs must, to avoid betrothal for three Seasons—so she had learned how to read people, especially men, in order to dissuade their attentions. She definitely would seek Richard out after she ate to ask about this bizarre footman who had turned up.

CHAPTER 11

*R*ichard sat at his mahogany desk, reading his neglected correspondence of the past few days. He was to meet with Halmesbury that afternoon at one of their mutual clubs, White's. He could do nothing more about the note planted on his person at the musicale the night before. All he could do was attempt to address his mounting work before the meeting.

He heard Perry's distinctive gait enter his study, then loiter near his desk. Richard bit back his irritation and looked up to find his brother looking disconcerted. *Hades, has something else happened?* He did not think he could handle any more surprises this morning.

Perry fidgeted in discomfort before opening his mouth to speak, then shutting it.

"What is it?" Richard asked in the most patient tone he could manage, not quite daring to hear the answer.

"You know those print shops? The ones that display caricatures in their windows, like the ones Thomas Rowlandson and George Cruikshank draw?"

Richard closed his eyes in trepidation. Despite his dissolute life up until now, he had mostly avoided being the victim of such drawings, unlike the new king who was plagued by unflattering illustrations depicting his libidinous activities. He feared his luck might have turned, based on his brother's lack of composure.

Perry continued. "I was walking past some of those shops this morning, and I saw a great quantity of these displayed." He tossed a paper on the desk as if he wished to be parted from it as quickly as possible, then swiftly stepped away.

Richard opened his eyes to stare down at the colored print. It looked like himself in nightclothes and several light-skirts tangled around him. Across from his likeness stood a woman who must be Sophia, based on the flowing red-blonde hair. He huffed in agitation before lifting it to read the caption.

Somerset earls and their licentious habits. "I swear I did not invite these women to our wedding night."

Richard dropped the print like it was scalding hot. Exhaling heavily, he pushed his chair back to rise, running his hand through his hair in agitation.

Perry ventured a question. "Do you suppose one of the servants tattled about what happened?"

Richard stopped to think. Recalling the threatening note in his pocket, he shook his head. "Nay, the man who let the doxies into the house. It must be him."

Perry tilted his head. "What do you mean? This is another prank?"

Richard scowled. "Not a prank. I believe whoever let those women in wished me ill. I received a threatening note, so it must be linked because it is too many situations converging at once to be a coincidence."

"But who?"

"I do not know. A jilted lover? A cuckolded husband? The potential for enemies is vast, considering my prolific bedding of women the length and breadth of England. Damnit, why could I not keep my falls buttoned?"

"May I read the note?"

Richard tugged it out of his coat and threw it at Perry, who caught it deftly. He resumed pacing, thinking about how he had decided not to tell Sophia about the note yet. He must alert her to the caricature, however. She might be a laughing-stock, and it was only fair to warn her to expect trouble the next time she left their home.

Perry whistled after reading the page. "What will you do?"

"I am meeting with Halmesbury this afternoon to discuss it. This is larger than my experience, and I need an outside perspective. In the meantime, I increased security for Sophia and Ethan. *Damnit!* The woman married me for safety, and all I have done is bring her chaos!"

His brother came over to hand the note back. "Halmesbury is a good idea because I find myself quite unprepared for this. But what can I do to help, brother?"

Perry's face reflected genuine concern. Richard sighed in relief. His brother's recalcitrance of the past few days appeared to have passed, for there was no evidence of it now. His help in dealing with the matter would be valuable.

"Perhaps you can attend your clubs and listen for gossip. Any clues to who is tormenting me would be helpful."

Perry nodded. "I can do that. What will you tell … your wife?"

Richard dropped his gaze. "I will need to warn her about the gossip, but I do not want to scare her about the note. I must take care of it, but she will be safe. I made sure of it."

Sucking in a calming breath, Richard went to his desk to take up the horrible print, then left the room to find Sophia. He tried a couple of rooms before locating her in the breakfast room where she sat with a full plate, raising a strawberry to the sweet mouth he had kissed so passionately the night before. A blaze of hot desire accompanied the memory.

"Richard!" she called out in delight, dropping the strawberry.

"Good morning, Sophia. Did you sleep well?" A pretty flush covered her cheeks, and he recognized that she was thinking similar thoughts to his own, a fact that caused his loins to twinge in reactive desire.

"Yes, my lord."

Richard grinned for a moment, suspecting he was being 'my lorded' because she was embarrassed and nervous.

"Can you clear the room?" He directed the command at the footmen, who quickly left and closed the door.

Sophia's features reflected worry when he walked over to pull out the chair next to her. "Is something wrong? With Ethan?"

"Ethan is fine. I have a bit of news this morning. Bad news. I wanted to share it with you before you became aware of it ... some other way." He offered her the print he was carrying. Perplexed, she accepted it and scanned the print.

"Oh my!" She made a snorting sound and her shoulders shook. Richard's heart sank. He was causing his bride to sob not three days in to their marriage.

Then the snort turned into ... laughter? Sophia howled, wiping tears of mirth from her eyes. Had she lost her mind? Had he driven her to hysteria with one too many problems? Thankfully, he had not informed her of the threatening note or—

"This is priceless!" Her exclamation marked the end of her laughter. Richard raised his eyebrows. Noting his expression, she raised her own. "Never say this concerns you?"

"Of course it does. I made you the object of gossip and—"

"Pish! Marrying you has made me interesting for a minute. But next week someone will draw yet another print of King George and that silly rumored trial of Queen Caroline. All will be forgotten of the Saunton household, and we will move on. Whatever we must contend with will be no worse than polite society's reaction to Ethan living in our household. If I can cope with that, then I can cope with this, too ... but I appreciate the warning," she finished in a cajoling tone, as if she was comforting him.

Richard had not realized he was holding his breath. At her words, he exhaled a sigh of relief. "What did I do to deserve you?"

She coughed delicately into her hand. "Quite a few things I do not wish to mention." Richard grinned at her reference to their fiery evening together.

Grabbing her hand, he raised it to his lips. "You are a marvelous woman! Beyond compare."

She blushed in response before waving him off so she could eat her meal. Richard was determined to prevent any more crises from arising before his wife ever discovered that he put the valued security she sought in jeopardy with his immoral past. He would finish his correspondence and then it would be time to meet Halmesbury to discuss the note burning a hole in his pocket.

* * *

SOPHIA HELD her skirts aloft while climbing the stairs to the nursery. She planned to take Ethan out to the gardens to enjoy some sunshine, and perhaps share some hothouse fruit with the boy. Reaching the landing, she turned in to the corridor leading to the nursery. Out of the corner of her eye, she noticed a flicker of movement and spun around in surprise to see that the new footman, John, was climbing the stairs behind her. He quickly stepped over to the banister, pulled out a dust cloth, and started wiping at the grooves.

Sophia frowned. She thought the chambermaids did the dusting. The man was behaving suspiciously, and she did not trust him. Perhaps she needed to talk to Richard about it when he returned home. News of the print had caused her to forget her desire to talk with him about the new footman earlier. Turning back, she made her way to the nursery, where she found yet another footman dusting picture frames in the hall. Stopping near him, she looked him over, noting she had not met this servant either. He gave her a quick bow. "Milady."

"Are you new?"

"No, milady. I ... am recently arrived from ... one of Lord Saunton's country estates." The man spoke like he was remembering lines in a play. Sophia's suspicions mounted once more.

"And your name is?"

The man, who was very similar in appearance to the footman she had met at breakfast, looked uncertain for a second. He was slightly taller, but his livery was just as disheveled and his collar was crooked.

"John, milady."

"John?"

"Yes, milady."

"Like the other footman just arrived."

His expression was strained. "Yes, milady."

"Two Johns?"

He gave a nod.

"Both arrived from the Saunton country estates?"

He nodded again, appearing to be tongue-tied.

"Well. Good to meet you, John. I hope you enjoy London."

Sophia abruptly opened the door to the nursery before he could reply. If he offered her another lie, she was going to vent her frustration, so she strode away.

When she entered, she found Ethan drawing on a page

with a graphite pencil while his nursemaid, Daisy, sat across from him. His sweet face lit up at the sight of her. "Mama!"

Sophia froze in surprise. His small face scrunched. "May I call you Mama? Papa said he thought you would like it."

Sophia's eyes prickled, a lump in her throat while she nodded with enthusiasm. "Of course! I was just surprised. If you want to call me ... that ... I would be most honored." She turned her face to dab at her eyes. When she turned back, Ethan was right before her, having crossed the room as silently as a cat.

"I have never had a mama before," he said earnestly, his small face angled up to look at her.

On the verge of weeping, Sophia swallowed the thick emotion and dropped to her haunches.

"Now you do." She reached out to hug him, and he ran into her arms, embracing her with his small arms. Sophia rested her cheek on the crown of his head, his thick curling hair tickling her nose, and she did her best to fight back the tears welling up. Across the room, Daisy caught her eye and gave a wide smile in encouragement.

Sophia leaned back to look Ethan in the face. "Have you eaten?"

"Yes. Daisy and I had breakfast early. Not as early as the farm, but early enough."

"Good. Would you like to go with me to the gardens?"

He nodded vigorously. Sophia smiled, rising to her feet to take his little hand. Daisy rose to follow her out of the room.

Exiting into the hall, Sophia came to a stop when she found the two Johns both waiting outside the door. She frowned, mistrusting that the two men were, in fact, footmen when she noted how they were slouching against the wall, quickly straightening when she had opened the door and surprised them.

There was no doubt in her mind that they were up to something. She resolved to seek Richard out.

* * *

STILL WORRYING about the unexpected note, Richard strode into White's for his meeting with the Duke of Halmesbury. He soon found his cousin sitting at a table with two fresh drinks on it.

The duke always put Richard in mind of a Norse god, with his powerful frame, broad good looks, and full blond hair. Although Richard was no lightweight at six feet, his cousin topped him by several inches. But Halmesbury possessed a friendly manner, and he was a true gentleman, which acted as a counter-weight to his intimidating physical stature.

Richard collapsed into the chair next to his cousin, the stresses of the day weighing him down.

Arching an eyebrow, he indicated the drinks with a nod of his head. "I thought you did not drink."

"We are sitting at White's. It is always easier to order a drink to avoid being constantly pestered by the servers. You can have mine, if you like. I have not touched it."

"My bride prefers if I do not drink. Something to do with her father, I think. It is the least I can do, given the chaos of the past few days."

"Indeed, it quite surprised me to read about your nuptials, considering you made no mention of courting the lady at our last meeting. When we discussed your list of paramours."

Richard flushed at the recollection of that meeting. Fortunately, he had made amends to several of the women on the list since then. "The union was unexpected. I planned to court her, but on my first visit, she interviewed me for the position of husband, then threw herself in my arms at the moment her uncle entered the room."

Halmesbury bit back a smile. "The countess compromised you?"

"After verifying I was serious in my pursuit, she blurted something about her uncle never agreeing to the match and kissed me senseless."

Halmesbury snorted, trying not to laugh. "An apropos manner for such an accomplished rake to be caught."

"Rake no more. Laugh, if you will, but she is a unique and intriguing woman."

Halmesbury frowned. "And my Annabel was not?"

Richard grimaced. It was a fair question. One he had asked himself repeatedly since meeting Sophia. Why had he not altered his ways when he had asked Annabel for her hand in marriage? His cousin was his best friend, other than his own brother. It was still awkward after nearly two years that Halmesbury had stolen his bride because of Richard's philandering ways. "I … I was not ready to change then. I was dishonest and incapable of forging a true connection with her. You made the right choice when you took her from me. Annabel deserved to be with you."

Halmesbury leaned back in his chair, astonished. Richard squirmed, unsure what to say next. "Well, it would seem quite a change has been wrought since I saw you last?"

"I have been meeting with the women I wronged and setting matters to right with them. In fact … I met with Caroline Brown and made matters right with her."

"The maid whom Annabel … witnessed you with?" Richard gave a nod. "Annabel will be pleased. She has expressed worry about the girl from time to time. They were apparently close."

Richard stuck a finger behind his tight collar, attempting to ease the pressure restricting his breathing. This was so dashed awkward to discuss with the husband of the woman he had wronged so unjustly. He caught the moment Halmesbury took pity and changed the subject.

"Tell me about your wife?"

Richard blew out a breath in relief. "She is feisty and intelligent. And more direct than I expected. We have experienced an outrageous few days, but the countess has shown great composure and presence of mind. I have met few women so impressive ..." He stopped, not wishing to reference Annabel again. "But now I fear I may have put her in danger when I married her."

Looking round to ensure no one was within earshot, and appreciating the duke's foresight in ordering the drinks so that the servers did not hover close by, Richard quickly filled his cousin in on the events of the past few days. There was much to discuss, including the discovery that he had fathered a natural born son who had arrived in his home, and that someone had placed a threatening note in his pocket, most likely at the Lawson musicale. When he was done, he leaned back in his chair to hear what the duke would advise.

"So, you have found a woman you can love."

Richard sat up, knocking against the table and nearly upsetting the untouched drinks. "I admire her. With her help, I believe I can remain on the path to regain my honor. I did not mention love."

Halmesbury stared at Richard without a word. After a deep silence, he spoke. "You admire the woman. It is my understanding from our last meeting that overhearing her at the Astley ball prompted you to begin this quest you are on. You are attracted to her, and you appear very concerned with her well-being. It is not love?"

Richard shook his head in denial. His family history proved that Balfours were incapable of love. The only one in his family who had possessed the capacity to love was his mother, but she had had no Balfour blood in her veins. Love had broken her heart and contributed to her death. Love was a foolish endeavor.

"Nevertheless, I brought you a wedding gift." The duke placed a small leather-bound volume on the table.

Richard picked it up. "Poems of Wedded Bliss?"

"The author is Lord John Pettigrew. Do you remember him from Oxford?" Richard nodded. "John's writing is the reason I met Annabel. The reason I was ready to risk marrying again after the death of my first wife. Since his own marriage two years ago, he has published his advice on marriage in the form of some very fine poetry. The poems contain exceptional advice about maintaining a happy marriage. The importance of honesty and such. I highly recommend reading it."

Richard's agitation rose at the repeated mentions of the duke's wife, the sheltered but fierce noblewoman who had jilted him because she had discovered him in the stables with her maid in an indecent tryst. He shifted the conversation before his discomfiture was revealed, because he was not yet ready to address the matter with Annabel. Hot shame about his behavior at the time—and after—made it hard to breathe each time her name was mentioned.

"Thank you." Richard put the small volume in one of his pockets and removed the note from another.

"The matter of the note, it is quite pressing. Sophia, and even Ethan, may be at risk. I have increased security, but I must take stronger action to protect them."

The duke nodded. "I understand. You feel the responsibility of your new family."

Family? He now had ... family? To protect and safeguard against the threats of the world around him. He shook his head in disbelief. He had not made that connection until the duke voiced it, but a wife and a son waited for him at home.

His need to defend them from this fresh threat filled him with resolve.

"May I see the note?"

Richard unfolded it to stare down at the ominous words inked on the page. So few words, yet so much meaning contained within the simplicity of two sentences.

You enjoy stealing the loved ones of other men. Perhaps someone should steal yours?

The duke pulled a face. "The note implies that you interfered in loving relationships?"

Richard was indignant. "Never."

Halmesbury raised a blond eyebrow in question. Richard avoided meeting his eye, instead staring at his own hand resting next to the brandy on the table. The confession he was being forced to make left a repulsive taste in his mouth. "It is far easier to seduce unhappy wives."

He glanced up and caught the flash of distaste that crossed his cousin's face before the duke composed himself, but Richard could not blame him for the slight reaction. Even he was experiencing a reaction to the shallowness of his past pursuits. He had awoken from the bad dream to realize that he was the villain of the piece. Now he wished to reinvent himself as an honorable gentleman. There was still much work ahead. But first, he needed to ensure his … *family* … would be safe.

Halmesbury pushed the note back across the table. "You need to tell the countess."

"But she married me for security. If she thinks I cannot provide it to her, she may turn away from me. Or leave me, to return to the Morelands."

Halmesbury shrugged. "I do not think you described a woman who is so inclined. Your priority, now that you have provided additional security to protect her, is to keep your developing marriage strong. You cannot withhold a secret of this magnitude without consequences."

Richard grabbed the note to put it away, irritated. This meeting was turning out to be most unhelpful. He could not frighten his new wife with this problem, which was his fault to begin with. It was mortifying how much she had been forced to contend with since the day they said their vows, and he could not reveal that she had put herself in danger by joining his household.

He knew she was an exceptional woman, but this situation was beyond the pale. Nay. He needed to deal with this matter without alerting her to what another of his past mistakes had exposed them to. Sophia deserved the safety she sought in marrying him, and he would move heaven and earth to provide it.

Halmesbury sighed. "I see you will not."

"I cannot. Eventually, my past will be too much and her patience will reach its limit."

"I do not think you give the young woman enough credit. From what you described, she entered this marriage with her eyes open, willing to assist you on your quest. But I cannot make your decision for you. I can only encourage you to think on it. There was a time you encouraged me to talk to Annabel rather than run from my feelings. I now encourage you to do the same because it is liberating to have a life partner. Someone who is always at your side, no matter what you may have done. Or have to do. I urge you to reconsider your decision to conceal this matter."

Richard gave a curt nod. He would think about it, but he doubted he would change his mind.

"Do you have any idea who could have sent it?"

"Any number of men who might consider themselves wronged."

"I suggest you make a finite list and then task your

runners to investigate. The goal would be to reduce the list down to a manageable list of likely suspects while maintaining increased security. Just realize that your countess would be better equipped to avoid danger if she is aware that she needs to be cautious."

"I agreed to think on it!" Richard quelled his rebellion. The duke provided excellent guidance in a matter where Richard's thoughts were compromised by the turmoil of fear for his new family, and he needed to keep a cool head. "I apologize. Your guidance is appreciated. I will do what you recommended and start listing out suspects to investigate until I uncover the source of this threat."

Halmesbury smiled. "I hope you uncover it swiftly. If there is anything I can do to help, do not hesitate to ask."

CHAPTER 12

*J*ust off St. James's Place, having failed to locate Richard earlier, Sophia wandered through the modiste shop her husband had recommended for her new wardrobe befitting the wife of an earl. Lily was accompanying her, animated in her exploration of the explosion of colorful fabrics to inspect.

"It is so exciting! You can wear so many colors now that you are wed. I am quite envious." Sophia smiled at her exuberant cousin. Lily was such a ball of energy, she never failed to lift Sophia's spirits or distract her from her worries. Worries such as the fact that one of the new Johns had joined her in the carriage for this outing.

The coachman and the customary footman had sat on the box, but the shorter of the two Johns abruptly entered the carriage behind her without so much as a by-your-leave. It was unprecedented, in her experience, to have a male servant inside the carriage. When he failed to explain himself, Sophia remained quiet and tensely observant. The only reason she had not leapt from the carriage to run back into the house was the sight of Radcliffe on the front steps. The butler had been watching closely, displaying no surprise when the footman embarked, which allayed her initial fear. Still, she resolved to talk to Richard the moment there was an opportunity.

When she had collected Lily from her home, her cousin had entered the carriage and then hesitated in dismay at the sight of a footman installed on the opposite seat, but his presence prevented her from questioning Sophia about it.

It had been a relief to reach the modiste shop and exit the carriage, but she noted that The Shorter John, which she had taken to calling him in her mind, followed them up to the entrance and was currently visible through the front window while her cousin chattered about which colors Sophia should consider.

Turning her attention back to Lily, Sophia leafed through the fashion plates they had been provided. Thinking about her husband, her thoughts strayed to how he had known to send her to this particular modiste.

The proprietress was an elegant Italian woman, dressed in a stylish but simple gown. This was unusual because most modistes were obsequious French women, and a large majority of those were English women feigning their French accents and names in an attempt to be fashionable to their clientele.

Her stomach tightened with jealousy when she thought of the women Richard must have brought here in the past to gift with expensive clothing. Mistresses? Widows? Possibly unhappy wives and courtesans? She dared not let her imagination run free because her gut felt hollow at the thought of it.

"How is it?"

Sophia looked up to find Lily's large brown eyes fixed on her. She had just quietly regaled her cousin with the events of the past couple of days, but her thoughts distracted her and she found she had lost the thread of the conversation.

"How is what?"

"Married life? Are you enjoying life with the earl?" Her petite cousin appeared to be holding her breath.

"His past has created some interesting situations to deal with."

"Pish! You knew it would. How are you enjoying him?"

Sophia hesitated, thinking. "I … like him. He has been most considerate, making a point to forewarn me about situations. He is learning to be a generous father, and he has spent a great deal of time with me and his son since I arrived." She checked the shop to ensure no one could overhear her before dropping her voice. "I very much enjoy the kissing and the bedding. Saunton is … I do not know … I am becoming very attached. I think this marriage may … may …"

"May?"

"He needs me so, and he treats me like an equal. I … may be falling in love with the earl."

Lily clapped her gloved hands in glee. "I knew it. I knew he was the one for you. And if anyone is capable of managing such a scoundrel of a man, it is you, Sophia!"

Sophia shook her head. Her cousin was such a hopeless optimist. There was much to deal with at Balfour Terrace before she could claim her happily ever after. *But you are on your way!*

She sighed. Lily's optimism was contagious, it would appear.

Over at the counter, Signora Ricci was conversing with two customers, waving her hands in the manner of the Italians. She did not notice when the bell on the door sounded, but Sophia was startled and turned her head to see who entered the shop.

She recognized two women she had been introduced to at the Yardley ball, one of whom was a young widow who wore her daring ball gowns cut so low and tight, Sophia had winced to consider the constricted binding of her stays. Noting the woman was currently attired in a scarlet dress, which was inarguably an indiscreet choice for a day dress and, in keeping with her implied character, the bodice was cut so low that Sophia feared on behalf of her dignity. Surely at any moment a breast would pop out right there in the shop?

The pretty blonde caught her eye and arched a perfect eyebrow, fixing her cold blue eyes on Sophia. A wave of pure malevolence crossed the distance between them.

"Lady Saunton. It is a pleasure to see you out and about. I did so hope that those vicious prints circulating the *ton* about your wedding night would not cause you to hide within Balfour Terrace."

Lily gasped, but Sophia found herself impressed—the woman's dig was well played.

"Thank you, Lady Partridge. I do appreciate your concern."

The succubus narrowed her eyes. "How is Richard? I have not yet been to Balfour Terrace this Season." Her companion, presumably a high-born jade of equally low morals, snickered at the prod.

Sophia kept her composure, but she could see Lily's delicate brown eyebrows shooting up to her hairline. The viper was not subtle. Richard was not known for holding events at Balfour Terrace, so there could be only one insinuation to draw from her remark. Lady Partridge had visited Richard's home for reasons that were quite obvious to conclude.

"He is well." Was there a polite manner to extricate herself from the conversation? No good would come from conversing with the wicked harlot.

"Please send him my regards. We enjoy a very special connection, and I am sure he will be pleased to hear I am thinking of him."

Sophia reached her limit. This ladybird was stepping far beyond the limits of good taste with her implications. Sophia needed to mark her territory regarding her husband, or his former paramours would devour her with malicious remarks in shops across London. Let the word get around that Sophia possessed teeth and claws.

"You are a widow, if I am not mistaken?"

"What of it?"

"And the time of your ... memorable connection with Lord Saunton, you were a widow then?"

The woman scowled in confusion. "Yes, what is your point?"

"Oh, I was just thinking ... You are quite young and of childbearing age. If your relationship with my husband was so ... *special* ... then he could have proposed to you, not so? Yet, he did not. He married me after several Seasons of hunting for his bride. Why is that, do you think? I hate to state the obvious, but ... Mayhap your time together was not as memorable as you claim?"

Both Lady Partridge and her friend gasped in wounded outrage, while Sophia maintained a politely interested expression. The she-devil struggled to find a retort, apparently not quick enough to engage in verbal sparring. After a few seconds passed with her mouth opening and closing in the manner of a fish, Sophia took her cousin by the arm. "Look, Lily. I see celestial blue silk near the back wall. Shall we examine it more closely?"

Lily appeared agog over the scene she was witnessing, but she managed a nod, accompanying Sophia away from the speechless women.

"We are to remain in the shop with them?" her cousin whispered beneath her breath.

"I am in need of a wardrobe. If I depart a shop every time a small-minded woman enters the door, I will never get rid of these debutante gowns your mother made me wear."

"I cannot believe what you said. You are so brave."

"Not brave. Just determined to live my life without strumpets interfering."

* * *

WHEN SOPHIA FINALLY REACHED HOME, she stalked toward Richard's study. Pausing by the door which was slightly ajar, she heard his brother, Perry. "No, not him. He slipped and broke his leg over Christmas, so he is languishing at his Derbyshire estate until he recovers. It was a bad break."

"I will cross him off the list, then," Richard replied.

Sophia pushed open the door and stormed in. Her husband leapt to his feet, distracting her for a moment. He looked very fine in a green tailcoat that picked out the color of his eyes. "Sophia, you are ba—"

"Did you hire guardsmen for Ethan and myself?"

He glanced away. "What do you mean?"

"The two *Johns* in the ill-fitting livery? Both of whom are *coincidentally* recently arrived from your country estates?"

"*Four* Johns," piped Perry from behind her. She turned to find him sprawled in one of the ivory armchairs, nursing a drink in his hand.

"Four?"

Perry gave a flippant nod, lifting his tumbler to sip on his brandy with his distinctive Balfour eyes fixed on hers.

Sophia spun back to Richard. "Did you hire *four* guardsmen?"

Richard glowered at his brother. "I did."

"Why have I met only two, then?"

"Two of them are on night watch."

"And *why* have you hired guardsmen?"

She saw something in his eyes. Shame, perhaps? "No reason. I am an important man, and I now have a new son and bride in my home. It seemed best to be cautious."

She narrowed her eyes at her lying husband. He was having difficulty meeting her eyes, and he moved his hand to cover a list he had been writing when she entered.

"Are you hiding something, Richard?"

"No."

"I don't believe you."

"It is simple. You and Ethan are my responsibility, and I am taking precautions to ensure your security."

Sophia tilted her head, recalling her mention of security the day before. Was it possible that conversation had prompted him to do so? She felt slightly mollified until her attention returned to Richard, who, she noted, was fidgeting like a schoolboy caught in a lie. Then, no. Something had happened, but he elected not to inform her. Sophia flushed with resentment. He had promised that they would be honest with each other, but now, after a mere three days of marriage, he was keeping a secret.

He did not trust her! She thought they had made so much progress, but ... *He does not trust me!*

Taking a deep breath, she tried again. "Are you sure there is nothing you wish to tell me?"

Richard looked like a guilty child, shaking his head in dissent. The resentment in her chest burst into flames. She wished to claw him in her anger—the stupid, glib idiot.

"I met your dear friend, Lady Partridge, today." Richard visibly flinched. Behind her, she heard Perry choking back a laugh.

"She is very eager to renew your *special* acquaintanceship." This time, there was no concealing it. Perry laughed out loud.

Richard held out his hands in appeal. "It was two or three years ago—"

Sophia did not wait for his excuses. She was already heading out of the room, ignoring his response.

RICHARD LEFT his brother in the study to follow Sophia. When he could not find her in the library or lower rooms, he eventually tried her chambers and found her sitting on a window ledge, seething. Her eyes were directed out to the street, but he sensed she was not seeing anything, instead lost in her thoughts.

He wished to tell her the truth, but more than that, he wanted to maintain her esteem and admiration. How could he tell her that, despite the fact she sought security by becoming his wife, not three days into the marriage, he had brought the enemy to the gates? He could not. He thought about what the duke had advised him, but he still could not bring himself to risk losing her regard.

Instead, he would need to use his well-honed charms to coax her out of her mood. A little misdirection to restore her good humor. "I apologize for not informing you about the guardsmen."

She turned her head to scowl at him.

"You and Ethan are too important. Having a family depending on me is an unfamiliar experience. I promise I am being cautious because I care about you."

His knees went weak with relief when her face softened to its normal composure. "I appreciate that. I appreciate that this is new to you."

Richard moved over to stand beside her. "I have never

had a woman like you in my life. And a child ... such a tiny child. Sometimes I feel overwhelmed with the sheer responsibility of it all."

She tilted her head back to look at him, her iridescent blue eyes speculative. "This is quite a change in circumstances, is it not?"

He nodded, running a hand through his hair. "I had no idea one's life could change this much in such a short period. I had to step in when I inherited the title. But this ... this is different. This is ... real. Living, breathing *family* under my roof, depending on me to make the right decisions to keep both of you safe."

Sophia reached out a slender hand to capture his own. "I understand. I apologize for my impatience."

He looked down at their clasped hands, and something stirred in his chest. Mayhap Halmesbury was right. Was it possible that a Balfour was developing a true depth of feeling for his wife? What horrific timing to have his emotions entangled for the first time in his adulthood, just when he needed to keep a clear head and find the source of the machinations plaguing his life.

He raised her hand to his lips and placed a gentle kiss on her fingers, relieved that he had distracted her from her suspicions.

CHAPTER 13

Sophia knew her foolish husband believed he had distracted her from her suspicions, but she merely relented when she noticed the strain visible in the tense lines of his face. For a man of just seven and twenty, his worries were aging him before her eyes these past few days. If only he would share the burden with her, but the oaf was keeping secrets. Most likely because of ridiculous male pride. However, she had promised him patience while he grew used to having a partner in his life, so she would provide it. Within reason.

She set aside her suspicions to enjoy dinner with him. Afterward, he had proved his devilish reputation was well-deserved when he joined her in her bed for the night to debauch her twice, after doing unspeakably wicked things to her with his tongue. Her blood heated at the recollection of the peaks of pleasure he brought her to. She could practice further patience if he continued to do such entrancing things to her body.

But now it was morning. And practicing patience, fortunately, did not mean she could not take steps to investigate what he was hiding from her. Which was why she currently pressed her ear to the door of his study to eavesdrop while he discussed the secret problem with his brother.

"… the night guardsmen reported they saw a man out in the square until late who could have been watching Balfour Terrace."

She heard Perry whistle. "So, it is true, then? There is one perpetrator for your wedding night fiasco, the spiteful print, and the note?"

Note? What note? She knew it! Richard was hiding something from her.

"It would appear so. I think I should increase security. If this continues—I will do whatever it takes to keep Sophia and Ethan safe."

Just then, Sophia heard the clip of Radcliffe's shoes approaching. She straightened up in haste and smoothed her skirts before lifting her hand to knock on the study door. Her husband called for her to enter.

When she walked into the room, she feigned surprise to see Perry sitting in one of the plump armchairs and bid him good morning before turning back to her husband. Her deceitful, prideful idiot of a husband. Keeping her face composed, she greeted him pleasantly, certain her cheeks were flagged with color at the memory of their night together. Richard looked happy to see her, at least.

"I was wondering if you and I could take Ethan to the park this morning? The boy is used to living on a farm, and I think it would be good for him to enjoy the outdoors."

Richard appeared torn for a moment, clearly thinking about the threat to their safety that he refused to discuss with her. He looked over at Perry. "Would you like to join us?"

"In the park? You must be funning—" Perry stopped abruptly at the expression on Richard's face. Her husband must want an extra presence with them, but he was unable to state it with her present, so he threatened Perry with a vicious glare. "I would be … delighted"—the younger brother grimaced—"to join you. It is high time I met my nephew."

Richard turned to smile at her. "We will all go to the park with Ethan, then."

She smiled back. Sophia wondered how her former scoundrel of a husband had got under so many skirts in his past. She saw no evidence of the subtlety required for such endeavors. Perhaps he was losing the glibness of his shallow charms? Or perhaps most people were too unobservant to notice what was happening right in front of them. She did know she was learning to read him like a book. She would allow him to think he fooled her, but only for a little while. And only if it was something mildly dishonest, such as not disclosing the mysterious note. Heaven help him if he tried to stray from her. She would take him apart with her bare hands if he attempted it.

So it was that Sophia found herself in a very crowded carriage. Her husband and his brother sat on the bench across from her, while she, Daisy, and Ethan were jammed together on their bench. Besides the coachman and the customary footman on the box in the front, the two Johns were crammed onto the rumble in the rear.

Apparently, one woman and one small boy required six men and a nursemaid to protect them. She would be exasperated with Richard for being overly cautious, but it reminded her of how she had recently gone to extreme measures to defend herself from Leech—which had turned out to be the exact right amount of caution, or she would now be wed to the murderous lord. She could not blame Richard for being a little overzealous. Nay, she blamed him for failing to inform her of the note.

Squashed into the corner of the squabs, with a pelisse

adding bulk over her walking dress and a large bonnet blocking her peripheral vision, she compared the brothers. She knew her husband was two years older than his brother, but it was hard to believe. Perry was a fraction taller and slimmer. They both possessed the artfully cut brown curls, deep green eyes, handsomely symmetrical faces, and strong jawlines, but Peregrine's face was that of a sulky, indolent spare. Richard displayed a lightness of spirit and smiled frequently, while his brother often looked cold, haughty, or sarcastic—sometimes all three at once. His immaturity was obvious to her sharp eyes.

Thinking of Richard's request on the morning of their wedding, Sophia observed that Perry's greatest issue appeared to be his lack of purpose. While Richard maintained several estates, overseeing thousands of tenants as well as several successful investments that had grown the wealth of the Balfour family, Perry had no discernible or worthwhile activities that he engaged in. Sheer boredom was likely the cause of his sour moods.

When the current situation settled down, she would mention to her husband that, despite the fashionable *ton's* ideas, Perry needed to find an occupation of some sort if he was going to find his way in life.

Perhaps Richard should involve him in his estates or teach him how to handle investments. It would do the spoilt young nobleman a world of good to have a greater purpose to steer his days. She had never thought much of the idle lives of most of the peerage, or their neglect of children relegated to servants' keeping.

In her experience, the most competent, purposeful members of their world appeared to be the most satisfied. Not to mention, the most interesting. Her own uncle and aunt were quite productive. She did not always agree with them, but she had observed that they conducted life with a stable, predictable character unlike her own temperamental parents who lost their unstable lives far too young.

"Mama, which park are we going to?" Ethan's youthful voice cut into her thoughts. He was on his feet with his face pressed against the opposite window. Richard watched him closely, clearly ready to grab the boy at the slightest hint of danger. She sighed at the expression on her husband's face. It was obvious he was on edge. If only the stupid man would share his burden with her, perhaps together they could find a solution.

Perry quirked an eyebrow in sarcastic comment, presumably because Ethan called her Mama. Sophia ignored it. She appreciated that Perry was assisting her husband with recent events, but she felt she had more to contribute. She knew she would be the better choice of confidante.

Did her husband see her as a weak-minded female despite his assurances that she would be his partner in life? Is that why she was being kept in the dark, while he conspired with his brother?

"We are headed to St. James's Park, Ethan."

"Where the *pelly-kins* live?"

She gazed at him in surprise. "How do you know of the pelicans?"

"Emma said if I was good in London, then I could ask to be taken to see the pelly-kins at St. James's."

"Yes, we will probably see the pelicans in the canal."

"Emma would be so jealous if she knew." Ethan's little face became mournful. Richard must have noticed, too, because he scooped the boy into his arms and plonked him down on his leg. The child giggled and squirmed in delight while Richard jostled his leg up and down to simulate riding a pony. Perry grimaced in displeasure, trying to move away but finding no room to do so. He was forced to endure the play of his brother and his nephew with his lip curled in disdain.

Not for the first time, Sophia wondered if her husband had handled Ethan's move to London in the most considerate manner. The little tyke kept bringing up this Emma of whom he was so fond, and despite making time for the child every day, she was unsure they were providing the same level of attention he had received on the working farm where he had lived amongst a large family.

Her well-meaning, hulking idiot of a husband was mishandling her, so surely he must have mishandled the situation with Ethan? She should seek details on how Ethan's familial transference had been dealt with so that she could assess what else the boy might need from them as parents.

The carriage came to a stop, and Sophia was grateful to climb down onto steady ground. The additional weight of so many passengers had made the journey rougher than usual. Richard waited for her while holding Ethan's hand, stepping forward so she might slip an arm through his free one. Together, they set off to the canal.

Perry joined the guardsmen and was scanning the vicinity, while Sophia did her best to ignore the large men, and perplexed nursemaid, following them en masse. A veritable army surrounded them to protect them on a simple walk in the park. She sighed. Richard felt it was necessary, but that did not prevent it from being irritating.

They walked along a path with rolling green lawns spread in every direction while above their heads mature trees laden with fresh spring leaves cast shade. Couples and groups of ladies passed by, and at the canal in the distance, boys were floating toy boats under the watchful gaze of their nursemaids. Nearing the canal, Ethan's excitement mounted, and he tugged eagerly on his father's hand to walk faster.

"Are those boats, Papa? Where did they get them?"

"From a toy shop, I should think. Would you like one?"

Ethan's eyes widened in delight. "My own boat? That I can put in the water?"

"If you would like. We can find a shop and return here in a few days."

"But ... I do not know how to sail it."

"Would you like me to teach you?"

Sophia listened to her husband and her adopted son chattering about sailing toy boats and skimming stones, her heart melting in her chest. Richard might be a half-wit who did not include her in his troubles, but he was a sweet half-wit who was proving to be a doting father. The stubborn ox was worth a little patience, she supposed.

Just then Ethan cried out in delight, pointing a tiny finger at a pelican that landed in the water nearby. Both she and Richard grinned at his obvious thrill before Sophia sank back into her thoughts.

She would appreciate it if he found his way to telling her about his troubles soon. She was certain she could offer a perspective that might help resolve the situation. Not to mention, an honest conversation would alleviate the recent development of grinding her teeth in vexation to maintain her forbearance.

* * *

AFTER THEIR VISIT to the park, Ethan went upstairs to play in the nursery and Sophia disappeared into the library. The outing had been a welcome respite, even with his brother and the two Johns skulking in the background as guardsmen.

Richard was thankful that he had a wife in his home to guide him regarding his son. She had instigated all the activities with Ethan over the past few days, and Richard was growing to know his son as a result. There was little doubt that without her help, he would be horribly mishandling the boy without a clue of what to do.

With this in mind, he took time from penning his lengthy list of potential enemies to pick up the small leather-bound volume of poetry the duke had gifted him. Leafing through the poems, he thought about Halmesbury's advice, to be honest with Sophia about the shameful note in his pocket.

But the note was so despicable a remark on his own character that even His Grace, Philip Markham, the magnanimous Duke of Halmesbury of legendary philanthropic works couldn't help but judge Richard after reading it. He had seen it on his cousin's face. On the other hand, the guilt of hiding it from Sophia was weighing on him. He thought back to how understanding she had been about everything that was occurring, and how impressed he was with her composure in the face of adversity.

Pulling the note from his pocket, he stared at it for some time while he thought about his options. Finally, he placed it back into his pocket. He must tell her. He *would* tell her—immediately after his meeting with his man of business.

Radcliffe appeared at the door, announcing Johnson's arrival. The man scurried past the butler and took a seat when Richard gestured to the chair. The trusted steward of his business affairs appeared quite nervous today. Beads of sweat dotted his bulbous forehead, and his navy eyes were evasive. He pulled out a handkerchief and dabbed at his face while Richard began to worry that the man was bringing him bad news, but he said nothing while Johnson scrambled through his papers. Perhaps the man was harried from all the extra work Richard was giving him?

"Mr. Long and I managed to investigate all the women on the list, my lord. We still need to approach the remainder, but you will be pleased to hear that there does not appear to be any more ... offspring."

Richard exhaled a deep breath of relief. "That is something." It was fantastic news. It was a mercy he had not inadvertently abandoned more children to their fate. There was only Ethan, who had fortunately been well taken care of by his extended family, so his father's unintentional neglect had done no lasting damage.

Johnson went through the list and reported what he had found. To his great relief, Richard could complete his apologies and suitable reparations over the next few weeks and close the door on his past. He stood up, ready to end the meeting. Johnson remained seated, his eyes averted. Richard felt his heart plunging into his boots. There was more.

"What is it?"

"I was at my offices preparing my report. On my way here, I passed by those print shops ..."

Richard resumed breathing in light-headed relief. He already knew about the caricature. He waited while Johnson leafed through his leather portfolio and pulled out a page. The man's hand was shaking when he reached forward to place it on the desk between them. Richard glanced down, prepared to dismiss the man, when he noticed the illustration. It was not the same one. This was a new drawing.

His body suddenly felt quite heavy, so he dropped back in his chair. With a fortifying breath, he picked the print up to look at it closer, his heartbeat pounding in his ears.

The drawing depicted two ladies calmly sipping tea. One of the women was meant to be Sophia, colored with her unique red-blonde hair. Around them stormed a horde of children—at least a dozen curly-haired devils with green eyes and demonic expressions—over the sofa where the women were seated, running amok between the furnishings, and climbing the draperies like monkeys spawned from the depths of hell. In fine, slanting print below, there was a caption.

"Lady S., are any of these children yours?"

Richard growled, his gaze transfixed on the page. From a distance, he heard Johnson making his excuses and fleeing the room while he continued to stare down at the offensive drawing. It took several minutes to gain control over himself, and he found himself alone in his study when he finally dropped the print on his desk and stood up. He walked over to the window and stood staring out at the enclosed gardens in the middle of the square, seeking a clear head. When he found out who was behind this, he was going to tear the man apart, limb from limb.

The prints were coming out too quickly to be anything else but calculated attacks. If this mysterious enemy wanted to attack Richard, he could do so. He could call him out for a meeting at dawn. He could demand reparations for Richard's sins. But there could be no excusing the blackguard for threatening his new family. Until this moment, he had believed the threatening note from the musicale was intended to target Sophia, but this print proved that the mystery perpetrator was aware of his son, too. Which meant the note was a warning aimed at both his wife and his son. Whoever this man was, Richard wanted his blood.

Once Richard's anger cooled sufficiently, he retrieved the print and went to find Sophia. Just as before, there could be no hiding the print because she would soon learn of its existence in a manner that could wreak more havoc. He resolved to show her the print and then inform her about the note. This situation was becoming as dangerous as he had feared when he initially read it. The duke was correct. It was time to tell Sophia the full truth, so she would be prepared to defend herself.

It took him a while to track Sophia down, but he eventually found her in the nursery, reading a story to Ethan. The boy was enraptured, staring at Sophia with a besotted expression on his young face. Richard understood how the boy felt because he, too, was experiencing it. She felt like home, with her calm presence, and she exhibited an endless well of patience and concern for himself and the boy. He could not believe his fortune in stumbling onto the terrace to hear her parody of his morals. The chance encounter had changed his life, abruptly, to one worth living.

Sophia's blue eyes found him standing at the door, listening to her tale. A single blink was the only sign that she noticed something was amiss. Gently, she ended in the middle of the story and promised Ethan they would read the rest together soon before she extricated herself to exit the rooms.

Richard offered her his arm, which she took, and they walked down the stairs to the library. The room was long and narrow, with shelves of books towering up to the tall ceilings. Sophia never said a word, just waited for him to speak when they took a seat at one of several library tables.

"What is it?" she finally asked in a quiet voice when he failed to speak.

"My man of business brought me another print."

Sophia looked relieved. "Is that all? I thought something serious had happened."

Richard handed her the print he was holding. He hoped she would find the humor in it as she had done before.

She took it from him and looked down. She was deathly quiet for some time. Suddenly, she exploded to her feet in a shriek of rage, knocking over her chair. "How dare they!"

Richard clamored to his feet, rounding the table to calm her, but she broke into a storm of agitated pacing. "How dare they! He is a child. This is unforgivable!" She spun to glower at him. "You must do something! Sue them ... or ... or purchase their shop and tear down the presses!"

Richard felt panic descending when he saw her blue eyes awash with angry tears. His dear wife was frantic in her desire to protect his son, whom she had only just met days before. He felt like such a cad. He knew he could never tell her about the shameful note and how he put not only her sought-after security at risk with his past misdeeds, but he had jeopardized the safety of his tiny child with his actions, too. She was correct. It was unforgivable.

He must make it right. She could not be forced to live with the burden of fear he now carried with him while he fought to protect his wife and child. It was clear he would need to keep the note to himself, but he would hire every runner in London if he had to. He would make this right and protect them.

He hurried over to fold her in his arms. She was quivering with rage and grief, dropping her head on his shoulder and sobbing in earnest. For the first time, Richard found himself comforting *her*, which was a novel experience.

"Sophia, I will make it right," he promised in a soothing voice, gently stroking her back.

"He is a child! A tiny, innocent little boy," she wept.

"I know, love. I will take care of it. Whoever is behind this will regret it." Her gasping sobs eased and her trembling body slowly relaxed into his arms while he continued to calm her with soft assurances.

Richard felt the worst kind of scoundrel for creating this situation, but he knew he must keep his promise. He did not care about the print shops that sold the illustration. Nay, he was going to hunt the instigator because he knew in his gut this was a campaign of terror with a single, vengeful cuckold or lover behind it.

The individual may have just cause to pursue him in this manner, but there was no excuse for attacking his wife and child who were innocent of wrongdoing. He would find the man and tear his beating heart out of his chest, before displaying it to the worthless, dying bounder.

CHAPTER 14

*S*ophia felt foolish over her display of emotion. Now her husband would be convinced she was a weak-minded female and never share the details of the mystery note he was hiding from her. It was her fault for making an utter cake of herself and behaving like a temperamental child.

Why the cut at Ethan scrambled her wits so thoroughly, she could not quite say. She cared not one wit about the malicious print aimed at her, but when she had seen the one aimed at the little boy in her care, her soul shattered and it had taken several minutes of sobbing in Richard's arms to gather the pieces back together.

It would not do. She must find a method of coping with attacks on Ethan, or the vicious gossips of the *ton* would eat her alive. Showing such weakness in elite society would leave her and the child exposed. She supposed she should be thankful that only Richard had witnessed her reaction, and that she had the opportunity to prepare her composure for contending with the contentious subject in the future. There was no doubting that eventually it would, and she owed it to Ethan to remain calm in those inevitable encounters.

There was no denying the drawing had caught her by surprise. It was so willfully disparaging of Richard's child that it physically hurt to think about it. Perhaps that was the key? Perhaps she should predict the type of confrontations or snide remarks that she might find herself in regarding the boy and plan out possible responses with a clear head, so she was not caught unprepared again?

The idea had merit. Planning strategies for dealing with members of polite society and the cross-purposes of her family was precisely how she had avoided matrimony with an unwanted suitor for so many years. If one handled these matters poorly, it doomed one to re-experience them over and over again, but if she made nothing of it, like her encounter with Lady Partridge at the modiste, people lost interest in their taunting and cruel gossip. Once she made up her mind that she refused to feed the gossip, Sophia felt her composure return.

With a calm face, she peered at her reflection in the full-length mirror in her dressing room. Her first delivery of the gowns she had ordered from the Italian modiste had arrived, so she finally possessed an evening gown suitable to attend the theatre. The one she wore now was a deep blue lace in a leaf pattern over a silk slip with the longer waist of this Season's fashion. A wreath of leaves covered the bodice and the puff sleeves were ornamented with rich lace and two bunches of leaves, while the hem of the skirt appeared to be two layers of skirts due to skillful bias and lace work.

The front of her hair was dressed in loose curls to fall low to the sides of her face, while the rest of her hair was loosely fastened with a pearl comb. Signora Ricci had recommended the lace color, and Sophia was pleased with how her hair shone in contrast and the hue of her blue eyes was picked out by the shade of the gown. She did not recognize the woman in the mirror in the fine colors not permitted to debutantes. The woman in the reflection looked elegant and high-born, just like a countess. Her pulse quickened when she thought of descending the stairs to meet Richard. Would he be proud of the woman on his arm when they attended Drury Lane tonight? She knew he looked especially fine in evening clothes, which was why she had been relieved to see the gown amongst those delivered earlier that day.

She pulled on her evening gloves, and the maid assisted her with a shawl before she headed out the door while the tall case clock down in the entrance hall announced the hour.

Richard was waiting at the foot of the stairs when she descended. His jaw dropped when he looked up to find her.

"You are ... ravishing." His voice was thick with emotion. She stopped on the last step, the extra inches bringing her almost to eye level to gaze at him. She picked up his hand and brought it up to clasp against her breast.

"I am glad we married."

A flash of pain crossed his face. "Why? I have brought you nothing but chaos since the first night."

"Because you are an honorable man who is doing his very best to change. Because of how you give Ethan your attention and make him smile. Because of ... the pleasure you have brought me."

Richard smiled lasciviously at the last. "I am rather excellent at that endeavor, am I not?"

"Thank you for taking me to the theatre tonight. I think it is a good idea for us to take these moments to enjoy ourselves."

"You mean before the next crisis presents itself?"

She grinned, pressing a quick kiss to his warm lips. "Exactly."

* * *

THE JOURNEY to the theatre district included the two Johns, the coachman, and a footman. Richard informed her that the additional two guardsmen, the men she had not yet met, stayed to guard the nursery, so it was clear he was not relenting regarding security. She shrugged it off. At some point this would pass, and in the meantime, she was happy to help give him peace of mind by cooperating with the measures he was taking.

They watched the first half of the show from a private box that he maintained, and she recognized many of the chattering patrons sitting in the opposite balconies who appeared to be using their lorgnettes to observe the comings and goings of other patrons under the recently installed gaslights. On either side of where they sat, she could hear the gossip spilling from noble lips in the adjacent boxes.

Sophia always found the theatre most enjoyable. She had never understood the inclination of the *ton* to use such events to tattle because the performance always riveted her.

Consequently, when the intermission arrived, she found herself quite bemused, taking a moment to realize that Richard was waiting for her to join him for refreshments. He stepped out into the corridor ahead of her, likely to ensure her safety on the short walk to where the two Johns stood waiting, when she heard a commotion. Sophia exited the box in consternation to find Richard embroiled in an argument with another patron, a young lord who was vaguely familiar.

Her senses reeled with confusion when she noted that a crowd of society's most important members was forming to observe the scene. Turning to Richard, she gasped when she saw he was holding a handkerchief to his face, spotted with crimson drops. She raised her hand to his face, only to drop it when the tempestuous young man lunged forward, startling her into retreating a step back at the same moment Richard angled forward to shield her with his body.

"You stay away from Lady Partridge, you hear me?" The two Johns had grabbed hold of the man's flailing arms, preventing him from attacking Richard once more.

"Stanford, I do not know what you are referring to! I have not spoken to Lady Partridge since before my betrothal to Miss Ridley. It must be at least two years since I even spoke to the widow!"

That was it—the young man is Lord Stanford!

"Your friend informed me he saw you visiting her home in January of this year, while I was in Paris on family matters. I know your reputation, Saunton!"

"In January I was in Somerset, hosting a house party with several witnesses! I could not possibly have been seen in London because I was nowhere near! What friend told you that?"

Sophia could tell Richard was keeping a tight leash on his temper, rage glinting in his narrowed eyes and his chiseled jaw set in an angry line. Stanford, who must be Lady Partridge's current paramour, refused to be placated, nor would he betray the confidence of the friend who had informed him. He finally stalked off in outrage, while Richard held his head back to stop the blood.

"We should leave. Your nose might be broken, and we need to summon a doctor."

Richard's eyes found hers, his face still tilted back and his white handkerchief spotted with red.

"Sophia, I swear I have not spoken to that woman in at least two years."

She watched him for a moment, noting the sincerity and concern in his eyes while he waited for her response. She believed him, but would he finally be honest about the threat that plagued them? "Do you think that the friend he mentioned caused this trouble on purpose? Used the facts of your past to cast aspersions about the present?"

Richard looked away, staring at the ornate ceiling. "I am sure it was a case of mistaken identity."

Sophia found herself grinding her teeth once more. Her vexatious husband must think her a cretin. It had long since become obvious that there was an imminent threat, but he continued to pretend that they were suffering from a string of coincidences. What would it take for the infuriating lummox to admit there was a problem?

* * *

BY THE TIME they boarded their carriage, the bleeding had stopped, so Richard stuffed the ruined handkerchief in his pocket. He could see the ire in Sophia's eyes and the way her jaw firmed after he brushed her concerns aside. He realized it was not working to try to fool her, but he would not reveal the note. Perhaps he could admit that he had concerns the events might be connected, which was why he was taking precautions while the matter was investigated.

He looked up to find her staring out the carriage window, but like once before, he sensed she did not see the roadway or buildings but instead was fuming about his behavior.

"Sophia, I admit I had the same thought. That the recent problems plaguing me might be related."

She swung her gaze to meet his.

"I will ask my man of business to investigate."

Her eyes fell. She looked disappointed in him.

"Sophia?"

"That is all? There is no other information? Do you suspect someone is doing this deliberately?" She would not look at him. Richard's chest tightened. His wife was an intelligent woman, but it was his responsibility to protect her. He brought this into their lives, and he would solve it without burdening her with unnecessary fear.

"I do not know, but I will have it investigated. The guardsmen will continue to protect you and Ethan until I am certain there is no further threat." He reached out a hand to cover her fingers. "Please, Sophia. I apologize you are being exposed to these situations. Know that I had a very different idea of how we would begin this marriage, and I have every intention of setting this right, so you and Ethan are safe."

What a confusing muddle of ideas. He knew he was alluding to a threat, but then pretending there was no cause for alarm in the same breath. The evening had begun as a smashing success and collapsed into disaster. His nose was throbbing, he had the metallic taste of blood in his mouth, and his temper still ran hot because he had wanted to pound Stanford into the theatre carpeting after the man surprised him with a sudden punch to the face.

He wished to take a hot bath and make love to his wife. It was yet another hellish day—and night—at Balfour Terrace, and the constant fear for his family with no specific target to attack was keeping his nerves on edge. Not to mention, he was lying awake at night trying to work out the most likely source of the menace in their lives.

He did not want to talk; he wanted to cut off the endless thoughts running through his head while the investigation into the source of all this pandemonium proceeded.

Sophia turned her face back to him, scrutinizing him. She gave a deep sigh. "I will leave the matter to you, but know that I am here and ready to discuss *anything* you need to discuss."

He gave a nod. "First thing is to summon the doctor. Then we should rest."

She turned her hand to clasp his. "That sounds lovely."

* * *

RICHARD BATHED while they awaited the doctor's arrival. It soon turned out his face was badly bruised, but his nose was intact. He had suspected this was the case, but he allowed the doctor to be summoned as a small mercy to his wife. She appeared relieved at the doctor's pronouncement and agreed that it was time to go to bed.

He undressed with the help of Shaw before donning his nightclothes and robe to join Sophia in her chambers. When he entered her rooms and saw her lying in the bed, the light playing across her face and golden-red hair, he experienced a moment of revelation not for the first time since he had met her.

Sophia was an angel. He would do anything to defend this woman, who had come to mean so much to him. He had been a fool when he denied his love to Halmesbury, because in that moment he knew his heart would stop beating in his chest if anything happened to her because of him. Just as he knew, he was not worthy of such a woman. She brought peace and grace to his home, where he had only ever brought fallen women and pursued his own selfish pleasures.

It was no longer about hiding his shame. It had become about proving himself worthy of her so that she might one day grow to love the gentleman he aspired to be and not the rascal he currently was. One day, he would be worthy of the title husband—and father—and until that day came, he would not rest in ensuring he completed his reparations and uncovered the threat that was plaguing their household. This was his duty to take care of, and until he did so, he was not worthy of earning her love.

Blazes! Maybe he needed a drink to clear his head of these maudlin thoughts?

Fuck! No, he was reforming and this small request from

his wife was the only one he could currently honor. He must bear the burden of his past actions and soldier on, one step at a time.

His wife raised her head. "Are you coming?"

To his relief, she seemed in a lighter mood than she had been since the predicament at the Drury Lane Theatre. When he approached, she drew a deep breath and blurted out a question.

"Do you think there will be another caricature of what happened with Lord Stanford?"

Richard threw his head back and groaned. "I guess that would be better than the last one. Mayhap it will distract the gossips from Ethan?"

She furrowed her brow in thought. "That is a good point. Well, in that case, I hope there is another print!"

They chuckled together while he disrobed and pulled back the covers to slip into her bed. She turned onto her side, a hand tucked under her cheek. "It is good to laugh about it. I now look forward to another illustration depicting the infamous Balfours."

He smiled, happy to see her relaxed again. The way she had been the first couple of days of their burgeoning marriage. She lifted a hand and trailed it over his chest, tracing the curves and indents of his muscles. His pulse increased in response to her exploration, and he was reminded of their first morning together, when she had explored him in this manner before Radcliffe interrupted them.

Was she remembering the same, caressing her fingers over his pectoral muscles before splaying her delicate hand over his abdomen and sliding it down to his belly? Her slight touch stirred his loins, blood rushing in when her hand slipped even lower to fire his lust once more.

He might be exhausted beyond belief, but his wife was an

irresistible minx. Her sweet curiosity mixed with the sensual admiration in her eyes called to something primitive in his soul. There were lovers in his past more experienced, more adept at the art of lovemaking, but Sophia's sincere interest in him made his heart beat like a drum. The primal urge to devour this woman, *his* woman, beat rhythmically through his veins while he held himself still under her searching fingers. There was something fundamentally healing in experiencing this sweet demonstration of her curiosity in him as a man.

So he waited while she played her fingertips with incredible, heart-stopping tenderness over every inch of his torso. Each pass of her delicate hand brought her exploration lower, lower, until he found himself holding his breath, his shaft straining in anticipation of her touch.

When her fingers brushed over his hardened length, he could no longer lay quietly under her ministrations. With a growl, he grabbed her hand. She looked up at him with a question in her gleaming blue eyes while he lay panting with intoxicated desire. "It will be over too soon if you continue in that direction," he explained.

Thinking for a second, he pushed the covers back to find that his wife was naked. He groaned, his greedy eyes consuming the sight of her silky skin. Her pert breasts. Her rosy, pebbled nipples.

His head swam with lust. Reaching out, he stroked his palms over her soft curves, brushing up to cup her creamy globes where he thrummed his thumbs gently over the hardened pink tips with an ardent hunger that he was still growing accustomed to since he wed this intriguing woman.

His wife was far more captivating than he initially predicted when he had decided to pursue her. She had become a vital part of his very being. Reverently, he leaned down to take a turgid nipple in his mouth, swirling his tongue and flicking it over her swollen bud to growl his craving when she moaned and grasped his head tightly to her bosom in yelping delight.

Richard reared up, yanked his cotton nightshirt over his head, and threw it away. His hands gravitated to her curved hips to lift her over him. Her face scrunched in brief confusion before she straddled his body, her slim legs bracketing his hips while her slick core descended to make contact with his hard cock.

Sophia's eyes widened in response to the contact, and she emitted a sensual purr, leaning down to lick playfully at his lips in an echo of his previous kisses. His lips parted in invitation, and she wasted no time tangling her velvet tongue with his in hungry enthusiasm. His wife was savoring the reversal of roles, the heady power of taking the lead in their bed sport, her breathing ragged while she gyrated over the ridge of his arousal.

Richard smiled in anticipation. She had no idea how good this was going to feel, how much *more* she was going to feel when he reached down between them and guided his shaft to her wet entrance to impale her with his length.

"Ride me," he commanded in a hoarse voice. She looked puzzled, but after a brief hesitation, she moved her hips in a bobbing motion. Flinging her head back, arching up, she hissed in delight. Richard chuckled, knowing she had just discovered the advantages of their current position; the exquisite friction of her nub against his pelvic bone while his straining length filled her tight channel.

He pushed up into her, but she quickly took the motion over, her hips beating a frantic tempo to rub against him. The sight of her, of her curved body undulating above him while her breasts and tight nipples drew his gaze to the magnificence of her womanly form, was overpowering. Richard had enjoyed the position with his former paramours, but no one like Sophia. She was a goddess in her sensual beauty and sincere passion. The flames of his craving consumed him as he watched her, felt her working his body toward her orgasm, growling when she hit her peak, her intimate muscles milking his shaft in the aftermath before she collapsed back down onto her haunches.

Richard reached down, taking firm hold of her hips, and used the power of his upper body to move her back and forth on and over his length. He was so close, fascinated by her hissing exhalations that revealed her renewed pleasure at the rocking motion. Lost in the vortex of sensation, moving her body in a frantic rhythm over his, he reached his own shuddering release.

Slowly, he descended back to earth, wrapping his arms around his perfect wife and holding her to his chest in a tight hug. He lifted his head and kissed the top of her head, breathing in the entrancing fragrance of rosewater while their labored breathing gradually returned to normal.

He accepted in the dark place where his heart resided that there was nothing he would not do to protect Sophia. She was the very heart of him, and he would tell her so when he eventually earned the right to do so.

CHAPTER 15

*I*t was early when a sound disturbed Richard from a deep sleep. So early that a single thread of morning light crept through a gap in the draperies.

"Richard?" It was the lowest of whispers floating through the air of the large, quiet bedroom. It sounded like Perry. Richard turned his head in awakening confusion, his eyes bleary from sleep. The connecting door to his rooms was slightly ajar, and a blurry face was peering at him.

"Richard?"

His heart sank. This could not be good. He gave a nod of acknowledgment, and the door closed.

Sitting up in Sophia's bed, he rubbed his eyes to restore his vision before easing quietly from under the covers. Once he was on his feet, he searched around for his nightshirt and robe. Dressing hurriedly, he crept from the room back to his chambers, opening and closing the door with the greatest of care. He did not wish to disturb Sophia after the athletic evening they had engaged in.

Perry stood at the fireplace, his forearm leaning against the mantel while he waited for Richard to gather his wits.

"What is it?" Richard was afraid to hear the answer, steeling his nerve for what new crisis his brother had come to inform him of.

"I was just returning home when one of the Johns called me into the hall. It would seem that a rock was thrown through the window of your study about thirty minutes ago. The window is shattered, but the servants did not wish to disturb you. You have an injury of some sort, from what I gather?"

Richard raised his head to stare at the ceiling in agitation. "I was at Drury Lane with the countess. When I stepped out of the box, Lord Stanford was walking by. With no warning, he turned to punch me in the face, accusing me of knocking boots with his ace of spades."

"Ace of spades—he is involved with a widow? Never say you mean Lady Partridge? I thought you decided to stay away from that vicious strumpet when she tried to convince you to—"

"I know why I avoid the deviant woman. Her tastes are far too … eclectic for my sensibilities."

Perry choked back a laugh. "Eclectic! My, what a gentleman you have become."

"I would have no soul to redeem if I followed the dark paths she wished to lead me down. She and Father would have made perfect bed partners in their degenerate tastes. But that is beside the point because Stanford said a friend informed him that they saw me leaving her home in January."

"But we were at Saunton Park for the entire month of January!"

"Precisely. It would appear the enemy I have made is not above fudging the details in the interest of causing trouble. I only ventured to the woman's home on one occasion before I discovered what a deviant she was, and that was during the Season of 1818. Either my villain is investigating deep into

193

my past, or just using bits of idle gossip collected over the years to pose plausible lies."

"Given the frequency of these attacks, I would say he is posing plausible lies. How could he have the time to do otherwise? Unless he is well-financed and has a team doing his bidding?"

"We are going about our own investigation the wrong way. It is too slow, and I need results. We should make a short list of who would be this energetic, vicious, unrelenting, and angry. Then direct the runners to investigate those men first."

"Agreed. There is no predicting what this lunatic will try next."

Richard stood hesitantly in the middle of the room. He was so weary, his body felt like it was being crushed by the weight of failed responsibility. Walking over to the bed, he dropped down and asked the question which had been haunting the dark recesses of his mind these past weeks.

"Perry, am I our father?"

"Good Lord, no!" His brother's reply was so utterly vehement that Richard was distracted from his worries. "Lord Saunton—*ahem*—I mean, our father was the devil incarnate. Why would you think you are him?"

"I have been chasing skirts these many years, and now my wife and son suffer for it."

Perry laughed, the sound hollow. "Chased skirts, perhaps. Our father surpassed chasing skirts before I was even born. The man had no conscience. No morals of any kind. I rejoiced when he finally died. You, however, I would miss if something happened to you, which is why I am aiding you with this situation. Do you think I would offer my help to the fiend who sired us? Nay, brother, I would be out on the street helping to lob rocks in the middle of the night. You are a far better man than he ever was."

Richard groaned. "Blazes, Perry, now you provide me with new worries! Do you think, mayhap, once this is over, that I will need to determine if we have siblings out in the world?"

Perry shuddered, his head falling forward in his pained despair to rest on the forearm balanced on the mantel. "I had not stopped to think, but I would say it is almost a certainty."

One step at a time, Richard. "Never mind that thought for now. We will settle this disaster first. Once it is done, we can discuss if we wish to investigate the sins of our father."

Perry raised his head and nodded. "I will inform Shaw to come and assist you. We can meet in your study once I find some sustenance."

* * *

KNOCKING on the door of Richard's study before entering, Sophia stopped in dismay when she saw that one of the windows facing the street was boarded up and a maid was sweeping up glass from the floor.

Perry rose when she entered and made to leave the room. "I will look into this, brother." With that, the Balfour brother left the study.

Richard dismissed the maid and came around his desk to gather Sophia's hand in his. Once the door was closed, he led her to the armchairs and had her take a seat before settling in the opposite chair.

"What happened?"

"Someone threw a rock at the window in the early hours of the morning."

Sophia's fear and irritation soared. "Are you going to continue to pretend this is not a campaign of some sort?"

Richard contemplated her for a moment. "I should have

known better than to attempt to fool you. Perry and I believe this is the work of one person."

"So you finally admit it!"

"I apologize. I did not wish to alarm you while I investigated the matter. But I should have realized you are too clever to not make the connections." He looked away, his expression pained. "I feel terrible about this. My past behavior is plaguing our household, and it is not fair to you. I hope you will forgive me while I try to sort out the havoc I have caused."

"That is not what upsets me. I thought we agreed to work together, and now you finally admit that you have been shutting me out. I could have contributed to solving this situation, but instead you decided to keep it from me like I am some sort of witless fool!"

Richard brought up his hands to rub his face. She finally noticed the weariness. His lips were pinched, and he was pale. Was he sleeping, she wondered with a sharp pang of guilt at the recollection of the hours they had burned away in each other's arms. She wished to ease his suffering, but she also wanted to hit him for being dense.

"I apologize, Sophia. None of this has been about your wits. It has been my shame to visit this on you and Ethan. My dark past has exposed the two of you to danger, and I am having difficulties with my conscience. But there is no time to sort it out because I must find the culprit behind this to protect you and Ethan. What if this worsens and the attacks become more dangerous ... more lethal?"

Sophia stared at him. "We will work together to resolve this. We will increase our vigilance. Have you told me everything?"

That was when her dear, wonderful, exasperating husband looked her straight in the eye—and lied. "Yes."

Sophia ground her teeth in frustration, forcing a smile

onto her face. The lying reprobate still would not inform her about the note.

"I am going for tea with my aunt and cousin this afternoon. I will take the shorter John and a footman."

Richard inclined his head. "Of course."

* * *

SOPHIA FORCED herself to endure the formality of tea with her aunt, while in the back of her mind, she continued to fume. How was she to assist meaningfully if Richard insisted on keeping secrets from her? The question could not be answered while they sipped on tea and Lady Moreland informed her of the latest *on dits*.

I do not care! My family is in danger and my husband will not talk to me, she wanted to scream. But she smiled and nibbled on dainty biscuits and sipped her tea from a delicate cup while her aunt's words flowed over her like water over a rock.

Lily gave her a light pinch. Sophia realized that the room was quiet and her elegant aunt was staring at her. "My apologies. I was woolgathering for a moment. What was the question?"

Her aunt, a handsome woman, tilted her head in bemusement. She had the same enormous eyes as her daughter Lily, and her hair was a deep chocolate brown with only a few strands of silver to mark her age under her jaunty turban. After a moment, Lady Moreland's mouth curled into a knowing smile, and she discreetly picked at her bodice with slender, graceful fingers. "I recall that I had a tendency to woolgather in the first few months of my marriage to Uncle Hugh."

Out of the corner of her eye, Sophia saw Lily wince and stick out her tongue to simulate gagging. Sophia herself did her best not to grimace at the thought of what her aunt alluded to. Her cousin cleverly interjected to change the subject. "Mama asked why you left the theatre early?"

"Oh. I was not feeling well, so Richard insisted we leave early."

"Lord Stanford punching your husband in the face during intermission was not the cause, then?"

Sophia shut her eyes in defeat. She should have known her aunt had already heard the gossip. "Yes, Aunt Christiana. That is the true reason for our departure."

"Well, not to worry, Sophia. I hear Richard has barely been seen about town since he married you. The speculation is that the rake has finally reformed and spends his evenings with his bride."

That was good news, at least.

"I never had any doubt, niece. You are the perfect wife for the gentleman. I believe the earl has been bored, but a clever girl like you will keep his attentions at home where they belong."

The sentiment rather touched Sophia, who smiled in acknowledgment.

Once the tea was over, she and Lily made their way to the garden. The spring air was pleasant, and the privacy of the garden afforded them an opportunity to talk. With a little coaxing from her cousin, Sophia confided all that had happened since the wedding, including the infernal note her husband kept from her.

Lily's expression was perplexed when Sophia finished telling her of what occurred that morning, and the fact that Richard still withheld the note.

"Why do you not ask him? It is quite out of character for you to not do so?"

Sophia felt glum admitting the truth. "I suppose it was

some sort of test. If he told me, I would know he truly considered me an equal and trusted me, so I could trust him."

Lily pulled a face. "That is most dishonest of you."

"What? I am not the one who is dishonest!"

"Sophia, Lord Saunton is under great strain. I do not think it is a good idea to be testing his sincerity at this moment. Inform him you were eavesdropping and you are aware of the note. Ask him why he has failed to inform you of it."

"Lily, you are most unfair!"

"I am not, Sophia. You have a terrible habit of trying to solve matters on your own without any help. Look how you suffered under the threat of kidnapping from Leech but failed to obtain assistance from your own family. You did not even tell me why you were sleeping in my chambers. In fact, you outright lied to me about that. If you want Lord Saunton to trust you, then you need to extend the same courtesy to him. Ask him about the note."

"Zooks, Lily, when did you get so demanding?"

"I care about you, cousin, and you know I speak the truth. I will not stand idly by without speaking my mind. Would you prefer I clutch your hand to commiserate and weep about the awful men of the world, or would you rather receive some useful direction on how to resolve the matter at hand?"

Sophia muttered her answer in resentment. "Useful direction, I suppose."

Lily's face lit up, her customary enthusiasm restored. "Perfect! Now you should go home and ask him about the note."

WHEN SHE RETURNED HOME from visiting her unsympathetic cousin, Sophia found Richard dispatching letters with his quill in hand. Smoothing her skirts with fluttering hands, she approached the desk and waited for him to complete the letter he was writing. Once he was done, his head came up, and he flinched in surprise.

"How long have you been standing there?"

"Just a few moments. You appear to be tired."

"I have had little sleep since we married. I must find the source of this threat. With your safety, and Ethan's, at risk, this cannot continue."

"Yes, that is why I am here. This morning you admitted that this is a campaign, and I asked you if there was anything else I needed to know."

"I remember."

"Why did you not tell me about the note?"

"Which note?"

"I do not know which note! That is the point! You did not tell me about the note I overheard you discussing with Perry the day we went to see the pelicans in St. James's Park with Ethan."

Richard's face was blank for a moment, then his hand went to his pocket. "That note. I would have told you about it this morning, but so much happened in the past few days it slipped my mind. It was not intentional, I assure you!"

"It was intentional not to inform me of it when you received it!"

Richard lowered his gaze. "I apologize for that. Halmesbury warned me it was not well done of me."

"So you spoke with Halmesbury about the note—and Perry—but you did not see fit to inform me of it?"

"I wanted to spare you the worry."

"Is that the full story?"

Richard's cheeks turned a ruddy shade. "And I am

ashamed I have caused this situation … and the contents of the note."

"Let me see the note, then."

Richard patted at his pockets. "I do not have it on me. I must have left it in my clothes, so Shaw will have it somewhere. Perhaps it is in my dressing table in my chambers."

Sophia huffed in irritation. The walk up to their chambers was interminable in this gigantic house, and she was too impatient to make the journey. "Well, tell me about it, then. Where did it come from?"

"Shaw found it in my tailcoat after we returned from the Lawson musicale. Someone snuck it into my pocket when I was collecting refreshments."

Sophia blanched, her legs were unsteady, and she reached for a seat to settle down onto. That night had been special for her, but he had been disingenuous, hiding a secret from her. It cast a new light on how they spent their night after the musicale. "You bedded me for the first time that night knowing about the note?"

Richard's consternation was mollifying. "No! I did not know about it then. Shaw gave it to me the following morning."

Sophia drew a deep, fortifying breath in her relief. "What did it say?"

"It threatened to harm someone I love."

"Me?"

"Or Ethan. The caricature of all my supposed children confirmed the scoundrel was aware of him, too."

Sophia felt empathy for her husband's plight. Since the day of their wedding, he had been grappling with one upheaval after another while knowing there was a hidden enemy planning the next disaster.

Richard cleared his throat, causing Sophia to tense. It appeared another downturn was to be announced, from the expression of discomfort on his face. "Which is why I have reached a decision to send you and Ethan to Saunton Park until this danger has passed."

Sophia jumped to her feet. "No!"

"It is best—"

"No! We are a family and we must stick together."

"Sophia, be reasonable—"

"I will not! You promised me." Sophia lowered her voice, quoting in a husky tone, "'I will allow you your freedom. As my countess, you may do anything you want and I will support you, as long as you are at my side.' That is what you said the day you visited me at my uncle's home! I will remain at your side, as we agreed that day."

Richard grimaced. "Please, Sophia, I must keep you and Ethan safe. I could not live with the guilt if something happened to either of you. I can barely live with my guilt for exposing you to this because of my shameful past."

"It is illogical, husband. If Ethan and I leave London, it will expose us while we travel for days to Somerset. Not to mention we will have to divide the men we have to split off. There is no guarantee that the villain dogging you will not observe our departure and follow us in order to ambush us. Here in London, the resources are combined, and we are protected behind the walls of Balfour Terrace. I will not leave! If you attempt to force me, my cooperation will end." She banged his desk with her open hand.

Richard's jaw fell open. "Bloody hell, you are a magnificent creature!"

"Do not attempt to charm me, husband."

"Sophia, you have made some fine points, but—"

"No but. I am not leaving! And I expect you to show me the note!" With a flurry of skirts, she stalked out of his study. If she remained any longer, she could not be responsible for what she might do to the infuriating oaf.

CHAPTER 16

*P*erry loped in to collapse with a negligent air into one of the ivory armchairs. "I thought that went rather well."

Richard picked up his empty water glass and threw it at his sardonic brother, who quickly ducked so that it hit the wall behind him in a shattering spray of shards.

"My, my, brother. Your emotions are taking over."

"Quit finding amusement in my troubles or I will blacken your eye, *brother*."

"The countess made several good points. I agree with her assessment that a journey to Somerset would be fraught with peril."

"I must do *something*! This is my fault!"

"Richard, this may be easier to resolve if you have a clear head. You may have done something to cause this situation, but a man who targets an innocent woman and child is deranged, which is beyond your control. And, thus far, nothing but gossip, threats, and minor incidents have occurred, so calm yourself."

Richard groaned, leaning his elbows on the smooth finish

of his desk to drop his head into his hands in a gesture of agony. "Perry, do you not understand? It is only a matter of time before the blackguard heightens the stakes."

"Your wife is losing her patience. Be careful she does not leave our household to return to the Morelands. Currently, she is cooperating with you, but you will push her too far and complicate the threat further."

"Why do you say that? How would you know?"

"It is what I would do in her position."

Richard stared at his brother. The possibility of Sophia leaving him was … It made his heart ache in his chest and his breathing shallow. "I will think on it."

Perry left him to his thoughts, and Richard sat staring sightlessly at the street through the window, aggravated by the boarded-up window in his peripheral vision.

He felt lost. He wanted to rant and rage and use his fists to sort out this turmoil, but on whom? Whom had he angered in this way? And why now? It could not be a recent situation, because he had ended the arrangement with his mistress in December the year before. It was five months since he had lain with a woman because of his decision to wed this year and he could not bear a repeat of his betrothal to Annabel, who had discovered him *in flagrante delicto* in the stables with Caroline Brown. At the time, he thought that once he wed, he would be free to return to his philandering ways, but that had been before he met the provocative minx whom he ultimately married.

This situation made no sense. Who could be so angry with him, yet they waited a minimum of five months to enact their revenge? Had his nuptials triggered their anger? And how had they known or reacted so swiftly? He himself only knew he would wed mere days before the event. Unless they had known about his search for a bride and been lying in wait to pounce.

Richard's head swirled with the possibilities. *Blast*, he needed a drink! Not the damn water he had been sipping since his wedding day, but a real damn drink!

* * *

SOPHIA WAS SO livid when she stormed out of Richard's study that she took herself back to the Morelands', inviting herself to dinner because her earlier visit had disclosed the family's plans to stay in for the evening.

Smiling and forcing small talk gave her a megrim. Light glinting off the silver and crystal at the dinner table caused it to worsen into a sharp, throbbing pain until she was forced to massage her neck despite her aunt's disapproving stare at her unladylike behavior.

The moment dinner was finished, she grabbed her cousin Lily by the hand to drag her to the library, where the last slivers of sunlight were visible through the windows.

"Lily, the man is so frustrating! Attempting to send me to the country to rusticate with Ethan while he remains in town. Is he trying to get rid of me?"

Lily's face showed her concern. "I do not think so, cousin. I think he fears on your behalf."

"Did I make a mistake?"

Lily's elfin face scrunched in confusion. "What mistake?"

"Should I not have married him? Did I make a mistake in my choice of husband?"

Lily sighed. "I do not think so. This situation will resolve, but you need to give it time—give Lord Saunton time to straighten it out. Why so impatient, Sophia? You are one of the most level-headed people I know."

Sophia sighed, lifting a hand to knead the stiff muscles in her neck. "I am afraid. My feelings for the earl are growing.

At first, his crusade to redeem his honor was so exciting, but now I fear …"

"What is it?"

"I worry that the only reason he married me was that I somehow represented this crusade. What am I to him, merely a talisman or a … moral compass of some sort? An ethical lodestone, if you will? What if that is all I am to him? What if he resolves his quest and loses his interest in me once he no longer needs me?"

"Silly goose! No man could lose interest in you once you got your hooks in him! You are one of the cleverest, most interesting people I know. Your mind bends around problems to solve them. Look how you sorted out the debacle with Lord Leech. It was perfection. The man was thoroughly outwitted. Nay, your husband will only grow more attached to you over time."

Sophia shot a sideways glance at her petite cousin sitting beside her on the library sofa. "Truly?"

Lily snorted inelegantly. "Of course. When will you inform the man that you are in love with him?"

Sophia stiffened in ire. "What do you mean?"

"You are independent and do not care a whit about other people's opinions on how you should live your life. But here you sit, lamenting about what you mean to the earl, and will he lose interest in you? Clearly you have fallen in love with the man, just as I predicted."

"No … it is not true. I merely care about him …" Sophia squeezed her eyes shut in agony. Her cousin was correct. She did love her stupid husband. It had been inevitable from the moment he had expressed his desire and will to change. When he stated his admiration and admitted how she had inspired his crusade to redeem his honor, she was smitten with the daft man.

She admired his courage and his drive; and she appreciated his fine looks and his sense of humor. He made her feel safe when she had never allowed herself to rely on anyone because of the havoc her parents had wreaked on their lives. And his affection for his son, whom he acknowledged without hesitation despite the scandal it brought into his life, was commendable. Richard accepted the mantle of responsibility without complaint, and even now worked tirelessly to find a solution to their troubles.

And he does not trust you to assist him.

It saddened Sophia that he would not accept her help, but she admitted her cousin had made a good point earlier that day. She must accept his help if she expected him to do the same. They needed to engage in a proper discussion.

Lily prodded a sharp elbow into her side, causing Sophia to yelp in pain. "But enough about you and your woolgathering. I have a problem of my own."

"You shame me, cousin. I have forced my problems on you for days now."

"Do not be ridiculous. There was no force. But this is about me, so are you ready to stay silent and listen to my troubles?"

Sophia gave a nod. Lily settled deeper into the sofa and sighed. "Mama is relentless. Now that you are married, she has turned her full attentions to me. If she had her way, I will be married to a gentleman I barely know by the end of the week. I am not strong like you, Sophia!"

"Stuff and nonsense!"

Lily wrinkled her nose to stare up at Sophia, who felt like a veritable giant towering over her delicate cousin.

"Do not be daft. You just doled out advice to me throughout the day. You forced me to go confront Richard about the note and just persuaded me I was in love with the man, despite my resistance to the news. You have plenty of backbone."

"But … I want to find a genuine connection with a man. I do not wish to be pressured into marriage, but I do not know how to stand up to Mama without hurting her feelings. She wants what is best for me, but her ideas are old-fashioned and too rooted in society's expectations."

"Uncle Hugh will never force you to marry a man you do not want. Just stay strong and wait for the right gentleman."

"I am not as wily as you, cousin. She will get the best of me."

"This is a silly conversation. Lily, you are just as clever as I am. Just prepare yourself to contend with her demands. Think of what her arguments are and prepare counter-arguments. When dealing with Aunt Christiana, I usually find that distraction is the best technique. You have observed me doing just that for three Seasons. Lord Francis Bacon once wrote that knowledge is power. You must use your knowledge of Aunt Christiana, but do not engage in direct debate with her because it invariably does not work."

Lily's mouth hung open in astonishment. "How did you discover all this?"

"I read a book by a Chinese general that was translated into French. Would you like me to find it for you?" Sophia gestured toward the annex behind them where the shelving was laden with heavy tomes.

Lily nodded, an expression of awe on her face as Sophia scrambled to her feet to search for the volume. "You were applying military tactics to my mother? You are such a blue-stocking, cousin."

"Nay, I study what I need to know. I am not interested in study for study's sake. I must have a question to answer before I will plow through these sedate books. I found *L'Art de la Guerre* in my first Season when the pressure to marry was causing me distress." Sophia looked back to find her cousin's face pinched into a puzzled frown. "It means *The Art of War*, Lily. You will need to brush up on your French if you wish to employ military strategy, but your instincts are excellent. I will find a dictionary to assist you."

She mounted the library steps to pull leather-bound books from the shelves, then set them on the table for her cousin to read.

Shortly after that, they said their goodbyes. Sophia stood outside near to the family carriage that had brought her from Balfour Terrace. She hesitated on the steps of the Morelands' home and stared at the Saunton coat of arms gilded on the carriage door, thinking about the current state of her relationship with Richard.

Lily was right. It was time to make an effort at a proper discussion. She needed to stop playing games and tackle their issues directly. This was a marriage they were building, and it would not do to use wily misdirection and military tactics with her husband, or pose tests without his knowledge.

Sophia hovered on the steps in a state of bemusement, hugging herself in the chilled night air. She admitted to herself that she had brought the accumulated disappointments of her past and laid them at Richard's feet while he struggled to protect her and his son. Every time her charming father had made a promise—only to break it when he disappeared for days into his gambling hells to fetter away their income—in those reoccurring moments, she had realized she could not trust her beloved father, and that his words were empty of intent. Those final days, she had decided to grow up far too young and accept that he was irresponsible and would never change. And then came the night they were informed of his untimely death while sitting at a card table. All had taken residence in her mind, taunting her, challenging her to devise tests to disprove Richard's sincerity.

"Milady?"

Her husband was mostly blameless. He was ashamed that his past was haunting their present and had withheld some information to protect his pride and ease her worries, and in return, she had set him a test without his knowledge to prove to herself that he would fail.

"Milady?"

Sophia chewed on her lip, lost deep in the memories. She had not intended to compare her husband to her glib father, but she had done it all the same. It was not well done of her; the earl did not know what—or whom—he was being measured against, which meant Lily was right. She was being dishonest with him.

"Milady?"

Sophia returned to the present to find her footman gazing at her with perplexed concern. She realized the liveried servant had attempted to gain her attention several times.

"I wish to return home. To Balfour Terrace."

The footman appeared puzzled by this specification, but Sophia paid no heed. She had reached a decision.

I shall sit Richard down and talk to him honestly. Share my concerns, so we can reach an understanding.

Her mind made up, she gathered her skirts in one hand and accepted the gloved hand of the footman with the other to step up through the open door of the carriage. When the shorter John climbed in behind her, she accepted it without resentment. Her husband was taking strenuous action to defend her, and it was time she acknowledged the concern he was displaying. They would need to talk and come to terms, but this time she would not get frustrated with him. She was confident that if they worked together, they could find a solution to navigate the danger they were living under.

* * *

RICHARD VISITED with Ethan in the nursery and read him a story, then returned downstairs at dinnertime to wait for his wife, until Radcliffe informed him that her ladyship had left for the evening. He had not expected to be so disappointed by this news, but it was the first time since they married that they were not taking their evening meal together.

Sitting in his study, nursing a cut crystal glass of water —*blech*—he thought about what she had said earlier that day. Perry concurred with her conclusion that it was safer for her and Ethan to remain in town rather than undertake a long journey.

Perhaps she had a point. Mayhap he had not involved her sufficiently, and treated her like a coddled child. But he had never confided in a woman before. This was all so new to him. Perhaps she needed to be more patient with him.

He stared down into his water, wishing it was a fine French brandy, and admitted to himself that perhaps he was not making the effort that he should. If she left him to return to her family, as Perry suggested, he would be utterly lost. Why this was, he could not fathom. They had known each other for less than three weeks, but he grew mawkish at the thought of her absence. He did not want to send her away, truth be told. He wanted to eat dinner with her in the evenings before joining her in her bedchamber. The decision to send her to Saunton Park had been reached because, more important than his time in her company, he wanted her to remain alive.

He could not believe how much he missed her at this moment, merely because she had abandoned him to dinner on his own. The only conclusion he could draw was that he now looked forward to the nightly ritual in her company, only to have it yanked away because of his own failure to include her.

When she returned home from her family, *if* she returned home, he would do better. And if she did not return home, he would haunt the Abbott household every moment of every day until she agreed to come home.

BANG. A loud thud shuddered the wooden floor beneath his feet, causing him to flinch in surprise. Richard sprang up to find out what had been dropped, but when he reached the study door, he hesitated when he heard a loud, agitated voice he did not recognize. He cocked his head to listen closer, but he could not quite make out what was being said. He only knew it was not a member of his household sounding off.

The commotion was coming from the vestibule. Briefly, he hoped Sophia had still not returned home. His body was on high alert while eerie calm descended over his mind. Instinct told him that, as he had predicted earlier to Perry, the stakes had just heightened and it was time for him to act. He finally had something—someone—specific to address.

Bending down, he removed his boots, concluding that his stockinged feet would allow him to investigate what was happening without announcing his presence. Stealthily, he crept into the corridor outside his study and moved toward the disturbance. When he reached the vestibule, it surprised him to glimpse a well-dressed couple facing away from him toward the grand staircase.

Richard stopped short, noting the thickset gentleman who appeared to be embracing a vaguely familiar woman. She was slumped at an awkward angle, and Richard could not make out her face until her head fell to hang forward. With dawning horror, he realized the gentleman was not embracing, but clutching his former paramour, Lady Evaline Wood, around her waist with her arms pinned under his, and she appeared to be swooning.

Richard caught sight of the shorter John behind the Woods, lying in a heap at the foot of the stairs and bleeding. Radcliffe stood to one side of the stairs with his hands raised outwards at an odd angle, as if he had been instructed to show them.

"That is when my wife decided that what is sauce for the goose is sauce for the gander and in a fit of pique engaged in an adulterous affair with YOUR HUSBAND!" Lord Wood roared.

Richard's heart skipped a beat. Sophia was here? Of course! That was why the shorter John was unconscious on the floor.

"But"—the man turned to Lady Wood to yell directly in her face—"you are not a GOOSE! Men dally. WOMEN BEHAVE THEMSELVES!" he bellowed at the top of his lungs. The man's wife appeared to be unresponsive, evidently having descended into a state of shock. Suddenly, Richard was able to see between the clasped couple, their bodies slightly parted by the new angle. Sophia was revealed to be standing stoically on the bottom stair, her gaze fixed on the ornate dueling pistol in Lord Wood's hand.

Blood thundered in Richard's ears and his eyes riveted to the pistol Lord Wood waved about while he ranted at his pale wife. With sharpened focus, he noted that the lord's bloated index finger rested on the side of the barrel, not the trigger, which meant Richard could attempt to disarm him.

One step at a time, Richard.

"Fortunately for me, a friend informed me of what was happening. Did you know Lord Saunton was spotted sneaking into my home last evening? I knew it was all fluff and propaganda that the rake was reformed. Men dally! It is what we do! No man can be expected to remain tied to one woman. We marry a respectable woman to sire our children,

213

and we visit our mistresses to have our fun. It is a good system! It WORKS!"

The man's ranting was despicable. Despite the danger of the moment, Richard could not help but be repulsed that he had once thought of women and relationships with a similar disgusting attitude as this vile reprobate who aimed a weapon at innocent people. Never had it been more clear that walking away from his past immorality was the correct decision. The only decision.

Slowly, Richard inched forward. If anything happened to Sophia because of his own debauched behavior with the unhappily married Lady Wood, he would find no redemption for his wicked soul. Damnation, what if his wife was killed tonight believing that he had engaged in an illicit affair *after* their wedding, rather than six months before he had even met her? He must save her because Ethan needed her. *He* needed her. He must save his wife!

Richard approached the dimly lit spot behind the couple. Lord Wood was in the midst of shaking Lady Wood, whose cracked lip was bleeding from an earlier blow.

Radcliffe's eyes flickered, noting Richard's arrival. His wonderful, clever butler imperceptibly straightened and lifted his chin, clearly steeling his nerves and preparing to divert Lord Wood's attention.

"My lord, perhaps a calm discussion might—"

"SHUT UP!"

"But, I assure you—"

"You speak again and I will end you, you insufferable *serf*!"

Radcliffe's ploy to distract the irate husband from Richard's approach succeeded as he crept up behind the couple. Fortunately, the angle of the light thrown by the chandelier above was in his favor, so no shadow announced his arrival. At this proximity, the raving nobleman reeked of hard liquor, which offered some explanation for his unbalanced behavior.

Verifying that Lord Wood's finger was still resting on the barrel, Richard spoke behind his ear. "I believe you are looking for me?" Simultaneously, he swung his clenched fist down on the man's pistol-wielding right arm. Sophia immediately swung herself around the curving banister and dropped to her haunches behind the staircase. Radcliffe stood hesitant, plainly unsure whether to retreat or leap forward to help, while Lord Wood was so startled that he released his wife. Lady Wood crumpled into a heap but still possessed enough presence of mind to crawl away to where the butler hailed her toward him.

All of these events occurred in mere seconds, but Richard observed the scene with the same eerie calm, perceiving the position of every actor in the unfolding melodrama concurrently with the heightened focus that descended on him when it was time for him to spring into action. He fought for control of the weapon now pointed down between them in Lord Wood's hand, while Richard gripped the barrel. He was younger and fitter, but the beefy lord he was wrestling had the advantage of mass and a large, powerful grip. Lord Wood was renowned at their pugilistic club for packing a devastating punch—Richard knew he must avoid the man's club fists while fighting for control of the firearm.

If the unthinkable happened and he lost … the damned weapon would only be loaded with one bullet, so Radcliffe and Sophia could protect themselves in the event of his demise.

Perry will take care of my family if he must assume the title, was his last coherent thought as the two of them stumbled and Richard took a ringing punch to the side of his head, holding on to the barrel of the pistol like his life depended on it while his vision spotted from the blow.

CHAPTER 17

A shot rang out.

Sophia screamed in fear and clamped her hands over her ears. Then she scolded herself for being a scared little mouse, stiffened her resolve, and carefully peered around the curving banister of the staircase, which afforded a little protection.

Both men were prone on the floor, Lord Wood on top of her beloved Richard. *Please,* she prayed, *please let Richard be unhurt.* Neither man moved. Were they both dead? Panic clawed at the thought that her wonderful, foolish husband might be gone.

Slowly, she reached behind her onto a table to grab a vase as an impromptu weapon and then, crouching down, she scampered over to where they lay. Lord Wood rolled off Richard, and Sophia panicked, her eyes filling with tears until she realized it was Richard who had pushed the large man off, causing him to roll as if he were still alive.

She wept in relief, taking in Lord Wood's sightless eyes and blood seeping through the gold brocade of his waistcoat.

Richard scrambled to his knees to grasp Sophia in a hard embrace while she sobbed out her relief into his shoulder, the vase she held in her hand trapped uncomfortably between their bodies.

Sophia gasped. "You are hurt!" she exclaimed, touching his blood-soaked jacket.

"Nay, it is Lord Wood's blood. Sophia, my love, I must take care of Lady Wood. Can you be strong for me while I check on her?" Sophia realized she was still sobbing. Calming herself, she nodded.

He let her go and crawled over the few feet to where Lady Wood lay near Radcliffe, who had collapsed in a stupor. His butler noticed Richard's arrival and exhaled in deep relief. "My lord."

"Are you all right, Radcliffe?"

"Just a little dazed. I will collect myself back together, my lord."

"Take your time, Radcliffe. This is not a typical evening."

The butler bobbed his head, drawing in a deep breath while Richard turned his attention to the slight form.

"Evaline?" He touched the trembling woman on her shoulder and she flinched, cowering in a huddle.

"Evaline? Are you all right?" She shuddered and then looked up at him.

"It is over?" she whispered, her eyes unfocused and her face as pale as a white sheet.

"Yes," Richard assented. "But, my lady, Lord Wood … I am afraid … he is no longer with us."

She stared up at him with empty eyes until, in a hollow voice, she replied, "I could do with a strong drink, if I may?"

"I will take you to my study in a moment, as soon as I check on John over there."

Sophia watched her husband move over to the shorter

John, carefully turning him over from the position he had fallen in after Lord Wood surprised him with a blow to the head with the pistol. The guardsman mumbled, to her relief, opening his eyes to look up into the earl's face. He bore a nasty gash on his temple that was bleeding profusely, and his gaze skittered about.

"Your lordship?"

"Yes, it is I. Radcliffe is calling for a doctor." Richard glanced over to the servant, who gave a quick nod and clamored to his feet.

Sophia dried her eyes, taking pride in the man she had married. Her heart had nearly stopped when her husband hurled into Lord Wood, but he had succeeded in his heroic antics and now ensured the well-being of each person, despite the ordeal he had just faced.

Richard had just saved her life.

And killed a man.

* * *

RICHARD PLACED his wife and Lady Wood in a carriage to return to the Woods' residence, promising to follow the two women later.

Then he dispatched footmen to dig Perry out of whichever club or hell he was gambling in that evening in his bid to gather intelligence.

Finally, Richard sent for the authorities.

When the Bow Street Runners arrived, he informed the grim-faced strangers that Lord Wood and himself had been playing cards together the day before and that Lord Wood had shown up that evening to accuse him of cheating before attempting to shoot him. Richard had been forced to wrestle him for his pistol, and the man was killed in the ensuing struggle.

Fortunately, Richard outranked the dead peer who had a reputation for drinking, an irascible temper, and violence with his fists. He recalled hearing of the man brandishing a pistol at a prize fight sometime in the past year, so he had high hopes that his version of events would protect Evaline over the coming days.

Radcliffe told the same story, forgoing any mention that the two women had been present and altering the accusations the lord had thrown to mumblings about a game of cards. Richard knew he could trust the longtime family servant to never speak on the matter.

The shorter John had been unconscious from the moment Lord Wood knocked him out with a crack to the head with the pistol the peer brandished after the couple had gained entry to the entrance hall. When the runners questioned the undercover guardsman, he corroborated that Lord Wood had been out of control upon gaining entrance to Balfour Terrace.

Richard worried if his story was weak, only having had a half hour to prepare it and gain Radcliffe's cooperation, but the runners appeared to accept what he said. Apparently, they were aware that Lord Wood was infamous for routing and fighting. The decoy tale was the least he could do to aid Lady Wood.

Perry arrived moments before the coroner. His brother was pale when he stepped through the front door, his eyes resting on the corpse before he strode over to Richard and grabbed him into a firm embrace.

"Thank God! You daft arse, you nearly got yourself killed!" His younger brother's sardonic ennui was not in evidence, his voice gruff with distress.

"Just think, you could have inherited an earldom tonight." Richard's jest was halfhearted, his tone sounding thick to his ears.

"Fuck, that would have been awful! Please promise me you will sire an heir soon. I have no wish to shoulder the responsibilities you carry. How will I find time to spend my allowance and frolic my days away?"

Richard chuckled, releasing his brother. "I am working on it."

They sat on the stairs while the coroner investigated the scene. Richard answered his questions and then, finally, the body was removed and his brother joined him in the study.

Perry made for the sideboard, poured two drinks, and walked back to where Richard sat in one of the plump armchairs to stare sightlessly into the hearth.

"Here, drink this."

"No, I am no longer drinking."

"Make an exception. You just killed a man and you look like hell."

Richard hung his head, bringing up a hand to rub his face in despair. "I killed a man."

"Drink, brother. You are in shock."

Richard took the tumbler and downed the brandy in a few gulps. Warmth spread through his chilled body, and he noticed Perry was correct. Shock had rendered his limbs cold and sweaty, while his pulse fired too rapidly and his breathing was too shallow. As the spirits spread through his system, his body eased and he became more aware of his surroundings.

"I killed a man," he whispered.

"I only pointed that out so you would accept the liquor. I think you should focus on the fact that you saved someone's life tonight. That bullet was inevitably going to find its way into one of the people present. All things considered, the right person was on the receiving end of that shot."

"I doubt his wife would agree."

"I am certain his wife would agree. Lord Wood was infamous for using his fists to win his arguments. Do you not think his wife was included in his violence? Nay, I think she strayed with you last year for a reason and you freed the tragic woman from the confines of a hellish marriage. Now the important question—is the threat over? Was he the source of these recent attacks?"

Richard's hopes soared at the possibility before sinking like a stone into a pond.

"Nay, when I first arrived on the scene, he ranted that a friend informed him they saw me sneaking into his residence last night."

Perry snorted. "He claimed you are currently having an affair? Good Lord! I hardly see you out of your bedchamber, or even leaving Balfour Terrace, since you married the countess. I am most impressed with Lady Saunton's stamina. Any other woman would be worn out by now."

Richard glared at his brother, who threw up his hands in surrender. "I shall not mention the countess and her bedchamber again, but clearly your hidden villain has struck once more. What are we doing to end this living nightmare?"

Richard leaned forward, his elbows on his knees, and dropped his head into his hands to ponder the question. "Lord Stanford knows the man's identity. He refused to name the scoundrel out of misguided honor."

Perry sprang to his feet, his jaw set in a determined line. "I will locate Lord Stanford and compel him to reveal the identity of this troublemaker even if I have to drag him out of Lady Partridge's bedroom of iniquity and beat it out of him."

Richard thought about it, then nodded. "Take one of the barking irons with you." He gestured to the carved walnut box that housed his pistols on a top shelf.

Perry frowned in puzzlement. "I was not planning to kill the man or call him out."

Richard groaned. "For protection, you cretin! You will carry one and I the other until we settle this matter."

"Oh, that makes more sense." His brother flashed him an impudent grin. "I am happy you are still with us, blighter." He ducked the cushion thrown at his head to walk over and take the box down. Resting it on the desk, he opened the box to remove one of the pistols. Carefully, he prepared and loaded the weapon before slipping it in the overcoat he still wore. Giving a quick salute, he left Richard alone to his thoughts.

After a few minutes contemplating the hell of this night, he stood up to make his way over to the Woods' residence, his carriage waiting for him when he exited the front door.

When he reached the Mayfair home of Lady Wood, he found Sophia waiting for him alone in a drawing room with an untouched cup of tea on the table in front of her. She jumped up when he entered the room, running over to fling herself into his arms.

Richard wrapped his arms around her, grateful that she was safe and alive while he rested his cheek on the crown of her head and breathed deeply the scent of roses.

"Richard, I cannot believe what you did. My heart stopped when the two of you tumbled to the floor. I thought you were dead!"

"Who would bring trouble into your life, then?"

Sophia pulled back to look up at him. "The trouble does not concern me. I need you alive."

Richard let her go, pulling back to walk over and drop onto one of the rickety, elegant sofas, which juddered under his weight. "I do not see why. I have brought nothing but pandemonium and peril into your life. You were more protected before you married me."

His heart squeezed in agony at the deep silence following his pronouncement. After many moments, he heard her light footsteps approaching. She sat down on the sofa beside him and reached out a hand to cover his.

"We are both exhausted and I can no longer think straight, husband. But please know my relief that you survived is most profound. Could we go home to rest and then we can discuss things in the morning?"

Richard bobbed his head. He could not deny that in the aftermath, his body was heavy with weariness. He had forgotten to rid himself of the jacket, and the smell of blood aggravated his senses.

"How is Lady Wood?"

"She downed a strong drink, showed me some bruises beneath her garments. Before she went to bed, she asked me to thank you. Evidently, she believes you saved her life this evening. Lord Wood has not permitted her to leave her home without him in several weeks, so she has been trapped in this townhouse since March. Some of the bruises ... they were ... much older and ... and ..." Sophia broke off, overcome by what she had seen. Richard grimaced and put an arm around her.

"Do not fret, Sophia. I will visit Lady Wood and ensure she is well taken care of. And I will have Johnson look into her circumstances to ensure that proper provisions were made for her. Hopefully, her father negotiated good terms for the eventuality of her bereavement."

Tears welled to slip down her smooth cheeks. She turned her head into his shoulder and flung her arms around him in a tight embrace. "I am such a watering pot tonight."

Richard gave her a squeeze and rose to his feet, holding out a hand to her. "Let us go so we can get some rest."

SOPHIA CLUNG to Richard the entire night. Each time he stirred, he found her form draped over him in different angles as if she could not bear to let him go. It warmed the depths of his soul where he still sought to come to terms with the fact that he had taken the life of a man he barely knew. Nothing could prepare a man for such an event. However, if he had to do it again, he would not hesitate to protect the woman who was lying in his arms, emitting a bleating snore from the awkward angle her head tilted so that she could nestle into his shoulder.

Carefully unwrapping her arms, he eased her onto her side, ensuring her neck was not cricked. He curved his arm around her sleeping form and went back to sleep, content to lie in bed with Sophia for the entire day if he could.

It was early afternoon when Richard and Sophia finally arose. Dressed in their nightclothes and robes, they ate breakfast from trays at the table near Sophia's window, too wrung out from the night before to bother with dressing or going downstairs to break their fast.

Once Sophia had swallowed down her eggs, sipped on her tea, and sat quietly contemplating the garden from her window, she broke their deep silence.

"May I see the note now?"

Richard huffed in mild amusement. He swallowed down his toast—he was surprised how ravenous he had been when the meal arrived—before rising to walk into his rooms.

After several minutes of searching, he found the note folded neatly with his things in a drawer of his bureau and returned.

Sitting down across from his wife, he stared at her for a while. She looked beautiful with her tousled red-blonde hair, her large eyes weary but prismatic with striations of light and dark blues reflected in their depths. And, more importantly, she was beauty itself because she was *alive*.

"I planned to talk with you when you returned last night. I wanted to apologize. Now I find I have more to apologize for."

"Apologize?"

"I thought about what you said, and I realized you were right. I should have included you in what was happening. Instead, I treated you like a child."

"More like a weak-minded female."

"From the moment I overheard you on the terrace disparaging society, I knew you were strong and independent. I admire you greatly, and I have never thought of you as weak-minded. Only a fool would overlook your presence of mind and strength."

She gazed at him, a smile of joy playing on her lips. "Thank you."

"I should have told you about the note. Halmesbury told me I should tell you about the note. I was foolish to hide it from you, but it had nothing to do with my thoughts on you and everything to do with how I felt about myself. I was ashamed to have exposed my wife and my son because my selfish nature angered someone to this degree. And the note does not cast me in a favorable light." He grimaced. "Not that I deserve to be cast that way."

Sophia nodded. "I understand. I was on my way to find you and apologize, too."

Richard felt his jaw drop in astonishment. "What could you have to apologize for?"

"My cousin Lily had the audacity to point out that I had been testing you rather than be honest myself. Most men in my life have been a source of disappointment. I agreed to marry you with the best of intentions, but proceeded to be cautious and guarded with you. I did not confront you, but rather stewed in my anger that I was proven correct. Lily asked me if I would prefer we complain together about how men are terrible, or for her to advise me to take control over my situation. She made fine points. You are not comparable to my father. Look at what you did on behalf of our household. You were present, and you acted. You asked me to be patient with you, but I was not."

Sophia was flushed with the force of her opinions. She looked magnificent.

He coughed into his hand, unsure how to respond. "I cannot say I agree. Perhaps I need to understand more about your family history. I appreciate the thought you have put into … us, I guess."

Her lips curved into a smile. "Thank you."

Richard glanced down at the note in his hand. "Please do not think less of me." He held the note out for her to take, then dropped his gaze down to stare at his hands. Working up his nerve, he finally said what had been in his heart for the past few days. "I have come to realize that marrying you was the most important decision I ever made. Sophia, I … I love you."

Deep silence followed. He waited, but she had nothing to say. *I made a mistake! I told her before she is ready!*

More silence continued. Finally, he found the courage to look up and confront her reaction to his proclamation, but he found Sophia frozen, white as a sheet, staring at the note in her hand.

"What is—"

The door to the hall flung open, banging on the wall as Perry rushed into the room. "Brother! Lord Stanford gave me the name of the man who told him of your tryst! It is Cecil Hayward."

"Cecil? I do not know any Cecil."

"But you do know a Hayward." Perry jerked his head in the direction of the woman sitting behind him. Richard's brow furrowed, and he turned around to find his wife staring at him with wide, shocked eyes.

"The note … it is written in my brother's hand. He has attempted to disguise it, but … Cecil … he is sly but not intelligent. Too many years of hard drink have addled his brain. He used his customary stroke through the o. The trouble plaguing your household … I brought this to your doorstep. This is all my fault!"

CHAPTER 18

*S*ophia felt like she had exited her body and observed the events in the room unfolding from a distance.

From the moment she had taken the note, she ceased to hear or see anything but the handwriting on the page, realizing that *she* had been the cause of the danger. Richard could have been killed. Even Ethan was in danger because she selfishly sought safety in the Balfour household and inadvertently brought her troubles with her.

Richard blamed himself for everything that had happened since the day of the wedding. He was so certain he was the cause that Sophia never stopped to observe the patterns. The bully tactics of the caricatures. The alteration of facts that caused angry paramours and husbands to target Richard. Even the rock through the window of Richard's study carried the mark of her brother's hand, but she had failed to see it. Failed to inform Richard of the danger she represented.

She rushed back into her body with a crash. Her hand dropped the note, and she crumpled over in anguish, sorrow and regret coalescing to slash through her soul. Emitting a wail of deep despair, she dissolved into a blubbering mess. Richard's arms engulfed her, but she tried to wrench herself away. She did not deserve his solace because she had risked everything the man held dear to protect herself. And she had not even warned him of the danger.

Sophia had underestimated how vindictive her brother could be.

* * *

RICHARD GATHERED Sophia into his arms. She tried to pull away, but he was not having it. He hugged her closer, attempting to soothe her. It was devastating to see her anguish, his strong woman, who brought peace into his household, reduced to heaving sobs.

"Calm yourself, Sophia."

"It is all my fault!"

"Sophia, I need you to calm down. Please, my love. Whatever this is, we will sort it out."

"I could have caused your death!"

"My love, Lord Wood could have caused my death. And your brother might have put him up to it. But you did not do this, Sophia. Please, calm yourself."

Sophia sobbed in his arms with such gut-wrenching pain, he wanted to hunt down Cecil Hayward so he might pound the man into the ground. He had no idea what the black-guard was about, but he did know he wanted to kill him. Meanwhile, he must be content with making soothing sounds and caressing his hands up and down her slight back while she wept.

Finally, her storm of tears eased, and her head hung limp against him.

Perry walked over to hand him a handkerchief. Richard

gently pushed Sophia back and used it to wipe gently at her downcast, swollen eyes. She would not look at him, an expression of guilt pasted across her face.

"Why would your brother target me? Did I cuckold him in some way I am unaware of?"

Sophia shook her head.

"Was he targeting me?"

Again, she shook her head.

"So, the doxies in my bed, the caricatures, manipulating Lord Stanford and Lord Wood, the rock through the window, and the threatening note—these were misdirection to hurt you?"

She nodded.

"I feel I am missing some vital information—"

"I should leave! I will go to Saunton Park, and my brother will surely follow me there! Then you and Ethan will be safe!"

Richard took her face between his hands and gently turned her to look at him. "My love, I am not leaving you vulnerable. Now that we know who is behind this, we will find him and end it. But Sophia, you have to explain what this is about."

Sophia looked at him with such guilt and pain, it tore through him. He wanted to comfort her, to make her feel safe. It was his duty as her protector, but he knew she needed to explain the situation. Not just so that he and Perry could take action, but because she carried some unnamed burden that wreaked havoc on her usual composure. His wife needed him to listen.

"Would you like Perry to leave us alone?"

She shook her head. "I put your household in danger. Perry should know what hangs over our heads."

"Why would Cecil target you in this manner?"

She exhaled in a shaky breath before pulling out of his arms. She stood and went to stare out the window.

"I am not sure how to start. Where to start …" She paused. "Ten years ago, my father died. He was a prolific gambler, and he drank too much. I was told he died of some sort of apoplexy while playing cards in the early hours. My mother was not a strong woman, and she died from a laudanum overdose within days of his death. Cecil is my father's son from his first marriage. He was sixteen and became very angry after our father's death."

Sophia stopped, raising a hand against the glass as if she were peering into the past.

"What happened?"

"Lord Moreland, my mother's brother, and his wife took us in. Cecil is not a blood relation of the Abbott family, but they have always valued family above all else, so they took my brother in along with me. They were not aware that Cecil started drinking quite heavily. Perhaps he was drinking before my father's death. It is possible my father encouraged it when they spent time together. I … I did not know what to do about it. He is my brother … the only one I had left after my parents both …"

Richard struggled to understand where the story would lead and how it related to their wedding, which had apparently set her sibling off on this rampage, but he remained silent to allow Sophia to find her way through the tale.

"Uncle Hugh provided him with an allowance, so Cecil started wagering. Playing cards, betting at disreputable clubs. The Abbotts were not aware of his descent. He fooled them with gracious manners, and they are not accustomed to his sort of depravity …"

His heart skipped a beat. He did not like the direction this was going. Had the brother hurt her in some manner?

"When I turned eighteen and came out, Uncle Hugh gave

me a generous allowance. Cecil needed to pay his gambling debts, and I had money. So he took it from me. When I threatened to tell my uncle, my brother ... made it clear that I would regret it if I ever informed on him."

Perry and Richard both stiffened, his brother casting him a questioning look. Richard shook his head to indicate he did not know, but he disliked the tone of her voice when she stated it.

"Sophia, my love, can you explain, how did he make that clear?"

"He beat me."

Richard jumped to his feet, agitated. Sophia needed to tell him the rest, which meant he needed to stay calm and let her finish.

Perry, noting his distress, asked the next question. "How ... did your uncle not notice?"

"Cecil was very careful to slap me across the face or punch me in the stomach. Evidence was minimal."

Richard ran his hand through his hair and gestured for Perry to stay quiet. His stomach was in knots thinking of his sweet wife being abused by the brute she was related to. The man who should have been protecting her. "Has he done it all these years?"

"Nay, after the first few times, I started reading military texts and working on strategies to outwit him. I hid items of sentimental value I did not wish him to take. I hid pin money, too, and told him that Aunt Christiana was making me spend it all on expenses related to the Season. He eventually stopped coming to me for funds, but I believe the gambling continued."

Richard drew a deep breath. Her resourcefulness was impressive, but he would have expected it from her. His sweet Sophia was no man's victim.

"How did we get to today? Why did our wedding rile his wrath after all this time?"

"He uncovered the truth about my dowry and realized he could come to a financial arrangement with a fortune hunter. Stealing me from my bed and taking me to Scotland for a forced marriage was discussed."

Richard stared at her in horror. "Leech!"

"Leech?" Perry hissed. "The wife killer?"

Richard nodded. "I interceded that night at the Yardley ball, or she would have been compelled to dance with him. The coroners in the matter of his wives' deaths could find no evidence of foul play and the man has powerful friends, so he walks amongst us unscathed, but he must have orchestrated their deaths."

Sophia spoke in a low, sad voice. "Based on the conversation I overheard, he definitely had a hand in their deaths. He alluded to the possibility of my own."

Richard shook his head in dismay, pacing back and forth while he tried to settle his thoughts. "Is this what you meant when you said you needed protection?" Sophia nodded, her face still averted toward the window. "Blazes, I thought you meant in a general sense that a woman needed a protector, or that you had concerns about fortune hunters pursuing you. I did not know you needed *actual* protection!"

"I was uncertain how much of a threat they posed, but once we agreed to wed, I took to sleeping in my cousin's room and paid a footman to sleep in my bed. The night before our nuptials, Lord Leech attempted my abduction, but Thomas apprehended him."

Richard and Perry looked at each other, aghast. They considered their dead father to have been the worst kind of scoundrel, but yet even he possessed innocence when compared to Sophia's brother. Richard could not believe she had lived under such intimidation. He wanted to walk over to his wife and fold her in his arms to comfort her, yet he knew she needed to finish her story for her own peace of mind, so he clenched his fists and stayed rooted to where he stood.

"I was forced to tell Uncle Hugh about Cecil's involvement. I ... I thought it was safe to do so. I would marry you in the morning and then I would be beyond his reach. I did not know he would take it this far." Sophia's voice thickened with tears. "I am so sorry for dragging you into this. I hoped to spare the Abbotts, but I endangered your household instead!"

At that, Richard raced across the room to embrace her. "Hush, Sophia, the only regret I have is that I did not know. If I had known, I would still have married you." He waved his hand at Perry, who left the room and quietly closed the door behind him. "Sophia, nothing—nothing—could have dissuaded me from pursuing you."

* * *

SOPHIA WAS MORTIFIED that she had been weeping again. Since the moment she thought Richard had been killed, her emotions had been skittering out of her control. Just when she had regained her equilibrium, she discovered she was the one at fault for the jeopardy their household was in.

She had been willing to tolerate Richard's troubles because she entered their marriage with her eyes open, but to learn that she was the true cause ... The guilt was chewing her up from the inside. She had miscalculated the risk that Cecil posed and exposed Richard, Perry, and little Ethan to his diabolical revenge.

"Sophia?"

A shiver of apprehension scurried over her skin. She looked up but had trouble meeting her husband's eye.

"Sophia, I need you to look at me."

Her eyelids flickered. With reluctance etched in every line of her body, she lifted her gaze. Richard's eyes were blazing in their intensity, green with gold striations, catching her in a net of fascination.

"Sophia, you are not to blame. Your brother is a diabolical fiend, but we will take care of it. Together."

His words penetrated the cloud of guilt she was cloaked in. "You do not blame me?"

"I do not. However, I accept your apology from earlier that you were not forthright with me, now that I comprehend what you have been hiding." His lips quirked into a wry smile. Sophia chuckled despite her dark mood. It was one of the things that made Richard so special—his ability to make her laugh in even her darkest hours.

"If I knew that he would follow me here ..." She trailed off in wordless dismay.

"I know, my love."

Sophia stared at him, her beloved husband. Who was still alive. Impulsively, she leaned forward to kiss him on his perfect lips.

"Are you feeling better?"

She gave a brief nod. "I know you must work with Perry to find my brother, but could you wait? Last night I was so terrified you had been killed, and up until this moment, the only time we have spent together is to sleep. I am weary of dealing with earth-shattering revelations. I need a few quiet moments to stop and rest with you."

Richard pulled her into a hug. "Yes, I would like that."

* * *

THEY SAT TOGETHER IN SILENCE, Richard picking at the remains of his breakfast while Sophia drank tea. He thought about his earlier declaration of love. Had she heard what he said? Was she pretending he had not revealed his heart to her? Or had she been too distracted to hear him?

Dealing with the emergency that Cecil Hayward created was easier to his state of mind than the nerves that assailed him at the thought that he had announced his feelings—*blech*—but she said nothing in return. Did she desire his esteem?

This was not the appropriate time to press the matter. Emotions were running too high, while shock was still wearing off after the tragic events of the night before. But, Lord, the impulse to delve into it anyway was all he could think about.

"Richard?"

He looked up to find Sophia restored to her usual composure. Her blue eyes were calm, and her manner peaceful. Apparently, her request to slow things down and stand still for a moment was exactly what she needed.

"Tell me about your crusade. What have you been doing? I know you found Ethan because of it, but I do not really understand how you have gone about it."

Richard pulled a face. "Will you still like me if you know the details?"

She extended a hand to cover his own, rubbing a thumb over his knuckles. "I will like you more."

He blew a puff of air and told her. He told her how he had composed a list of the most vulnerable women of his past. How Johnson and Long had looked into the circumstances of everyone on the list, then he met with his past paramours to apologize for any irresponsibility on his part, and, where appropriate, he made financial amends to assist them. And how he had provided an unentailed property to Ethan's family for their generosity in sharing their home with the motherless boy. When Richard was finished, he finally returned his gaze to find her smiling.

"Your crusade is most commendable."

His spirits lifted at her encouragement. Oh, how he loved this odd woman he had married. He could think of no other woman of his acquaintance who would be so gracious about his past mistakes and his clumsy efforts to sort them out. *Except for one. You know of one other.* Richard squashed the voice in his head. He did not want to think of her. Since the moment of his revelation on the Astleys' terrace, he had made a point not to think about *her*.

It was as if Sophia picked the errant thought from his head because her next question was so unnerving that his stomach heaved when she asked it.

"Tell me about your first betrothal?"

Richard sprang to his feet in agitation, knocking over the heavy armchair with the juddering force of his movement. His heart fluttered in his chest, revolting at the subject she wished to discuss. Why did she have to ruin their nice moment?

"I think we should call for the servants. It is time to get dressed and deal with this Cecil debacle, I think."

"Richard?"

He righted the armchair to distract his thoughts, desperate to find a change of topic, but his mind was a blank. All he could think about was—

"Richard?"

He rubbed his hands over his face, panic setting in before he realized that withheld information had nearly resulted in Sophia being killed last night. That he himself was lucky to be standing there breathing. If he could survive an encounter with a dueling pistol in his own home, then surely he could survive a conversation in the privacy of his wife's bedchamber about the worst mistake he had ever committed. "Damnit!"

Sophia waited for him, calm and far too understanding.

Seething with—what, he did not know—just seething, he reclaimed his seat to stare at the table in front of him. Reaching up to loosen his cravat, he floundered at the recollection that he was dressed in an open-neck cotton nightshirt. He dropped his hand back to the table.

Why was he more afraid to think about what he had done to Annabel than he had been about leaping onto an armed man the night before? It was beyond comprehension how emotions and guilt could eat at one's soul. Emotions had no force, no tangible mass. Yet they could feel more solid than the walls of a prison, despite their intangible nature.

"Earlier you allowed me to talk. To explain about Cecil. It was not comfortable, but having finally shared the burden of what I have been living with … it helped. I will sit here and wait until you are ready, Richard. I care about you, and it is obvious you need to unburden your conscience. It is important, because we face genuine danger when we leave this room, and I think it best we leave with clear minds so we can operate effectively. For our sake, and the sake of your son upstairs."

Hell, I need a drink!

But he only needed a drink because his guilt had been tearing him in two since the night he had confronted the magnitude of his betrayal. And ever since the first inkling of guilt had presented itself less than three weeks earlier, he had desperately tried to push it down and seal it back in a box and bury it in the attic of his mind where it could not torture him.

Now it was time to unbury the box and bring it out to open it. Holy hell, it was mortifying.

Clearing his throat, he finally spoke. "Her name is Annabel."

238

CHAPTER 19

"*A*nnabel is the younger sister of a friend, Brendan Ridley. We met when we were children. She is intelligent and lively, the first female I ever genuinely enjoyed spending time with outside the ..." Richard waved his hand at the bedchamber, clearly unsure how to complete the sentence. Sophia nodded her understanding so he would continue.

"After my father passed away, I rescued our estates from the brink of financial ruin. Once I succeeded, I needed to ensure that our tenants would find themselves with responsible leadership in the event of my demise. Three or four years ago, I decided it was time to do my duty and sire an heir because Perry made it clear he did not wish to inherit. I started my search for a suitable wife, but after two stupefying Seasons of meeting tame young misses whom I could not tolerate for more than five to ten minutes at a time, I realized there was only one woman whom I could marry. Annabel was rusticating in the country because her father refused to bring her to London, and I realized I had an opportunity to marry an interesting woman."

Sophia experienced a slight twinge of envy, then reminded herself that he was not married to the other woman but was sitting in her own bedchamber recounting his history. She suppressed her jealousy and forced herself to pay attention to what was important.

"The problem was, I thought I could marry a close friend and continue my pursuits as a rake concurrently."

"I take it Annabel did not see it that way?"

"Correct. I had taken up with a maid on her father's estate, someone she cared about, and Annabel discovered us … well … doing something in the stables."

"Doing something you should not have been doing?"

Richard flushed in embarrassment and looked down at his hands folded on his lap, every line of his body stiff with tension. "I did not handle it well. She did. She let the maid go with references. She even helped the young woman find a new position. I … I did nothing. Except when Annabel said she wanted to cancel the wedding. Then I did something."

Sophia frowned, puzzled and trying to work out what he could have done. "Never say you refused?"

Richard's head sank lower, blushing so hard his ears turned a bright red. "And I convinced her father to proceed with the wedding."

"My word!" Sophia gasped. "Blast! I apologize. I am just surprised. Please continue."

"She begged me to change my mind, but I insisted the wedding would proceed. Annabel grew desperate, so she sought my cousin, the Duke of Halmesbury—"

"And married him!" Sophia clapped a hand over her mouth. "Please, I am sorry. It is just so ingenious of her."

Richard grimaced. "That is the short version of the story, yes. The long version is that she dressed herself like a lad and risked her life to ride alone through the night from Somerset to Wiltshire to seek him out. Apparently, she asked him to intercede with me, but he seized the opportunity to win my bride from me for reasons I will explain another day."

Sophia realized she was gaping at him, quickly pressed her lips together, then said, "It was not well done of you—what you did to Annabel—but why does it bother you so much after all this time? Given that it all worked out for her in the end."

Her husband lifted a hand to knead the muscles in his neck, his expression agitated while he thought. "I suppose ... all the other women I wronged were active, willing participants in my dalliances. Annabel was different. She was innocent of any wrongdoing, and I had no excuse to betray a friend in that manner. Then I compounded it by insisting she wed me when it was clear she did not want to. When I awoke to how wrong my past behavior has been, it finally dawned on me how poorly I treated her. If you told me a man had done this to you ... I would seek them out and pound them. It was pure villainy. My father was the very worst of rogues, far past the point of redemption, but what I did to her ... it ranked as one of the worst things a potential protector could do, and then when I was caught, I showed no remorse of any kind. If she had not gained assistance from Halmesbury, I would have proceeded with the wedding and she would be trapped in a marriage to me after I proved I could not be trusted."

Richard's face displayed his self-loathing, which made Sophia's heart ache on his behalf. She could not imagine the difficulty of repairing so many mistakes of the past and having to live with the consequences in the present. This morning, she had experienced her own guilt, which had been torturous.

"Husband, might I make a bold suggestion?"

He could not look at her, but he did gesture her to continue.

"I think if you had married her, something would have happened and you would have stopped chasing skirts."

Richard's head shot up, amazement on his face. "What? Why would you say that?"

"For one thing, less than three weeks ago, you made a decision to change, and you have done so. That infers that it was inevitable that eventually you would decide to do so, given the right circumstances."

"That is generous of you, but it was a chance encounter with you that did it, so—"

"And that is the other thing. You had to be seeking an opportunity to change."

"What?" Richard was genuinely perplexed, clearly at a loss for words because of her bold statements.

"Think about it. Why would a man planning on pursuing infidelity for the remainder of his days insist on marrying an intelligent and lively woman? It makes no sense. Unless …"

"Unless?"

"Unless he sought a strong partner who would make him change? Someone who could hold him accountable?"

Varying emotions played across Richard's face for a while. She waited for him to think it through until she finally saw understanding dawn. "I wanted to change?"

"And that is the trait I admire about you above all else— except for the courage to leap on weapon-wielding lunatics in order to save me." She shuddered at the memory of the night before. "The reason I agreed to marry you was that I grew up with two men in my life who each and every day made worse and worse decisions. They kept moving toward moral oblivion, but you—you came to me from the brink of moral ruin and decisively announced your intention to change. Not just in words, but with genuine action that you were taking. Until that moment, I was not aware that it could be done, but I saw the sincerity in your eyes and it moved me. It was … inspiring."

"I … inspired you?"

"More than any person I ever met."

Richard finally looked at her, his eyes filled with admiration. "You are utterly amazing."

With that, he raised a hand to cup the back of her head and tugged her forward to lay a searing kiss on her lips. She squeaked in surprise before parting her lips to meld her tongue against his in delighted response, pressing her curves into his hardness in anticipation of where this might lead. It seemed somehow life-affirming to lose herself in his arms while his hand traced down to rest on the slope of her neck where her pulse beat frantically.

* * *

RICHARD FOUND Perry waiting in his study when he went downstairs. His brother stood hovering near his desk.

"I have been thinking. I went through all of the recent events, starting the day of the wedding. The only conclusion is that the countess's brother gained access to the house through the library. Remember, he was standing by the doors that face the garden during the ceremony? He could have unlocked those doors to gain entrance later."

Richard took a seat at his desk, noticing a page covered with the timeline of events in his brother's untidy hand, along with a quill dripping ink on his smooth mahogany. Perry, who was so impeccable in his dress, had always been disorderly with his work. Richard nodded absent-mindedly while he pulled out a handkerchief to wipe the ink from the surface. He hoped the housekeeper or one of the maids knew how to clean the stain off the lacquer.

Perry pressed on. "So my question is, how did he know

about Ethan? In order for that caricature to appear at the print shops so quickly, he would have needed to know about Ethan's existence from the moment the boy arrived at Balfour Terrace. Unless you believe that Johnson, Long, or Radcliffe would have leaked the information?"

"Never. I trust those men implicitly. There were maids who prepared the nursery, but only that day when my son arrived."

"So how did this Hayward fellow know about your son? I thought about it, and given … um … your reputation …" Perry pulled at his cravat in discomfort. "Well, I do not know how to say this, but if I witnessed a young child arriving in the family carriage and put it together with your reputation, I might assume that your basta—I mean, natural born child was joining your household. And we know the scoundrel does not care for facts because of the lies he told Lord Stanford and Lord Wood, so let us assume he did not care whether he guessed correctly. His intention was to create as much trouble as quickly as he could."

"That makes sense."

"Well, how did he observe Ethan was here? The boy arrived, entered the house to eat, he spent time with you and went up to the nursery to sleep."

Richard scowled, trying to understand Perry's point while muddling through his emotions and thoughts about the discussion with Sophia regarding his former betrothed. Then, with sudden clarity, he realized what Perry was trying to point out. "He must have seen the carriage arrive with Johnson and Ethan!"

"Exactly! If he did that, then he must be consistently watching the house."

"Which means we might find him somewhere in this square!"

"Perhaps Hayward has been visiting someone here, or he

is staying as a guest. Or possibly he just broke into a home that is closed up for some reason. I propose that you and I go to meet our neighbors because no one is going to refuse an earl at their front door. What do you think? Are you tired of this situation yet? Should we take action?"

"It will certainly be better than sitting here waiting for his next strike. Do you still carry the pistol I lent you?"

* * *

WHILE SOPHIA DRESSED with the help of her maid, her mind worked over what Richard had told her about his failed betrothal. She wanted to do something for him. Last night, he had saved her life. At the time, they believed the danger had been caused by his past misdeeds, but that made it no less telling of his character when, to protect his household, he leapt onto a physically imposing man wielding a weapon.

Then it came to light that she was the one who had brought the villainous machinations to their doorstep. To which her husband had responded by giving her solace without a word of complaint. Even now, he had gone downstairs to plan with Perry how to locate her brother and end the threat.

He was doing all the work. What had she done except sit around useless? She needed to contribute in a meaningful way, and an idea had come to her after Richard left her chambers. An idea that took root and she felt driven to execute. Immediately. The moment she was dressed, she ordered a carriage be brought round. While she prepared to leave the townhouse, she saw the taller John hovering close by.

"Where is the other John? Is he all right?"

"He is recovering and well today, but his lordship

assigned him the lighter duties of the nursery and tasked me with taking his place."

"Good. We are going out." With that, she stepped out the front door and headed for the carriage.

A short drive to a nearby Mayfair home and then Sophia was standing in the entrance hall waiting to be shown in. She hoped the noblewoman would see her. She needed to do something useful, and this felt right. It would help Richard confront his inner demons, so he could finally forgive himself for his past sins.

The butler returned. In an unusually hoarse voice, he informed her that the duchess would see her and showed her into a drawing room.

Sophia entered the lavish drawing room, decorated in blue and gold, to find a young woman of her own age seated on an elegant sofa, with a tea service laid out on the table in front of her. She had a crown of curling chestnut hair, and warm eyes the color of brandy with glints of gold not dissimilar to the light catching in said drink.

"The Countess of Saunton," announced the very proper butler in his husky tone, startling Sophia so that she flinched ever so slightly.

The duchess stood and walked over to greet her. "Your Grace." Sophia sank into a curtsy, feeling a little in awe of the beauty and grace of the woman.

Her hostess smiled widely before exclaiming, "Pish! My name is Annabel."

Sophia smiled in return. She could not help it. Her mouth moved in response to the young woman's vibrant energy. Richard had said she was lively, but he had not mentioned how warm the woman was. Sophia felt like she was being wrapped in a sunny Saturday afternoon in the park, her overwrought nerves relaxing into an even state she had not enjoyed in some time.

"Sophia," she acknowledged.

"I was hoping I would meet you soon, Sophia. I wanted to see what kind of woman tamed the infamous Earl of Saunton and here you are. Shall we have tea?"

Richard was right. This woman's mind moved quickly. She could see a younger version of this woman haring across two counties alone on horseback to find an escape from her nuptials. Of course the duke had been immediately captivated.

She followed the duchess to take a seat, then watched as she poured another cup of tea and passed the cup and saucer to her. Sophia guessed it to be Twinings, breathing in the delightful fragrance before raising the china cup to her lips to take a small sip.

Annabel leaned back in her seat. "What is the reason for your visit?"

"May I speak frankly?"

"I would prefer it. I am still mastering the art of polite small talk and could do without it for a spell. We have much more interesting subjects we could talk about than the weather."

"Richard told me what happened between the two of you."

The duchess raised her chestnut eyebrows. "Indeed. The duke told me he believed a singular woman had finally captivated Richard. If your husband told you about The Stable Incident, then I know it must be true rather than merely my husband's hopes on behalf of his cousin."

Sophia smiled, feeling uncertain. They had a true marriage in the sense that they were now working together. However, the duchess appeared to believe that Richard loved her, and there was no evidence of that. He had not said so. He had not promised it at any time. She feared she might just be the medium for his crusade, but it seemed dishonorable to confirm or deny it, so she said nothing.

"I was wondering what it would take for Richard to receive your forgiveness. He feels much guilt over what happened, and it would provide surcease if he knew you were no longer angry."

Annabel sighed deeply. "I am no longer angry. Things turned out well for me. I met the man I love, and I have a wonderful baby boy upstairs in the nursery. If Richard had not been faithless, I would never have met Philip—the duke —under the circumstances that we met and I would not be wed to the most honorable man."

"So you forgive him?"

"No."

"But ... you said you are not angry with him."

"I appreciate that he finally took responsibility for what he did to Caroline Brown, but he has not done what is required to make things well with me. I am happy that he and my husband have been able to resume their friendship and I wish him all the best, but I will not forgive him. He knows what I require."

"I ... is there nothing I can do?"

"You can convince him to do the right thing."

Sophia put her tea down. She had hoped this discussion would proceed well, but now disappointment was rising in her chest and her hands were shaking from all the repressed emotions. Under ordinary circumstances, she would know what to say next, but nothing about the past couple of weeks had been ordinary. "Please, could you tell me what it is he needs to do so I can assist him?"

"I want an apology."

"An apology?"

"That is correct."

"An apology?"

The duchess nodded in agreement. Sophia wondered if she was dreaming because suddenly nothing made sense to her. "Are ... are you saying ... that the earl never *apologized* for what he did?"

Annabel raised her chestnut eyebrows, which Sophia took as an affirmation.

"My daft husband was too proud? Is that it?"

"Not exactly. At the time, he insisted he acted exactly as he should, that it was essentially a man's prerogative. Since that time, if he is now struck by guilt, I would assume it is pride that stands in the way of him coming to see me."

"So all he has to do to end this matter with you is simply apologize for his faithlessness?"

"That is correct."

Sophia bit her lip. "May I ask a favor of you?"

The duchess appeared intrigued, tilting her head in agreement. "You may."

"Before I do, perhaps I should tell you about some unusual events from the past few days and the heroics of my protector."

CHAPTER 20

*R*ichard and Perry returned after several hours of tiresome introductions, endless cups of tea, and dainty biscuits, which they nibbled on to extend their visits and establish if any of the residents in the square were hosting the Hayward scoundrel. Alas, the venture had been to no avail.

Entering the vestibule of Balfour Terrace, they removed their coats, hats, and gloves to hand off to the footman in attendance before Perry mumbled something under his breath about needing the necessary, and Richard made his weary way to his study.

Pushing open the door, he was astonished to find the shorter John standing just inside. The older man had a raffish air, sporting a taped gash over his right temple. Richard swiveled his head to locate the man's charge, Ethan, flinching in surprise at the sight that met his eyes. His nerves were too frayed to deal with any of it.

A nursemaid he did not recognize was holding an infant, bouncing the babe whose shock of familiar chestnut hair informed him that his cousin's heir was present. The nursemaid's low humming soothed her charge as she bobbed.

His own son's nursemaid, Daisy, sat sipping a cup of tea in a seat tucked in the room's corner while Ethan sat on the floor in front of a low table playing chess with his cousin, the large blond Viking of the Markham clan. It was a confounding scene of domesticated perfection.

"Halmesbury?"

The duke looked up from his position on the carpeting. "Just a moment, please." He turned back to the table. Ethan's little face screwed in concentration. He picked up a piece with his small hand and moved it, staring down at the board for several seconds, and then raised his head in triumph. "Checkmate!"

Halmesbury chuckled. "Well done, little cousin! I told you it would work!"

Ethan beamed before leaping to his feet and racing over to hug Richard's legs. "I beat the duke, Papa!"

Richard reached down to swing his son into his arms. "Well done, Ethan. What say Daisy take you to celebrate with something from Cook in the kitchens?"

"I want to eat biscuits," his boy proclaimed before squirming out of Richard's arms to land on his feet when he lowered his son down.

Daisy and Ethan left hand in hand, the shorter John dedicated to shadowing their heels as he exited and shut the door behind them. Richard turned to find the duke seated in one of the plump armchairs by the fire, striking an imposing figure against the bottle green of the wallpaper that framed him.

"What the deuce are you doing here?"

"Sophia invited us. She said to meet her in the mews when you returned."

Richard was lost. Halmesbury never visited his home.

Sophia had never met the duke, so why would she invite him and his infant son over to visit? Was this some sort of visit for Ethan? He shook his head in confusion.

"Go find your wife, Saunton." Philip's steady gaze revealed nothing. As usual, his kinsman appeared wholly composed, providing no clues to his thoughts.

Ballocks, my cousin can be infuriating!

Richard turned and stomped out, heading down the passage. He let himself out into the garden and crossed over to enter the mews, where he found the taller John standing at the entrance. *How the blazes did I think I would fool Sophia into thinking these rumpled guardsmen were actual footmen?* She would need to be blind and stupid not to notice something amiss. He blamed his lack of sleep and stress for his miscalculation of not informing her he had hired additional security.

"Where is her ladyship?" he demanded of the man, vaguely noting the distant sound of men at work in the carriage house.

"Down near the end in one of the stalls, milord."

Richard's mood worsened as he looked at the dim interior to the right. What was his wife doing here, and why had he been summoned to see her? He regretted his promise not to drink. He needed one to wash the taste of conflicting tea blends from his mouth.

He stomped down the corridor toward the workrooms at the other end of the mews, where he heard a woman talking, stopping mid-sentence at the sound of his approaching footsteps. He forced himself to relax his face into more pleasant lines before walking into the stall to unearth what this summons to the stables could possibly mean.

Where he came face-to-face with the one person he had been dreading he would encounter this Season.

"Annabel!" He winced. How was he meant to address her? "I mean ... Your Grace." He bowed stiffly.

"Annabel is acceptable."

Richard pulled a face before looking around to find his wife standing to the side with a sheepish expression on her blushing face. "What is this, Sophia?"

"I asked Annabel—Her Grace—Annabel ..." Sophia ground to a halt.

"Your wife informed me of your heroics last evening, Richard. She asked me if I would visit today so you could say what you needed to say. According to her, a conversation with me would ease some of your troubles."

Richard shot a look at his traitorous wife, who was studying her slippers in chagrin. "I see."

"I thought it would help." Sophia's voice was but a whisper.

"Why in the damn—I mean—blasted stables?"

"If I may?" Annabel interjected with an amused smile. Richard turned back to face her, finding it difficult to meet her eye, so his gaze settled on the brick wall behind her shoulder. "I would not come otherwise. I have waited for your apology for some time now, and I thought it would be appropriate to pick up the conversation where we left off. These are different stables, of course, but I think it lends an air of authenticity to the completion of this discussion."

Guilt, irritation, and resentment squirmed in his belly. He wanted to turn and run, but he would merely look foolish. Eventually, he would need to admit that he had made a horrendous mistake with the woman standing in front of him. Richard huffed in defeat.

"All right. I suppose I owe you an apology, and you are in your rights to demand the time and place, considering ..."

Sophia interrupted. "I will be standing right outside while you talk." She hastily walked out of the stall to stand a few feet away, a nervous air about her as she folded her arms to wait.

Richard turned back to find the girl whom he had known since he was a lad and who was now matured into a woman of elegance. Annabel had developed into a self-assured duchess of the realm while still retaining that spirited, intelligent glint in her brandy eyes.

He thought about what Sophia had pointed out earlier that day. How could he ever have believed he could fool this woman regarding his philandering habits if they had married? Even two years earlier, it now made sense that he had been making decisions that would eventually sabotage the depraved life he had led and force him to become honest. Somewhere deep in his heart, he must have sought to change his path. But what he had done to Annabel was ... There were no words adequate to describe how deeply he had betrayed the woman who was once his friend. His chest constricted with the burden of guilt he was carrying.

"I ... am ... sorry."

Richard was surprised to discover that a small piece of the weight chipped off, and he found his thoughts began to clear. "I am sorry I misled you into thinking I planned on having a genuine marriage with you."

More weight lifted, his breathing deepened, and air rushed into his lungs. "I am sorry I betrayed you with someone you cared about."

The sheer relief at his words made him feel light-headed. "I am sorry that I showed no remorse."

Finally, he shifted his gaze to look her in the eye. "My deepest apologies that I failed to respect your wishes or allow you control over your destiny when I refused to cancel the wedding."

Annabel smiled widely at him. "Admit you feel better."

Richard returned her smile, feeling ten years younger at that moment. "I do."

"Good! I am glad you did everything you did because it led me to Philip. But I also knew you needed to say this. To accept responsibility for your actions, and that is why I remained firm on the point."

She reached forward and grabbed his hands in hers. "I am so happy you found the right woman and that you finally found your way. I always knew you had it in you, Richard. You are a great man who influences many. I want you to live a long and happy life—"

"CECIL!" At Sophia's cry, Richard and the duchess froze. The sound of someone running could be heard.

Richard lunged out of the stall just in time to see his wife hurl herself at the legs of a groom, throwing her arms around his knees tightly to cause him to fall. There was a loud thud as his body hit the hard-packed earth. Then the man swung his arm back to cuff Sophia hard across the face, who bounced back with the force of the blow but held on firmly.

Rage rose in Richard's chest at the sight. Roaring his fury, he ran to fling himself over the scoundrel, pinning him to the ground while calling out for the taller John. Pulsing with anger, he swung a fist into the groom's kidney. *How dare the bounder assault my countess?*

He heard the taller John run up while Richard was still pounding his fist repeatedly into the knave's side.

"Your lordship, stop! I am here. Let me take hold of the man." Richard could barely hear the guardsman as blind outrage made him pull his arm back to throw another punch.

"Richard!" Sophia's voice penetrated his frenzied haze. Richard froze. His heart beat loudly in his ears while he slowly unclenched his fist. He used that hand to push himself up and look back.

Sophia was sitting on the blackguard's legs. The sight of

disheveled hair and her split lip, with a trickle of blood running down her chin, broke his heart—until he noticed that her face, her eyes, her skin were glowing. She was incandescent with unbound joy.

"Richard! I caught him! I tackled him to the ground!"

Richard reached over to wipe the blood off her chin, feeling reverence at the bravery of his young wife. He realized why she was so overjoyed—she had just bested the bully that tortured her these past several years. "You did, my love. I take it this is your brother?"

"Of course!" He forced back a smile at her wounded affront. "I do not make a habit of tackling strangers."

The taller John helped him hold the struggling man by the arms so they could turn him over. Richard reached down and pulled off the low-slung hat to reveal red-blond hair and defiant bloodshot eyes. The brother showed evidence of hard drinking, his face ruddy and his congested skin webbed with spider veins. For such a young man, his appearance was bloated and unhealthy.

Richard grinned with grim determination. "Mr. Hayward, I spent the day looking for you."

* * *

WHO WOULD HAVE IMAGINED that visiting his own stables to deliver the long-overdue apology would fortuitously lead to the capture of his foe? It was fitting somehow that the two events converged in such a manner. By accepting responsibility for his past, fate dictated that he solve his present troubles.

Now the scourge of their household was trussed to a chair in a little-used drawing room. The cursing man tugged at the ties in a futile attempt to leave while being guarded by the two Johns and Radcliffe.

"He certainly has a fixation on coin," commented the duke in a dry tone.

It was as if Hayward overheard the remark; the cursing increased in volume. "I do not see why that bitch should receive all the money and advantages! She leaves nothing for me!"

Annabel, the duke, Perry, Sophia, and Richard stood on the far end of the large drawing room, huddled in a group to discuss what to do while pointedly ignoring the brother's spitting vitriol.

Only Perry glared at the scoundrel. "I knew it! I knew he must have been observing Balfour Terrace! Who would have thought such a spoilt young man would take a post working as a groom? He must be quite dedicated to ruining this household!"

Sophia shook her head in disbelief. "He could be angry that I tattled to my uncle about his plot. Or he is simply enraged to be thwarted in his plans to exploit my inheritance. He seemed to think he had some right to the funds, so that might fuel his petty anger."

Richard nodded in agreement. "The stable master said one of the grooms disappeared the afternoon of the wedding —hopefully because your brother paid him off and not for more sinister reasons—and that Hayward showed up early the next morning with references, which I assume are faked. Or written by his cronies. He has been right under our noses the entire time."

Halmesbury's deep baritone interjected. "Yet somehow he found the time to sneak off to rile up Lord Stanford and Lord Wood."

"How intrepid of him. If he put half that energy into making a respectable living, he would have done well for himself," Annabel observed.

"Be that as it may, what do we do now?" Sophia's question made them all pause.

Minutes ticked by without any suggestions offered. Richard sifted through ideas in his head but came up with nothing worth offering out loud.

"We could have him jailed," Perry finally ventured.

"There is no evidence that he broke the law. The only offense we can prove is he provided false references, and an assumed name, but I would not want to take my chances that he goes to prison for a short time and then returns angrier to seek vengeance for having him arrested," Richard reasoned.

"Nothing for which he could be transported, then." Perry appeared disappointed.

Sophia hissed in dismay. "Not that! The journey could kill him, especially in his current unhealthy condition. He is … still my brother."

"So, burying him in the garden is out of the question, then?" Perry joked weakly. Richard saw Sophia's elbow come up to dig his brother in the ribs. It made his heart sing to observe their familial horseplay; they were becoming a proper family here at Balfour Terrace.

After a moment, Halmesbury spoke up. "If it were me …"

Richard waited, but the duke did not complete the sentence, clearly musing. "If it were you …?"

The duke turned his gaze to Richard. "I would want the man as far from my family as I could manage, even if I paid coin to ensure it. Say, New York or Boston. Australia, perhaps. Whatever destination he chose, I would pay for the privilege of knowing he was very distant from my family."

Richard thought. He wanted to mete justice on the brother, but more important was the need to protect his family. "I could have him accompanied. Long or Johnson could deliver him there and find a solicitor to manage a trust. Hayward would need to present himself each month to collect an allowance. If he has to collect it every month, he will never have time to travel back to British soil and return in time for the next payment."

Sophia clapped her hands. "That could work! Perhaps his escort could ensure that the solicitor knew Cecil's appearance and even provide a miniature of him to be kept on file, so he could never pull another of his sly tricks to collect the funds while not being personally present."

"I will do it! I will escort him to the Americas!" Perry sounded committed to the task.

Richard appreciated the offer, but he preferred his brother remained in England. The errand would take a minimum of four months to complete. "Nay, brother. I need you here. Without your assistance, I would have been lost."

Perry turned his green eyes to look at him with a hopeful glint. "Truly?"

"Aye." His younger brother seemed quite pleased at the acknowledgment. Mayhap Sophia was right; his brother needed purpose to fill his days. "Mr. Long will escort Hayward along with two of the Johns because Johnson has family to care for. I want my men safe from this trickster, so it will take more than one man to complete the task."

Annabel folded her arms in contemplation and added her thoughts. "It is unconventional, but it gets the job done. Pursuing justice is not as important as the peace of mind that your family is protected from this vengeful lunatic. With his predilections, he will be geographically tied down to that source of funds. Perhaps make their payment contingent on the countess being well and alive and ensure it is enough that he will not be willing to walk away from it."

Halmesbury nodded. "One could also remind the young man that his gambling debts will no longer plague him if he remains far from British soil."

Richard looked around at his ... his—what word would best describe what was unfolding around him?

Family!

His cousin and the duchess, his brother and Sophia, they were all family.

He sighed with deep contentment. Here they stood together at his side, assisting him to solve the predicament that faced him. Appreciation and gratitude filled his being. What an incredible change in his circumstances in such a short period, all because he opened his heart. These were the true riches of his life. Perhaps he should try telling Sophia he loved her again? It seemed almost certain she did not hear him say it before.

Damn, he was proud of his feisty wife for tackling her horrid brother to the ground!

CHAPTER 21

$\mathcal{T}$he duke offered to mediate with Cecil, which Richard accepted to Sophia's relief. Her husband's sleepless nights, the fact that he had killed a man the night before, and his belligerence toward the sibling who had laid hands on his wife suggested it was the wise choice to make.

The men headed over to parlay with the scoundrel tied to the chair, which left Sophia to show the duchess back to where her babe was waiting in the study. The duchess collected the boy and his nursemaid and took her leave when the Halmesbury carriage drew to the front.

After the duchess departed, Sophia found herself with nothing to occupy her attention. She dared not enter the drawing room where the negotiation was taking place. Her presence would only infuriate her brother, rendering him uncooperative.

She was too tense to read and too anxious to complete any tasks. Briefly, she considered visiting Lily to tell her what had happened, but cast that idea aside as premature.

Which was why she paced up and down in her bedchamber, wringing her hands. Now that the worst of the threat had passed, she had too much time to think.

Does Richard regret that he married me? He had said she brought him peace, but today's events revealed that was not the truth. He must now live with the fact that a man had died at his hand because the infamous Haywards had entered his life.

Did I make things worse when I tricked him into meeting with Annabel? She was having second thoughts about that decision. After the most traumatic evening of the man's life, she then deceived him into a confrontation that he perhaps was ill-prepared to handle. What had she been thinking? It seemed like such a good idea at the time, but in retrospect, it was terribly manipulative and controlling. She would be angered if he tried something similar. Hell, she *had* been angry when he attempted to interfere with her life by removing her to Saunton Park.

Now that he has confronted the worst, will he lose interest in me? After all, she had raised the possibility to Lily just yesterday that she might be some sort of ethical lodestone. Richard had risen as a hero from the ashes, reconciled with his cousin's wife, and even now was downstairs to conquer her villainous brother. What role would Sophia serve now that he had uncovered his true self? Would she fade into the role of nobleman's wife with her only duty to sire his heir?

What if I want more? Could their marriage grow into a true partnership despite her troubled past? She had returned home the night before intending to talk to him. To explain. Perhaps to disclose that … she loved him. But so much had happened since she had stepped through the front door and been accosted by the inebriated Lord Wood. This morning she had hoped they would find an opportunity to talk things out, but then she had been shocked to her core to see the note—realizing that she had missed all the clues that her brother was the secret enemy working against them.

Damn! This was harder than she had expected. Building a life with another person was quite an undertaking. Would Richard remember how she had accepted Ethan without complaint? Would that stand in her favor when they next spoke?

Sophia concluded that thinking was not the best use of her time. She was arguing herself into tighter and tighter binds. Something to occupy her attention was what she needed to find while she awaited Richard's return from the drawing room negotiation with her trussed-up brother.

Making up her mind, she left her rooms to find Ethan in the nursery. She would read him a story and discuss his day with him.

* * *

TWO HOURS LATER, Sophia returned to her bedchamber, stopping short when she found Richard sipping coffee on her settee.

"I have been waiting for you."

"How did it go with Cecil?"

"Quite well. I suspect that part of the reason he took the post as groom was it gave him somewhere to hide out. Those gambling debts of his are more prolific than is safe for a man of his current financial position. When Halmesbury proposed he leave English soil, he did not demur and then, when he heard about the trust, his relief was palpable despite his blustering to the contrary. The duke stipulated he would not be allowed to drink during the voyage, a rule which his escorts will not hesitate to enforce."

Sophia listened with only half of her attention. Her heart was pounding hard. She wanted to race into his arms and smother him in kisses, but she did not know if he would welcome them. "It sounds like Cecil has a very uncomfortable journey ahead of him, then."

"The hope is that sobriety might take hold if he is dry for such a long voyage. We can at least attempt to assist him to recover from his addictions before we set him loose."

"Where is he headed?"

"He chose New Orleans to be his new home. Perhaps he might find a wife and settle down with the allowance he will be receiving. But that is in his hands once Long sets him up. We have done what we can to give him a chance at a new life."

Sophia moved over to the settee, sitting nervously on the very edge. Her palms were moist with her anxiety, and she discreetly wiped them over her skirts as if smoothing wrinkles in the cloth. She was at a loss for words.

"Thank you … for making such an effort. He is an utter rogue, but it is still … difficult. I remember him as a young boy when he was different."

Richard reached out to take her hand, causing her to flinch in surprise, which he ignored. He gently ran his thumb over her fingers. "It is my pleasure to take care of this on your behalf."

Sophia sat in silence, enjoying his caress and wondering what came next now that the threat had passed.

Richard cleared his throat. "Sophia … If I may?"

She turned her head to look at him only to find that he appeared to be as nervous as she felt.

"This morning when I told you that I loved you … did you hear me say it?"

Her eyes widened in astonishment. "You love me?" she asked breathlessly.

"Of course! Your sharp tongue saved my life, and your gracious presence gave it meaning. Before our home was invaded last night, I had every intention of talking to you about it ... about us."

"Oh, Richard!" She flung herself into his arms and—*damn it*—her tears started falling once more. Mayhap she was a weak-minded female, after all? She lifted herself to wipe at the tears. "I am so sorry to be weeping again! I promise this is out of character."

Richard caught her chin with his fingers to lift her face. "Sophia, I am quite aware that you are a strong woman with her own mind. Hell, these last twenty-four hours have been so fraught with peril and potential loss, I am inclined to join you in your tears!"

Sophia laughed in surprise, batting him across the chest. "Damn you, Richard! Do not make fun of me."

"I do not! See!" Her ridiculous husband contorted his handsome face as if he was attempting to cry. Sophia giggled so hard that her stomach cramped. She threw her arms around him and pressed her face into the heated skin of his neck, listening to the rhythm of his heartbeat and scarcely able to grasp the magnitude of having this man in her life.

"I love you, too," she whispered. He tensed and then slowly relaxed to press kisses to her hair.

"My love, I am so very happy to hear that," he rumbled quietly, holding her close to his heart.

EPILOGUE

A FEW WEEKS LATER

*S*omething woke Richard from his sleep. His thoughts foggy, he tried to take stock of his senses. He heard breathing, not from Sophia who lay sleeping to his right, but another presence. He lay still, scarcely daring to breathe and alert the intruder that he was conscious.

"Papa?" Richard's heart skipped a beat in his chest when his son spoke almost directly into his left ear. He threw a hand over his chest, while he attempted to calm his breathing. The boy had frightened him out of his wits.

"Shhh ... Mama is sleeping. I will come with you to talk." Richard winced when he made to rise and realized he was stark naked beneath the covers. "Ethan, wait for me in my rooms."

The boy left his side, giving Richard the opportunity to search for his nightshirt. He felt around in the dark and found the garment, pulling it close with relief. However, when he attempted to put it on, he discovered he had merely found Sophia's discarded night rail and was forced to keep feeling around. The night rail would never fit over his broad shoulders.

Once he dressed, he loped carefully to his adjoining bedchamber to find Ethan sitting on the floor waiting for him. Closing the door gently behind him, he walked over and sank down beside his son.

"What is it, Ethan?"

"I was dreaming about Emma."

"Your cousin?"

"I miss her. Is she well?"

"I do not know for certain, but I did obtain a grand new farm for your family, so I know Emma is now living in Somerset near Saunton Park. Johnson told me that there are fine gardens."

Ethan smiled. "Emma likes gardening."

"See, then she must be well. The weather is very pleasant in Somerset, and I am sure everyone in your family is happy with their new home. Johnson told me the library is well-stocked."

His boy clapped his hands in joy. "Emma likes books."

"Well, then, it stands to reason she is very happy. Shall we go steal some of Cook's biscuits before I return you to your bed?"

Ethan shot to his feet. "She made York biscuits this afternoon, but she would not let me try them!"

"We will ferret them out."

Thirty minutes later, Richard descended the stairs from the nursery, having had a word with the panicked Daisy and the new governess who had awoken to find Ethan missing from his bed. Bleary from his interrupted sleep, he turned the corner to the corridor leading to the family bedrooms, only to knock into Perry on his way in.

They both panted heavily in the aftermath of the shock of

encountering each other in the dark.

"Did you just get home?"

"I am a fully grown man. I do not need to account for my whereabouts, do I?" Perry reeked of wine and cigars.

"Calm yourself, brother. I was displaying interest."

"The question is, *Saunton*, why are you prowling the halls at three in the morning?" his brother drawled with a sarcastic tone.

"Ethan woke me up. I just returned from the nursery."

"The little terror woke you up again?"

"He did. He worries over his family that he left behind."

"This is what comes of having children. And now you have another on the way. Soon there will be no peace left in this household."

Richard smiled at the reminder that his countess was *enceinte* with his babe. "It is not so terrible. He is a clever boy."

"He might be," Perry begrudgingly admitted, "but he is also a cautionary tale. Since I learned about your son, I am being most fastidious in ensuring I do not wind up in a similar position. I have no wish for children of my own nor a wife."

He mused on his brother's words for a moment before responding. Sophia had pointed out the path to what Perry needed, and Richard was paying mind to her advice. She was correct in her assessment that Perry lacked purpose in his life, which was why as the head of this household, he planned to alter that. It was why he had not allowed his brother to accompany Cecil Hayward to New Orleans the month before. He needed his brother close to hand if he was to intercede in the direction of his younger brother's path.

"You will change your mind, Perry. When you meet the right woman."

With that, Richard turned away from his brother to rejoin his beautiful wife in her inviting bed.

AFTERWORD

Restorative justice is highly therapeutic for both the perpetrator and the victim, no matter how large or small the offense. Planned out with good judgment, it can usually be a smooth process with a lot of gains to be made for everyone involved.

During the years of my nonprofit work, I was fortunate to assist many people with their restorative journey and to reclaim their lives as a fully contributing member of society, which was rewarding, to say the least. In that time, I received many reports of the recipients of unwarranted actions being moved to tears of joy with assertions that their faith in humanity had been restored by the simple act of a person confronting them to confess what they had done, and the offer to make amends. Most times, the amends requested was simply to make a charitable donation on their behalf. This type of activity helped both parties receive closure and restore their sense of belonging to the tribe of man.

Richard's journey was, of course, complicated by having a hidden enemy to thwart his efforts at redemption. If not for that unforeseen obstacle, the advice from his philanthropic ducal cousin would have resulted in his progress in a more orderly fashion. But then it would not have made a good story, would it?

I did not start out with a plan to write Richard's story, but as *The Duke Wins a Bride* unfolded, I could not help thinking about what would it take for a man of his sins to change? To change so much that he could be trusted to never revert or be unfaithful to his new wife despite his troubling history.

I hope I answered that question to your satisfaction, and that you enjoyed the trials and tribulations of pursuing honor after so many dishonorable deeds littering the past.

With the dissolutely charming Richard discovering the value of integrity, it is now time for his arrogant younger brother to discover the value of love and kinship in *My Fair Bluestocking*. Peregrine meets a very unsuitable country mouse who captures his attentions despite himself. Can the mysterious Emma Davis draw the damaged Perry out of the aloof shell into which he retreated so many years earlier? Find out in Book 3 of Inconvenient Brides.

Sign up for Nina Jarrett's newsletter to find out about future books as they are released and receive two books for free! NinaJarrett.com/free

DOWNLOAD 2 FREE BOOKS!

ABOUT THE AUTHOR

Nina has been an avid reader throughout her life. She started writing her own stories in elementary school but got distracted when she finished school and moved on to non profit work with recovering drug addicts. There she worked with people from every walk of life from privileged neighborhoods to the shanty towns of urban and rural South Africa.

One day she met a real life romantic hero. She instantly married her fellow bibliophile and moved to the USA where she enjoys a career as a sales coaching executive at an Inc 500 company. She lives with her husband on the Florida Gulf Coast.

Nina believes in kindness and the indomitable power of the human spirit. She is fascinated by the amazing, funny people she has met across the world who dared to change their lives. She likes to tell mischievous tales of life-changing decisions and character transformations while drinking excellent coffee and avoiding cookies.

MORE BOOKS BY NINA JARRETT

INCONVENIENT BRIDES

FRIENDS OF THE DUKE: PREQUEL ANTHOLOGY

A wealthy merchant's daughter and a struggling writer. A missing bride and her estranged husband.

Can these gentlemen woo the ladies they desire?

Anthology: Two captivating prequel novellas full of unrequited feelings and steamy romance.

London, 1818. Dinah Honeyfield can't wait any longer. In love with her family's long-term houseguest, she's determined to get him to reveal his affections before her rich industrialist father marries her off.

Lord John Pettigrew gave up his birthright to follow his dreams. And with nothing to offer a potential wife, the aspiring author despairs he'll never be able to win the hand of the one who's been his muse.

Can they rewrite their future and plot a path to forever?

Mrs. Lydia Lewis has given up on broken promises. Marrying her soulmate only to be attacked during his heartbreaking absence, she finds refuge as an incognito ducal housekeeper.

Captain Jacob Lewis is angry and hurt. Returning from military service to discover his spouse has vanished into thin air, he begins an almost hopeless search to bring her home.

Can this star-crossed pair reclaim newlywed bliss?

Friends of the Duke is the delightful prequel anthology of the Inconvenient Brides Regency romance series. If you like worthy heroes, fast-paced plots, and enduring connections, then you'll adore Nina Jarrett's charming collection.

Buy *Friends of the Duke* for twin tales of passion today!

* * *

THE DUKE WINS A BRIDE: BOOK 1

Her betrothed cheated on her. The duke offers to save her. Can a marriage of convenience turn into true love?

In this steamy historical romance, a sheltered baron's daughter and a celebrated duke agree on a marriage of convenience, but he has a secret that may ruin it all.

She is desperate to escape ...

When Miss Annabel Ridley learns her betrothed has been unfaithful, she knows she must cancel the wedding. The problem is no one else seems to agree with her, least of all her father. With her wedding day approaching, she must find a way to escape her doomed marriage. She seeks out the Duke of Halmesbury to request he intercede with her rakish betrothed to break it off before the wedding day.

He is ready to try again ...

Widower Philip Markham has decided it is time to search for a new wife. He hopes to find a bold bride to avoid the mistakes of his past. Fate seems to be favoring him when he finds a captivating young woman in his study begging for his help to disengage from a despised figure from his past. He astonishes her with a proposal of his own—a marriage of convenience to suit them both. If she accepts, he resolves to never reveal the truth of his past lest it ruin their chances of possibly finding love.

The Duke Wins a Bride is the delightful first book in the Inconvenient Brides series of steamy Regency romance books. If you like worthy heroes, strong heroines, fast-paced plots, and enduring connections, then you'll adore Nina Jarrett's charming novel.

Buy *The Duke Wins a Bride* for a tale of passion today!

* * *

MY FAIR BLUESTOCKING: BOOK 3

A young woman who cares little about high society or its fashions. A spoilt lord who cares too much. Will they give in to their unexpected attraction to reveal a deep and enduring passion?

She thinks he is arrogant and vain ...

The Davis family has ascended to the gentry due to their unusual connection to the Earl of Saunton. Now the earl wants Emma Davis and her sister to come to London for the Season. Emma relishes refusing, but her sister is excited to meet eligible gentlemen. Now she can't tell the earl's arrogant brother to go to hell when he shows up with the invitation. She will cooperate for her beloved sibling, but she is not allowing the handsome Perry to sway her mind ... or her heart.

He thinks she is uncouth, but intriguing ...

Peregrine Balfour cannot believe the errands his brother is making him do. Fetching a country mouse. Preparing her for polite society. Dancing lessons. He should be stealing into the beds of welcoming widows, not delivering finishing lessons to an unstylish shrew. Pity he can't help noticing the ravishing young woman that is being revealed by his tuition until the only schooling he wants to deliver is in the language of love.

Will these two conflicting personalities find a way to reconcile their unexpected attraction before Perry makes a grave mistake?

My Fair Bluestocking is the delightful next chapter in the Inconvenient Brides Regency romance series. If you like worthy heroes, fast-paced plots, and enduring connections, then you'll adore Nina Jarrett's charming novel.

Buy *My Fair Bluestocking* for a passionate enemies to lovers romance!

Printed by Amazon Italia Logistica S.r.l.
Torrazza Piemonte (TO), Italy

54204701R00161